HEADWATERS RECKONING

Book 3: Overdrive Evans Series

Patrick J. Hughes

BearLilly Press

To my wife, Paula J. Hughes. Without her love, support, encouragement, and understanding the creation of this novel never would've happened.

CONTENTS

CHAPTER 1

Trouble in Overdrive's Paradise –
Saturday; June 19, 1965; 9:00 AM

James 'Overdrive' Evans was six-foot-three, and unusually slender, wiry, and strong for a man of 47. Although still full of piss and vinegar, recent-year stress had sprouted a small bald spot up top and grey at the temples. He wasn't one to show much emotion, but the stoic facade masked an explosive temper, and those closest to him knew when to steer clear. The locals described him as set in his ways, and joked that he and his Cascade, Wisconsin, dairy farm were like a dog with a bone. From a place deep in his soul, Overdrive knew he'd been placed on earth to steward the family farm until one of his children took the reins. Though not much of a church-goer, Overdrive was spiritual in his own way, and had no intention of violating what he considered to be God's will.

The morning was sunny with a pleasant breeze, as Overdrive bumped down one of his farm lanes. He was driving the "cow car", so-named for its unmistakable scent of cow-manure. The car had seen plenty of rocks and ruts in its day, and given the jalopy's current state a few more jostles were of little concern. Overdrive's task that morning was to go from field-to-field, and inspect his crops. He surveilled the land as he drove along, but also stopped at each field. From experience, he knew walking the ground for a closer look was the only way to detect disease and insect infestations. As he worked, Overdrive ruminated over the unlikely series of events that'd led to this moment.

Overdrive and his wife, Mary, were happiest when left alone to run their farm. Since WWII, that's the way it'd been until 18 months ago when Rachel Wolf arrived on the scene. That women had other ideas for how their land should be used, and had demonstrated … twice … that she'd go to any lengths to fulfill her vision. In Wolf's mind, the law was merely a suggestion. So long as she remained free, Overdrive's earthly mission to steward the farm was in jeopardy. Left no other choice, Overdrive and Mary had committed themselves to putting Wolf behind bars. Fortunately, they weren't alone in that commitment. In fact, a formidable team had been formed. What was once a coterie of disparate individuals and entities, now stood united. Through her various misadventures, Wolf had inadvertently forged them into a unified team.

The team had formed in an ad hoc manner, purely by chance. When the troubles first started, the Evanses had engaged Ted Ritter, a country lawyer from Random Lake. As it turned out, Ted's lawyering ancestors and Wolf's, swindlers all, had crossed swords many times over the past century. Given this history, Ted quickly realized what he was up against. His family's archive of legacy case files gave him special insight into the Wolf clan's darkness, cunning, and total disregard for the law. With Ted's help, the Evanses survived Wolf's first attempt to force them off their farm. For years, Overdrive and Mary had relied on Cascade bank for their financial needs. When it came time to take out a large loan to double the milk herd, that's where they went. Although Cascade had been acquired by Wolf's regional bank out of Fond du Lac since their last dealings, the farm loan officer remained the same and Overdrive trusted him. It'd been a costly mistake. Under the new management, his trusted friend had been powerless, and the Evanses found themselves in a hole they couldn't get out of. If not for an eleventh-hour loan from Oostburg's small independent bank, arranged with the help of Ted, they'd have lost the farm. Having recently fought off their own hostile takeover attempt by Wolf's regional bank, Oostburg Bank viewed helping out as sweet revenge, which was why Ted had recommended them.

Takeover scare or not, Oostburg Bank's board had been split on whether to approve the Evans's loan. Some members had a hard time believing that a farmer's own long-time bank would deceive them, enabling a land grab motivated by a desire to develop a casino. But at the last minute, into the bank walked Darkwater Flint with the proof, and the bank moved forward. Darkwater, a close friend of Overdrive's father, Old Bill, was a member of the Potawatomi tribe of Forest County, Wisconsin. His band of the tribe had a sacred connection to burial mounds on land now owned by the Evans family. On the way to Oostburg Bank, Darkwater escaped an attempt on his life and eluded a manhunt. Both had been perpetrated by Wolf, in her desperate attempt to prevent details of her casino development from reaching the bank.

As Overdrive rolled these events over in his mind, he saw once more how foolish he'd been to stumble into the predicament in the first place. With the clarity of hindsight, he found it even more humbling that so many good and honest people had come to the aid of he and Mary in their time of need. It was unbelievable, and yet it had happened. And Darkwater ... Overdrive's eyes teared at the thought of what he'd gone through. Half-Potawatomi and half-Welsh, Darkwater had participated as a young boy in his clan's annual pilgrimages to the Evans farm each spring, which had continued into the 1920s. What're the odds that decades later, he'd remain one of Overdrive's father's closest personal friends? Even more astounding, was that he'd been willing to put himself in harm's way for he and Mary. Not many people would've had the courage to do that.

Only four months after the bank loan came through, the second shoe dropped. Overdrive and Mary found themselves caught in another of Wolf's snares. This time, dozens of other dairy farmers had also fallen into the trap. It was no coincidence that most of these farmers had loans at Oostburg Bank. Fortunately for everyone, Overdrive and Mary already had Old Bill, Darkwater, Ted, and Oostburg Bank on their side. If not for this ready-made team, Wolf's scheme would've succeeded all these farmers plus the next domino, Oostburg Bank, would've been ruined.

Ruining the bank had been a major interim objective of Wolf's. Causing dozens of farm loans to default at once was merely the means to push the bank into insolvency. She anticipated the bank would try to raise capital from existing stockholders to save itself, and had at the ready a plan to skuttle that too. Left no choice, the bank put 60 percent of its stock up for public sale. Poised and ready to pounce, Wolf put in a ridiculously high bid and bought it all, or so she thought. Once she controlled the bank, Wolf planned to call in the Evans note, and take over the farm when the Evanses failed to pay in full. Owning the Evans farm had been Wolf's primary objective all along. Instead of this dreadful outcome, the bank made a miraculous recovery and declined all offers received under its stock sale. The bank's recovery stemmed from quick action by the ready-made team, which enabled every farmer to pay what they owed, and bring their bank-loans current.

Overdrive had been over the details a million times, but they never ceased to amaze him. Wolf appeared to be obsessed with his farm. Without it, she couldn't build her dream ... the Headwaters of the Milwaukee River Casino. She had demonstrated, twice, she'd do anything to get it. Overdrive understood the motivation. He had no doubt the casino would be a gold mine. But even so, he found her approach deeply troubling. Never once did she try to buy the farm, fair and square. Instead, she tried to steal it, twice. It's as though she felt entitled to it, somehow. Well, she isn't.

As a simple farmer whose life had been detoured to Europe for WWII, Overdrive was well aware he probably wasn't attuned to the latest trends. Sometimes he wondered whether the world had passed him by, and Wolf-style behavior was now acceptable. But he always dismissed this line of thinking because it didn't explain the Ted Ritters or Darkwater Flints of the world. He refused to believe a pocket of humanity existed anywhere on earth where Wolf's behavior was okay. She thinks if she doesn't get her way, she's entitled to kill for it. Hell, it's even worse than that. When she tried to kill Darkwater that last time, she mistakenly thought Oostburg Bank was hers. In other words, she'll kill even when she does get her way. Killing Darkwater was ... what ... payback for screwing up her first run at the farm? What kind of person does that?

Overdrive interpreted the throb between his ears as a sign that he'd let his thoughts run free long enough. Bottom line, Oostburg Bank had eluded Wolf and remained independent. Darkwater had been shot three times, but survived. With the bank independent, the farm was in no imminent danger. In other words, Wolf once again initiated hostilities, but the team fought her to a draw. True, nobody enters a fight hoping for a draw. But when Wolf brings the fight to you, achieving one is a major accomplishment. Next time, maybe the team can bring the fight to Wolf.

Overdrive finished his rounds that day, in a much better mood than when he started. In general, his crops were out-competing the weeds, had good color, and he saw no telltale signs of disease or insect infestation. Second-cutting hay looked phenomenal, and was ready to harvest. Even better, concerning the Wolf problem, he felt more optimistic than ever.

Overdrive's last stop that morning was the Lemke place, a farm adjacent to his own where he'd purchased the land and farm-buildings years back, but the previous owner still owned and lived in the farmhouse. He was pulling out of the yard when old Mrs. Lemke stepped onto her porch, and waved him down. He liked his elderly neighbor, and gave her a wave and a smile as he parked, and got out of the car. After joining her on the porch, he said, "Well, hello Mrs. Lemke. What can I do for you today?"

With a hint of an Irish brogue, the widow said, "And hello to you, my dear sir. It's probably nothing, James, but seeing you jogged my memory. A while back, I drove to Cascade for groceries and noticed a car parked not far from the culvert on Rock Road. When I came back, it was still there. I didn't recognize the car, so it struck me as odd."

Overdrives brows went up, "Huh ... when did you say this was?"

Mrs. Lemke's eyes narrowed in thought, then she shook her head, "I'm sorry James, this is embarrassing. What day is today?"

Overdrive smiled warmly, and said in an encouraging tone, "No need to be embarrassed. I ask Mary the same thing all the time. It's Saturday."

The widow put a hand to her chin for a moment, then said, "Okay, then it must've been last Sunday. Yes, that's right. I go to Reinhold's Market after church. I'm sure I had groceries in the car." Then, she frowned, "No, wait a minute. I go to market on Wednesdays, too. So, it might've been on a Wednesday. Not just a few days ago, but the one before that. I'm sorry, James. I'm just not sure. It's either last Sunday, or the Wednesday before that."

Overdrive's brow beetled, "Huh ... strange time of year for a trespasser, if that's what it was. Usually they're after ginseng, hunting, gathering nuts, or looking for bittersweet to decorate for the holidays.

This isn't the right season for any of those." He thought a moment, "You didn't happen to get a license number, did you?"

Mrs. Lemke shook her head, "No, I'm sorry … never crossed my mind. Not exactly crime-central around here, you know. I did slow down to look, though." She paused to smile and wink, "Always been a little nosy, you know. Anyway, I saw a man walking along the edge of your field, back toward the car."

Overdrive frowned, "Did you recognize him?"

She shook her head again, "No, sorry. He was far off, and I don't see so well anymore. I'm really sorry, James. I meant to tell you sooner, but you know how it is. Sometimes my brain is like a bird trapped in an attic."

Overdrive ran a hand through his hair and said, "Do you remember what the car looked like?"

She scrunched her lips and looked up in thought, then said, "Well, I remember it being big and dark, black maybe. But that's about it. I don't keep track of cars these days. Sorry, wish I could be more help."

Overdrive said kindly, "Don't you worry. You've already been a big help."

About then Mrs. Lemke's dog, Butch, wandered over. She bent to scratch his ear, then bobbed back up with concern written all over her face, "You know, I'd forget my head if it wasn't attached. There's something else I meant to ask. Any idea what's going around among the neighborhood mutts? Butch here seems fine today, but yesterday he could barely stand up."

Overdrive shook his head, "No idea, but I'll ask Mary to look into it, and let you know." Then, he thanked her for the heads-up on the strange car, and went on his way.

* * *

After an early lunch, Overdrive left the farm headed toward Cascade on his Owatonna, the all-in-one hay cutter, crimper, and rake. His ultimate destination was the rented Courtland Farm, on the far side of the village and Lake Ellen. There, he planned to spend the afternoon mowing second-cutting hay. But first, he needed a private conversation with his father, Old Bill, so he stopped at his shack in Cascade along the way. He knew Old Bill would be home for lunch.

When the big reaper pulled up out front, Old Bill came outside to greet his son. As the machine fell silent, he asked, "To what do I owe this great honor?"

Overdrive hopped off, looked this way and that to see if anybody was within earshot, then said in a low voice, "Mary's running the baler this afternoon, so you'll be with Jumbo, unloading. I'd like you to have a conversation with him."

Old Bill stood back, appraisingly, "In other words, you need your silver-tongued father to deliver a delicate message to your son ... again."

Overdrive shot him the Popeye look, "Don't flatter yourself, Dad, it's unbecoming of a true Welshman. But yeah, that about sums it up."

Through a wry smile, Old Bill said, "You know, the thought of still being needed at my advanced age ... it kind of gives me a stiffy." Then, after a pause, "So, what's the message this time?"

Overdrive groaned at the pun, but then a wrinkle of concern appeared on his forehead, "Well, Jumbo graduated high school over two weeks ago, and he hasn't said a word about whether he's going farming or not."

Old Bill groaned sarcastically, "God forbid, two weeks out of high school and he's yet to decide on his life's work. What's the matter with that boy?"

Overdrive winced, "Come on Dad, you of all people should know how important this is. Jumbo's been avoiding me. I can feel it."

Old Bill put a hand on his son's shoulder, "I know how important this is to you. I do. But I also can't blame Jumbo for being a little dodgy. He knows what you want to hear, and apparently, he's not able to say it. At least not yet."

Overdrive, with nervous stress evident in his voice, "It's not just that. With the war in Viet Nam going on and all ... Mary and I just worry."

Old Bill gave his son's shoulder a squeeze, "You went off to war."

Overdrive caught his father's eyes, "WWII was different, and you know it."

Old Bill dropped his hand and nodded, "Yes, it was. I'll grant you that."

To strengthen his case, Overdrive added, "It's not just us. Lizzie Flint has her hopes set on a country life, too. The farm would be perfect for them."

Old Bill whistled, "Seriously? Life's work ... marriage ... good grief! It's only been two weeks. That's quite a load to put on a boy right out of high school, don't you think? Life decisions don't get any bigger, do they?"

After letting that hang in the air for a moment, Overdrive doubled down, "No, they don't. But I've been there, and so have you. Just do what you can to encourage Jumbo to be smart, okay? You'd be as sorry as the rest of us, if he came home in a body bag."

Old Bill slapped his son on the shoulder, and said, "I can do that."

✻ ✻ ✻

In Overdrive's view, haying was all about keeping up the tempo. As part of that, whenever a haymow approached full capacity, he moved Jumbo to the unloading crew. Today was one of those days. To backfill Jumbo, Mary would run the baler, which meant her corn cultivating would have to wait. Mary was plenty good on the baler, but kickoff balers weren't perfect. No matter how skilled the operator, occasionally on curves and hills they'd miss the wagon when they threw a bale. With Jumbo on the baler, retrieving errant bales manually was no problem. Not so with Mary, hence wagon-hauling duties fell to Joe. Aside from Overdrive and Jumbo, he's the only other family member strong enough to toss ground-level bales up into the tall-sided wagons. That left Old Bill, Jumbo, John and David as the unloading crew.

Jumbo's forte was to stand at the end of the elevator up in the haymow, armed with a three-tined fork. Using his superior strength and the leverage of the long fork-handle, he'd fling bales to the far corners of the mow as if shot out of a cannon. The other poor bastard up in the mow, was John. To avoid direct-hits from Jumbo's whizzing bales, he needed to keep a watchful eye. But once they safely landed, his job was to cram them into every available crevice, right up to the roof. Outside, David rolled or dragged bales to the back of the wagon, and Old Bill set them on the elevator spaced sufficiently so Jumbo and John could keep up.

Between wagons, the unloading crew would take a blow and shoot the breeze. Through the first two breaks, Old Bill kept the conversation with his grandkids light. But after the third wagon was emptied, he sent David for a fresh jug of ice water, and John to ride along with Joe, presumably to test his manhood on those errant bales.

Alone with Jumbo at last, Old Bill joked, "Big as you are, this might be a stupid question. But have you decided what you want to be when you grow up?"

Jumbo half laughed, "That's a tough one, gramps. I'm working on it. How did you decide?"

Old Bill smiled, and his eyes widened as he thought back in time, "Well, those were different times, of course. But my father, grandfather … hell, every generation before me had farmed, either here or in Wales. It struck me as a way to make a good living, without climbing all over other people to do it."

Jumbo's expression became serious, "I've heard Dad say that. But is it true anymore?"

Surprised, Old Bill took off his hat and ran his fingers through his hair to buy time, "Sure, I think it is. Your parents are making a good go of it."

Jumbo considered that for a moment, "But are they? Back when we added on to the barn and doubled the herd, as I recall, Mom and Dad really had to scramble. Hell, we all did. Then, milk prices dropped so they got involved in that NFO milk diversion … holy cow, what a shit storm that turned out to be. From where I stand, it's not so clear they're making a good go of it." During this time, the National Farmers

Organization, or NFO, was attempting to prop up milk prices through collective bargaining.

Old Bill, somewhat impressed, "I see you've been paying attention, and that's a good thing. But don't jump to the wrong conclusions before you have all the facts. Dairying got to the point where a farmer needed to get bigger or get out, so your parents got bigger. Once bigger, milk price became even more important, so they and others made keeping it fair a priority. One could argue your parents are making all the right moves."

Jumbo chewed on that for a while, "I suppose you're right. But farming just seems like a never-ending slog. If the deck is stacked against it, why not move on to something else?"

Old Bill doubled-down, "Look, farming is hard work, I'll not say it isn't. To keep their farms going, every generation has had its challenges. But when they're overcome ... I don't know, it's hard to explain ... it's just so damn gratifying. You realize that hey, all that hard work was worth it. Your great-great-grandparents left everything they knew in Wales, to seek a better life here. And they found it. Your great-grandparents finished clearing enough land to till, and when dairying took off, they hustled to get involved. And they did! Your grandma and I had to make it through the Great Depression. We did that, and nobody can take that away from us. What your parents are struggling with now ... well, it'll warm their hearts later. It'll be their contribution to the next generation."

Jumbo opened his mouth to say something, hesitated, then went ahead anyway, "I used to see things that way. But I don't know, after almost dying in the silo last winter, I've been talking to friends and doing some serious soul searching. Of all my friends, I'm the only one that's had a near-death experience. And get this, my friends actually go on vacations with their families. Here, well, as far back as I can remember, mom and dad only got away once, for about a week. We can never all go together … I mean, who'd milk the cows? As for me, I've been out of state once, to the Boy Scout Jamboree at Valley Forge. Hell, other than that, I've barely been out of Sheboygan County, a few football and basketball games I guess, and track meets. Even Dad got to Kentucky, and even Italy, during WWII. I feel like I need to see some of the world first, you know?"

Old Bill flinched, "During the war, your dad saw things he wishes he hadn't. That's why he won't talk about it." He studied his grandson for a moment, made a decision, and said, "But I understand what you're saying." Then, after a beat, "If that's your plan, seeing some of the world I mean, how'd you go about it?"

Jumbo stuffed his hands in his jean's pockets, looked down, and kicked a stone, "Well, I've been thinking about enlisting in the Army. I'd get to see some of the world. Then, when I get back, there'd be the GI Bill. If farming turns out to be what I want to do, I could take some ag classes and get a leg up."

Old Bill tried to stifle the gasp, "But they'd send you to Viet Nam, wouldn't they? Is that what you want?"

Jumbo kicked another stone, "No, of course not. But the recruiter said they're always looking for big guys like me, to be military police. He couldn't make any promises, but said for military police, the chances of going to Nam are much smaller."

After that sunk in, Old Bill laid it on the line, "You

probably already know this, Jumbo, but I'm going to say it anyway, just to be sure. Your father would gladly give his right arm, if you were to come farming with him. He'd give you time off for vacations. He'd find a way to pay for ag classes, if you wanted them. I know he would."

Jumbo squeezed the bridge of his nose for a moment, "I know how Dad sees things, and how he'd like things to turn out. Some aspects are appealing to me, but I'm just not ready to make that kind of commitment yet. I feel like I've got to be on my own for a little while first ... to find neutral ground to think things through ... before I can make a decision like that."

When their eyes met, Old Bill asked, "What about Lizzie?"

Jumbo's eyes widened, and his forehead wrinkled, "I hope she can wait for me ... you know, while I try to figure things out."

Old Bill shook his head, "I hope she can too. Lizzie is special, and it'd be a shame to lose her." He paused to let that sink in, then made one last run, "Look, I can see you've still got a lot of thinking to do. And having worked this farm myself, I can't claim to be neutral, any more than your father and mother can. But that doesn't mean we don't have your best interests at heart. Can you say the same about that Army recruiter? He's probably paid on commission to sign up recruits like you. My advice is don't believe a word he tells you, unless you get it in writing."

Jumbo winced, "I thought you'd be more understanding than this, grandpa. I guess I was wrong."

Old Bill exhaled heavily, "You weren't wrong. I do

understand. You're in a tough spot right now, and need to process things before making some big decisions. I respect that, I really do." He hesitated, then said, "I've got one more piece of advice, but I'll keep it to myself if you prefer."

Jumbo's eyes narrowed, then he shrugged and said, "Shoot."

Old Bill put a hand on Jumbo's shoulder, "Keep the Army thing to yourself, at least for now. In fact, never bring that up again unless you've made up your mind to do it, and there's no turning back. It's your life, and you can do what you want with it. But until you're sure, there's no point in hurting the people that love you the most."

Jumbo pulled him in for a hug, "Fair enough. I can do that."

That evening after milking, Lizzie cantered into the yard on horseback, and Jumbo took her and his younger siblings to Lake Ellen for a swim. Soon after, Old Bill drove in, and updated Overdrive and Mary on his talk with Jumbo. Midway through, Overdrive began kicking a gas can around the backyard. Mary heard Old Bill out, but then ran into the house crying. Convinced the conversation was unlikely to resume, Old Bill settled into his car, and drove back to Cascade.

❋ ❋ ❋

The next day, after morning milking and breakfast, the family deployed as it had the day before, and continued their assault on second-cutting hay. Overdrive and Mary carried-on as if they hadn't been told about the conversation between Old Bill and

Jumbo. By the end of the day, the current haymow was packed to the roof. After supper and evening milking, Jumbo and the younger boys moved the elevator to the next haymow, in preparation for the following day. Meanwhile, Overdrive and Mary, with Old Bill in the back, drove to Random Lake for a meeting at Ted's office. On the way there, not a word was spoken about Jumbo. None of them were ready to deal with it yet.

Upon arrival, they found Ted chatting in his conference room with Peter Nyenhuis, the president of Oostburg Bank, and Jason Binder, Ted's go-to freelance private investigator. After pleasantries were exchanged, Ted dialed Darkwater and put him on speaker, then got right down to business, "I know it's only been a few weeks since the bank ordeal and Darkwater's shooting, and we all could use a break from our private little war with Rachel Wolf. But unfortunately, that's not a luxury we can afford. Wolf moves fast. Only four months after we forced her to settle with Darkwater's insurance company, dozens of farmers voted to divert their milk to a phony cheese factory, as part of scam number two. You can bet she's already planning her next move. Now is our chance to put Wolf on the defensive. If we can get out in front of her, and keep her distracted, it'll buy us the time we need to collect evidence and put her away. Speed requires a dedicated team, which doesn't come cheap. Peter has some good news on that front."

Peter, eyes a-twinkle, "I've had one-on-one meetings with my peers at Verifine, Lake-to-Lake, and Golden Guernsey." During Wolf's second scheme, these three dairies experienced the troublemaker first-hand. Peter continued, "After giving them the full details about Wolf's recent shenanigans, they all agreed

Wisconsin's business climate would be better served with her behind bars. Consolidation in Wisconsin's banking industry had already been a major concern of theirs, and she's known to be a leader of that movement. But after hearing the rest ... well, that put them over the top. Between us, we've agreed to fund Ted and his team full-time until the job is done."

Ted, excited and unable to hold back, "This means I can essentially devote my entire office to this case, plus field two full-time PIs."

Mary eyebrows went up, "You've hired another PI?"

Ted winked, "Yes ... a man by the name of Darkwater Flint."

Old Bill gasped, "What? Darkwater, you're not even healthy yet, are you? And since when are you a private eye?"

Darkwater admitted over the phone, "I'm not fully recovered yet, but even in my present condition there's plenty I'm able to do."

Ted jumped in, "As for sleuthing skills, I think Darkwater's already proven his mettle. He may lack formal training and experience, but he's a natural."

Overdrive, in an earnest tone, "What about the guide business?"

Ted waved that away, "That's all been taken care of. The safest thing for Darkwater, is for people to believe he's dead. The only people up north that know otherwise are his girlfriend, Robin Thunder, the elder of his Potawatomi band, Make Wit, and Make Wit's two most trusted lieutenants, Round Wind and Cedar Root. They're all in on the secret. Darkwater, why don't you explain how it all fits together."

Darkwater, in a voice still weak but determnined, "Robin told everyone in Eagle River and on the reservation that I'd passed, and the small private service I'd requested had already taken place. She told the resort-owner my wish was for the guide business to continue, under a young Potawatomi hand-picked by me. Guiding brings in a lot of his business, so he jumped at the opportunity. Just between us, the new-guide is Robin's younger brother, and he's also in on the secret. Behind the scenes, I'll coach him on where to take the clients to fish and hunt. He'll go by my old moniker, Trophy Hound. We won't even need to change the brochure. The repeat clients will get used to it, and the new ones won't know the difference. When all this is over, Robin's brother and I will build the business large enough for the both of us."

Old Bill said, "Huh, sounds like a plan."

Mary, her arms akimbo, "But Darkwater, do you want to be a PI?"

Darkwater snorted a laugh, "Well, Wolf tried to burn me alive. When that failed, she had me shot three times. Let's just say I'm highly motivated. The sooner she's behind bars, the sooner Robin and I can start to lead a normal life."

Mary nodded, "Now that you put it that way, I can see your point."

Jason jumped in, "Trust me, Ted will keep us both busy."

Ted eyed the room, and for Darkwater's benefit, leaned into the phone and said, "I haven't even told Darkwater this yet, but there's another reason why he's the perfect fit for what we need. It'll take some time to run down the evidence, convince the proper authorities to indict Wolf, and for them to convict her. During this time, we'll need to keep Wolf on her heels and worried. Otherwise, she'll skin us alive. Up to now, Wolf hasn't had to worry about her partnership with the Potawatomi. What if Darkwater's friends were able to change that?"

As the meeting wrapped up, Ted told everyone they'd meet as-needed rather than on a regular schedule. He felt cross-communication was essential for success, and waiting for the next scheduled meeting wasn't an option, because things would move fast. Further, he expected everyone to attend in person, including Darkwater, once he was back on his feet. Who knew Ted had a crystal ball?

CHAPTER 2

Turning Up the Heat – Monday; June 21, 1965; 8:00 PM

The Evans family finished evening milking and chores in time to enjoy a pleasant Monday evening. There'd been no hay wagons to unload, so everyone had time off. Jumbo left in the cow car to hang out with Lizzie at the Flint farm. Joe drove into Plymouth in the family car, for a sheepshead game with high school friends. Kathy's boyfriend, Kirk Walcott, came for a visit, and they'd settled in front of the TV. Marie rode into Cascade with Old Bill, for a birthday party sleepover with the girls. Meanwhile, John toiled in front of the milk house, hurling his rubber ball at the strike zone marked on the wall, with a helmeted David in the batter's box.

Stranded without a car, and desiring to give Kathy and Kirk some privacy, Overdrive and Mary hung out in the machine shed. After cutting hay all day at the Courtland Farm, Overdrive had driven the Owatonna back home for service. As he greased the machine, Mary sat perched in the Owatonna's seat, holding his and hers bottles of Kingsbury beer. Between grease fittings, Overdrive would step over for a pull. All the while, they chatted about the work to be done the following day, who needed to do what, and the local goings on.

As part of that, Mary said, "Did you notice Duke was sick today? Strangest thing, he was wobbly on his feet in the morning, but got better as the day went on." Duke was the Evans's farm dog.

Kneeling to reach a grease fitting, Overdrive cracked his head when he looked up in surprise, "Ouch!" Then, after a few choice words, "You know, Mrs. Lemke told me Butch was ailing a few days ago. Asked me if some bug was going around among the dogs."

Mary exclaimed, "Really! I'll have to give her a call, and compare notes. Maybe there is something going around. Duke was definitely not himself ... slept late, wasn't hungry, and seemed unsteady-on-his-feet until afternoon."

As Overdrive worked, they continued to enjoy their beer and pass the time in pleasant conversation. After the greasing was finished, he topped up the oil, filled the gas tank, and then started replacing broken blades on the cutter bar. All was well, until it wasn't. First, came a loud thud, followed by an ear-splitting wail. Mary set the bottles down and jumped to the floor, Overdrive leapt to his feet, and together they streaked toward the commotion. Ahead, John sprinted toward David, who was rolling on the pavement in front of the milk house.

As she ran, Mary screamed, "What happened? What happened?"

When they arrived, Overdrive barked, "John, what the hell happened?"

Kneeling and trying to console his younger brother, John said over his shoulder, "Well, Davy was getting too comfortable in the batter's box … you know, no longer looking to bail on my curveball. So, I threw an inside fastball, to loosen him up a little. It kind of got away from me, and hit him."

Mary crouched, and in a tender voice, asked, "Honey, where'd you get hit?"

Still sputtering and initially unable to speak, David pointed to his left eye and managed to squeak, "Here."

Mortified, Mary sat and pulled the 10-year-old into her lap. Then, she hissed at John, "You hit him in the eye?"

John stood up, and said in a defensive tone, "Well, not on purpose, for Pete's sake! Besides, he just stood there and watched it come. Looked it right into his own face. How stupid is that? When the ball is coming for your head, you step back or duck. Everybody knows that."

Indignant, David screwed up his wet face and shouted, "Every pitch all night came at my head. You told me to stand in there, so I did! All the other ones curved over the plate."

John stood his ground and spat-back, "That's not what I said, stupid! I said stand in there IF YOU SEE THE SPIN. That means it's a curve ball. No spin, no curve … then you bail. You never listen to me!"

David cranked up a rant, "I can't see …" but Mary cut him off. "Now that's enough! Both of you!" She pushed David to his feet, stood, and held his hand, "I'm taking David in to get some ice on that eye." She pointed a finger at John, and said in a stern voice, "I'll deal with you later."

Overdrive waited until Mary was out of earshot, then in a voice almost bubbly, said, "So, the curve ball's working pretty good, huh?"

John's eyes widened in surprise. Wary, he studied his father's face for a moment. Convinced the coast was clear, he said, "Never better. Tomorrow, we'll cream them."

"Playing Batavia, right?" After John nodded, Overdrive slapped him on the back, and said, "Kick their asses, son. Never much liked Batavia."

John, using the three-finger Boy Scout oath sign, "You have my word."

Father and son walked toward the house. Overdrive asked to see John's ball, and tossed it up and caught it a few times as they went. Then, he suggested, "You know … it might be a little dark out here. I mean, for a batter to pick up the spin of these phony rubber threads. Plus, the white is all worn off. All you've got left is red rubber."

John's face lit up, "Did I just hear you offer to buy me a new ball?"

* * *

The next morning, the family resumed its quest to harvest second-cutting hay. After assigning tasks to ensure wasteful idleness among the family would be averted for another day, Overdrive mounted the Owatonna and headed to the Riley farm on the far side of Cascade, to cut more hay. At the Riley place, the buildings were abandoned, and Overdrive rented the land.

On the way over, Overdrive contemplated the various setbacks that might derail his haying tempo. Weather was always the prime suspect, but in this case the forecast was fine. Second on the list was baler reliability, which had become an issue of late. He probably should've traded it in for a new one last winter, but being a frugal man, he'd decided to squeeze another year out of it.

In addition to being frugal, Overdrive was impatient. Although happy with the John Deere dealer in Glenbeulah, the dealer served a large territory and sometimes responses to service calls were untimely. Hence, when the baler broke down, Overdrive preferred to fix it himself. This meant putting Jumbo or Mary on the Owatonna. Both were competent operators, but from experience, debris was more likely to be sucked into the machine with one of them at the wheel.

Since they'd taken first-cutting hay at the Riley farm, violent thunderstorms had passed through the area. At Riley's, large trees arched over the perimeters of the fields. Overdrive knew there'd be more downed branches than normal along the fence-lines. Since field perimeters were the high-risk areas, he decided to mow those first, for all five fields. Then, if the baler broke down, he could put Jumbo or Mary on the Owatonna without worry. Generally, field interiors could be mowed trouble-free with back-and-forth swathes, and 180-degree turns at each end.

Overdrive pulled into the first field at Riley's, and began to mow. As expected, downed branches were everywhere, and progress was slow. As he worked, Overdrive ruminated over Jumbo and his big decision. Truth be told, this mental ground had already been well plowed. In fact, he'd been chewing on it for years. After Old Bill's talk with Jumbo, Overdrive vowed to intervene no more. The ball was in Jumbo's court. Either he'd make a decision, or ask for further advice. Overdrive wasn't betting on the latter.

In some respects, Overdrive's thinking had already moved on from Jumbo. Over many years, he'd done everything he could to positively influence his oldest son's decision ... or, at least he thought he had. With the outcome still uncertain, Overdrive made the pragmatic choice. He decided to seriously consider his other children, and what could be done to make the farm appealing to them.

Joe, who'd be a high school senior in the fall, was next in line. The boy had a smart mouth, which had always gotten under Overdrive's skin. Sometimes he wondered if this unduly colored his thinking about Joe. Whether Joe could manage the herd, crops, and fleet of machinery for an operation this large, was an open question. His school grades were awful, but in all honestly, Overdrive's hadn't been much better and he'd done fine. At five-eleven and 185-pounds, Joe had the physical strength needed to endure the rigors of farming. In some areas, Overdrive had seen progress in Joe over the past year. Yet, the thought of Joe as the face of the farm still made him uncomfortable ... the way he held himself, the hat askew, the clownish expression. Maybe he's just being too nitpicky. In all honestly, he knew plenty of farmers that gave even a worse first-impression than Joe. Overdrive chalked Joe up as a definite maybe, and vowed to keep his fingers crossed.

Next, Overdrive's thoughts moved on to his oldest daughter, Kathy, who was a year behind Joe in school.

Physically, she resembled her mother in many ways ... five-eight, 130-pounds, toned and athletic. But unlike Mary, Kathy lacked the knack for stepping in wherever needed ... milking, cultivating, baling, mowing and so on. She once dissolved into the state of hysteria over the sight of a harmless dead garden snake sticking out of a hay bale. She'd had similar reactions to flies, spiders, mice, rats, and shit-splatter ... all hard to avoid on a dairy farm. For these reasons, Overdrive had all but dismissed Kathy as a possible successor on the farm. But that all changed when her boyfriend, Kirk Walcott, entered the picture.

Kirk had spent his childhood working summers on his grandpa's farm. Whenever he came to visit Kathy, it's as if he's looking for ways to help out. Unless Overdrive was mistaken, Kirk had both the skills and the interest to be a farmer. Kathy alone may not be an option, but the duo of Kathy and Kirk might be. According to Mary, Kathy would be great at running the house, garden, and orchard. Based on her grades, she'd probably be able to handle the books, too. Admittedly, her various aversions would leave Kirk shorthanded on the farm. But the thing is, Kirk and Joe got along well. With Joe as a hired hand, it could work.

✳ ✳ ✳

As forecast, the weather held through the next several days, and the Evans family made steady progress on the hay, garden, orchard, and everything else. On Thursday afternoon Ted's office called, informing them of a meeting in Random Lake that evening. After supper Old Bill begged off, humbly suggesting he didn't have much to offer. Overdrive was surprised, but let it pass.

After evening milking, Overdrive and Mary left for Random Lake. On the way, Overdrive filled Mary in on his latest farm succession scenarios. Always the good wife, Mary held her tongue and heard him out. They'd already pulled to a stop in Ted's parking lot, by the time he finished. On the way inside, Mary elbowed her big oaf of a husband, and said in a teasing tone, "James, you're not serious, are you? I mean ... Kathy and Kirk hardly know each other. And here you are, fantasizing about them taking over the farm. Sounds a little desperate to me."

As he opened the door, Overdrive winked, "It never hurts to think ahead."

A moment later, they joined Ted, Peter, and Jason in the conference room. Darkwater was already on the line. After the niceties, Ted jumped in, "I'd like to spend a few moments to get everyone on the same page. As you recall, our goal is to put Wolf behind bars. To do that, we'll need to identify specific crimes, and tie them to her. We know her primary motive is the casino, which makes the Evans farm a must-have. Her first run at the farm was done carefully. Although underhanded, no laws were broken until she feared Darkwater would blow the deal, and lashed out to kill him. Wolf's second run, trying to take down a bank to get to the farm, was bolder. Even more bold, was her second attempt on Darkwater's life. That wasn't even part of the scheme, it was payback. This tells us something important about Wolf. She's so vengeful, it can make her reckless. We might be able to use that against her down the line."

Peter picked up the thread, "If I understand

correctly, you think we might be able to bait Wolf, to make her do something rash in the future. But in the meantime, we focus on three crimes ... two attempted murders and conspiracy."

Ted nodded, "Exactly. And if she's reckless, those future crimes might be easier to prove."

Overdrive frowned and said, "I hear lots of talk about crimes, but no mention of the milk stolen from all of us farmers. Isn't milk theft a crime?"

Ted turned to face him, "It is, but it's not a crime committed by Wolf. We think the mob stole the milk."

Forehead wrinkled, Mary said, "But they were part of the conspiracy, weren't they?"

Ted put his elbows on the table, and said, "Yes, they were. But remember, our goal is to put Wolf behind bars. To have any chance, we need to stay focused. Bringing the mob to justice is beyond our means. Trust me on that." There was strong sympathy in the room for the victims of the milk heist, but after a few minutes of back and forth, everyone came around to Ted's way of thinking.

Ted sat back, "Okay, I'm glad we all finally agree on scope. Now let's move on to progress, there's been a lot of it since the last meeting. Let's start with the conspiracy." Ted got up and wheeled his large chalk board to the head of the table. Then, he continued "This gets a little complicated, so let me use this to help explain. Our working theory is that Wolf built and led the conspiracy. So, she's the circle in the middle labeled 'RW'. Now, I show a line going from RW, down to this box labeled 'BB aka AS', which stands for Bert Baker, alias Al Stone. This other line goes down to another box labeled 'EB', which stands for Ernie Baker, Bert's brother.

As part of Wolf's conspiracy, *BB aka AS* posed as an NFO roaming rep. He offered his help to the Sheboygan County NFO Chapter, and was welcomed into the fold on the basis of *EB*'s phony reference. Once inside, he recruited dozens of dairy farmers into the chapter, most having loans at Oostburg Bank. The chapter wanted to negotiate a higher milk price with Verifine, by temporarily diverting milk away from Verifine, to somewhere else. *BB aka AS* manipulated the chapter into diverting the milk to Papini Cheese LLC, which turned out to be a front for the mob. That's shown by this line going up from the *RW* circle to the box labeled '*PC LLC*'. There was never any attempt to make cheese from the milk delivered to *PC LLC*. Instead, the milk was hauled away to God knows where, by a mob-owned trucking company, named ABC Milk Hauling LLC. That's represented by this other line going up from the *RW* circle to the box labeled '*ABC LLC*'. Note, I also have a third line going down from the *RW* circle to a box with a question mark in it. Somehow two Oostburg Bank lists fell into Wolf's hands, and we don't know who made that happen. One, was dairy farmers having loans there, which we believe was used by *BB aka AS* to target his NFO new-member recruiting. The other, was the bank's shareholders, which we believe Wolf herself used to send an anonymous letter, and defeat the bank's attempt to raise capital through an assessment. The focus of our conspiracy investigation is on the *RW* circle in the middle, and the three boxes below it. Everything above the *RW* circle, we think is the mob. For those, we plan to do the absolute minimum required to verify it's the mob, and then back off. Does anybody have any questions?"

After a few minutes of questions and answers, Ted said, "Jason, why don't you start with the two boxes that have to do with Bert and Ernie Baker, and give us a summary of what's been learned so far?"

Jason Binder, Ted's go-to PI, was tall and slender with close-cropped brown hair. His wire-rimmed spectacles and dress gave the impression of a farm-country accountant, as much at home in a client's barn as behind a desk. From looking at him, you'd never guess he's ex-FBI. Legend has it he quit because wearing a suit and tie wasn't his thing. In precise clipped language, Jason said, "Be my pleasure. I returned to the Baker farm near Campbellsport, but this time Darkwater came along in his own car. When last there, I'd found a great stakeout spot on the ridge across the road. With Darkwater setup on the ridge, I knocked on the farmhouse door and Ernie answered. I could tell he was spooked, but he had the presence of mind to stick with the same lies he'd told me before. When I asked if he knew where Al Stone was, he referred me to the NFO. He claimed he hadn't heard from Al, since the NFO reassigned him. Then, when I switched tactics and asked to see Bert, he went all bug-eyed and began to twitch. Things went south from there, and he ordered me off the property. After I left, Darkwater continued the stakeout." He leaned toward the speaker phone and said in a loud voice, "Darkwater, why don't you pick it up from there?"

Darkwater, paused to collect his thoughts, then said, "Our plan all along had been for me to keep watching the Baker place, after Jason finished his pop-in visit. Everything Jason just said ... I witnessed ... using the binoculars. Within a few hours of Jason leaving, I had great photos of Bert and Ernie together in the yard. That telephoto lens on Jason's camera is unbelievable. The images are crystal clear. You can even see the worry on their faces."

Mary, impressed, "Well done, but I hope you're not overdoing it."

Darkwater chuckled, "Thanks, Mary, but I'm fine. I'll mend faster if I'm out and about, rather than lying around in bed."

After some thought, Overdrive suggested, "With those photos, dozens of farmers will be able to identify Bert Baker as the man they know as Al Stone."

Ted agreed, "That's exactly right." Then, he gestured to Jason, and said, "Go ahead and check off the box on Papini for us."

Jason nodded, consulted his notes, and said, "Okay, so my next task was to find and brace Vito Papini. I started my search in Kenosha County, because it came out at last February's Sheboygan County NFO meeting that he originated from there. Finding his house was no problem. I watched the place long enough to know he was home, then went to the door. At first, he tried to blow me off. But when that failed, his eyes started darting all around … you know, as if concerned to be seen with me. He sent me around back to the fenced yard, and joined me there. The man was scared shitless … pale, sweaty, jumpy. I couldn't get anything out of him. Instead, he referred me to a Milwaukee-based attorney. My local sources say the lawyer represents the Milwaukee arm of the Chicago mob."

From there, Ted picked up the story, "Since we're on the topic of the mob, let me check off the box for ABC Milk Hauling LLC. As you recall, after Papini abruptly closed his plant in May, ABC made the rounds to affected farmers, and offered to haul their milk to Chicago-area processors. There wasn't much interest at the time, but yesterday I posed as one of those farmers, and called ABC to say that I'd reconsidered. After several transfers, a surly guy got on the line to say that ABC no longer operated that far north. Afterword, under the same guise, I called all the big-name Chicago beverage milk processors, and asked if their haulers would make pickups in Sheboygan County, Wisconsin. Every processor identified ABC as their sole hauler, and referred me back to them. This reminded me of something our NFO friend, Otto Schwartz, said a few months back when he was helping us fend off the bank takeover. Just to be sure, I called Otto to verify. According to him, ABC is mob-run, and has Chicago-area hauling monopolies from farm-to-processor, and processor-to-supermarket."

Overdrive, with anger in his voice, "Well, that figures. Chicago haulers set the benchmark price for haulers throughout the region."

Mary, palm to forehead, "That's right. Our haulers always point to Chicago to justify how much they charge. No wonder we can't get a fair price for raw milk. When the middle man gets more, there's less leftover for the farmer."

In a no-nonsense voice, Ted redirected, "I hear you both, but let's stay on track, okay? We've checked off the Papini and ABC boxes. Both are the mob, not Wolf. We're not in a position to right all the world's wrongs, so let all that go."

Peter, mid-epiphany, "Reading between the lines ... is the theory then, that Wolf somehow hooked the

Milwaukee arm of the Chicago mob into her conspiracy? And then the mob brought Papini and ABC to the party?"

Ted, smiled at the on-point remark, "That's what I think, yes. And how she did it is no big secret. Given the mob's role in the Chicago milk markets, the opportunity to expand north would've appealed to them. And even if a permanent expansion north failed, they'd still bag a tidy sum from the one-off milk heist."

Still red-faced, Overdrive muttered, "Those bastards."

Ted pivoted in his direction, "James, I understand your frustration. I get it, but stay with me, okay?" When Overdrive nodded, he pressed forward, "Like I said at the chalk board, there's at least one more co-conspirator out there we haven't discovered yet. After Bert Baker, aka Al Stone, infiltrated the Sheboygan County NFO, he managed to recruit dozens of new dairy farmers into the organization. Most every new member had a loan at Oostburg Bank. The odds of that happening are one in a million. Bert must've had a list of names to go by. In addition, we believe Peter's shareholder list fell into Wolf's hands, and she used it to send an anonymous letter to skuttle his capital raising effort. Whoever gave Wolf those lists, is another co-conspirator."

Peter exhaled heavily, "I've been fretting over that one. I hope there isn't a leak at the bank."

Ted shrugged, "That's one possibility, but there're others too, so don't go jumping to conclusions."

Peter nodded, "Fair enough."

After consulting his agenda, Ted said, "Anyway, we've almost covered everything, but there's progress on one last front you all should be aware of. Darkwater, give us the short version of what's happening up north."

Darkwater, in an upbeat tone, "Well, after the stake out, Ted sent me back to my hidey hole near Eagle River. From there, I've been coaching the new Trophy Hound, Robin's brother, on the guide business. Word is, I'm not even missed. Robin checked in with the resort owner, and he says the guide business is almost back to normal."

Mary said warmly, "That's great news, Darkwater. It really is."

Darkwater, buoyant, "Maybe so, but the rest is even better. At Ted's urging, I had a long talk with Make Wit … you know, my Potawatomi band's elder. In the ten months since the tribe partnered with Wolf to develop a casino, absolutely nothing's happened. There'd already been grumblings among the tribe, so Make Wit was open to the idea of amplifying that discontent. Since our conversation, he's dropped a few hints here and there, and the idea of abandoning Wolf and seeking another casino partner has spread like wildfire. In fact, the elder of the tribe's largest band, Eternal Oak, has volunteered to serve as the pitchman, if and when this gets taken to tribal council. Just to be clear, they're talking about not only dropping Wolf, but switching to a different casino location. A working group has been established, so it sounds pretty serious."

Ted picked up his pen, "Darkwater, tell me when tribal council meets next, so I get it in my notes."

After some rustling at the other end of the line, Darkwater said, "Well … let's see … yeah, here it is. The next council is Tuesday July 13th at 6:30 PM."

Ted, thinking out loud, "It'd be good if we had an insider on the working group. Darkwater, please see if Make Wit can arrange for someone he trusts, to be a member. With an insider, we might be able to help. For one, we'd be able to make sure the working group understands the importance of secrecy, including staying away from tribal council until after everything is nailed down. If it's still half-baked when Wolf finds out, she'll go to war and it'll never happen. Also, if they've picked an alternate site, we might be able to hook them up with a nearby developer ... you know, help speed things along." The room exploded in high-spirited speculation for another ten minutes or so. As the meeting began to break up, Ted hinted he may be seeing them again in a few days.

CHAPTER 3

Pressing the Advantage – Friday; June 25, 1965; 6:30 PM

For a tween growing up a mile from nowhere, Marie was a fast-talking schemer. She'd gotten an A+ on her spring semester's family history project, presumably by picking grandpa's brain. After relentless badgering, Marie successfully negotiated with Mary continued over-the-summer sessions with gramps, to set her up for another A in the coming school year. Consequently, it became customary to invite Old Bill to stay for supper on Fridays, so Marie could catch a ride with him to Cascade after she'd finished the dishes.

Under that cover, Marie spent many a Friday evening walking the streets of Cascade with friends, meeting boys at the softball games in the park, and generally having a good time. If she didn't have a sleepover arranged, parents of friends would give her a ride home, or Overdrive, Mary, or an older sibling would come and get her.

Marie lived for these outings. Without them, she wouldn't have scored her first kiss, learned where the boys that interested her lived, or been privy to the latest village gossip. As thrilling as these experiences were for a girl her age, sometimes the most excitement came from actually spending time with grandpa. On the sly, he'd been including her in bridges with the ancestors. Motivated by these experiences, she'd put in the work and become fluent in Welsh. Recently, Old Bill had begun to teach her how to open and close the bridge, all by herself. Tonight, she was going solo for the first time ever. She couldn't wait!

On the drive into town, Old Bill said, "When we get to the shack, I'll come in with you, but only to observe. Go ahead and prepare the place for the bridge. When you think you're finished, let me know. Only then, will I speak. Do you understand?"

Jittery with excitement, Marie said, "Yes, I understand."

Old Bill nodded, "Good … good. Now, if I find something isn't right, I'll correct you. Then you'll put everything back the way it was, and we'll go back outside. When we re-enter, you'll try again. It's important that you remember everything, and do it just so. It may take a few times, so don't fret if you're not perfect right off the bat."

After a mumbled, "Okay," Marie began to visualize each necessary step.

As he drove, Old Bill risked a quick glance in her direction, "When you've got it down pat, I'll walk down to the Opera House to play some sheepshead. When you're done, put everything back the way it was, and come get me."

To this, Marie nodded absently as she replayed the ritual in her mind. To let her concentrate, Old Bill drove the rest of the way in silence. She was a bright girl, and he knew she'd do fine. Learning Welsh was the hard part, and she'd done that faster than he had. Upon arrival, they did exactly as Old Bill had instructed. Marie nailed it on the first try, and Old Bill went off to play cards.

Alone in grandpa's shack, Marie suddenly felt lost. Her mind blanked. She broke into a sweat, and felt her breathing quicken and heart race. Struggling to regain her grip, Marie's eyes darted around the darkened shack, hoping for something … anything … to remind her what to do. Finally, the dancing shadows caused by the dim candle light, captured her attention. As she continued to watch them, she found them entertaining in some ways, soothing in others.

Now relaxed, her roving eyes fell on the bottle of Welsch liquor, *Drysien Gwyllt*, and instantly she remembered what to do. She poured herself a jigger. Then, alternately sipped, and whispered the Welsh phrase *'a fo ben, bid bont'*, which meant *if you want to be a leader, be a bridge*. Within a minute, the bridge to the Welsh ancestors was opened.

Timidly, and with her fingers crossed, Marie began to speak in Welsh. After what felt like an eternity, she heard what would roughly translate to, "Marie, is that you? Where's that no-good grandpa of yours? Out carousing and gambling again, I'll wager. Never could keep that old coot home on a Friday night."

Eyes bulging, Marie asked, "Grandma, is that you?"

Chatter came back across the bridge, "Well, of course it is honey. Who else would it be? Hey gang, we've been summoned by Marie all by herself."

The isolated chatter grew to a rumble. As voices

talked over each other, Marie struggled to sort it all out. Here and there she caught snippets ... well I'll be, congratulations, welcome to crazy town, and so on. As the clamor subsided, grandma became more insistent about getting an answer to Old Bill's whereabouts.

Trying to be respectful to all concerned, Marie said meekly in Welsh, "I'm sorry, but I don't feel comfortable tattling on grandpa. Can I ask you some questions instead? I know that two William Evanses came to America, and settled in Sheboygan County. Who were the grandparents of William-the-elder?"

* * *

On the surface, the daily rhythms on the Evans farm appeared normal for late June ... haying, milking, and caring for the livestock, garden and orchard. But for Overdrive, internal machinations were competing for his attention. What weighed most heavily on his mind were the life choices that weren't his to make, but rather his children's. Although advance knowledge of what they might decide would be nice, but he wasn't a fool, and realized the impossibility of such a thing. Instead, he settled for becoming a more vigilant observer of his oldest children. He hoped paying more attention to their words, facial expressions, and body language might help him tease out their underlying thoughts.

Before long, Overdrive had already noticed something different in the way Jumbo carried himself. His oldest son used to be a prankster. For example, he used to enjoy giving Joe a vice-grip handshake, just to hear him squeal. Gathering rotten apples from the orchard, and chucking them at John and David just to see them flee, used to be a favorite pass time. These behaviors had been missing lately. Also missing, were the macho '*look what I can do*' displays. Things like carrying two bales of hay in each hand, or hefting a hundred-pound sack of grain on each shoulder. He used to enjoy showing off his extraordinary strength, but no more.

With Marie gone to Cascade and the milking done, Overdrive was curious what the rest of the kids had planned on a Friday evening. Soon he heard hoof beats pounding in the distance, which told him Lizzie would soon canter into the yard. Without fail, she always ended up in the orchard, where Jumbo would join her. Overdrive wanted to use the opportunity to observe them together, without being too obvious about it. He figured his best bet was to watch while servicing the tractor and baler. To make that possible, he quickly relocated them from the gas pump, to a spot in the backyard with an unobstructed view of the orchard. By the time Lizzie arrived, he was busy installing another spool of baling twine. She waved and flashed a smile on her way past, then dropped into a trot and headed to the orchard.

Overdrive watched with a combination of quick glances and peripheral vision. Jumbo had already been in the orchard, and turned back toward Lizzie as she entered. Overdrive was in the background, and could see his face clearly. It didn't light up at the sight of her, like it usually did. Though too far away to hear, Overdrive could tell their talk was less animated than normal. Their typical playfulness seemed missing. In their normal routine, Jumbo would bend over and lock the fingers of both hands together, making a place for

Lizzie to step up into. Then, he'd straighten up and raise his arms, elevating her to pick apples for the horse. She'd invariably lose her balance and scream, and he'd try to crab back under her. If that didn't work ... and it never did for long ... he'd remove a hand from underneath and pull her in before she fell. Overdrive thought the whole routine was a ploy to provide cover for what they really wanted, which was to touch each other. But tonight, there's none of that. Instead, an awkward stiffness replaced their normal ease and joy. It didn't take a genius to figure out why. Jumbo must've told her he's thinking of joining the Army.

Overdrive was still muttering to himself at the thought, when Kirk drove up the driveway and waved hello. As he swiveled his head to follow Kirk's car into the backyard, Joe came into view, walking around the end of the barn. The image was classic Joe ... silly smirk, rosy cheeks, ball-cap bill pointing up and left like a blind bird-dog, saggy-necked t-shirt, dirty jeans, and shit-kicker boots shuffling along in a duck-footed gait. Overdrive couldn't help but groan at the thought that this might someday be the face of the Evans farm. Though done servicing the baler, he pretended to have more to do. Kirk and Joe were about to greet each other, and he wanted a good look at how that went.

Overdrive caught side views of the boys as they shook hands and began to chat. They both seemed genuinely happy to see each other. To provide cover as he spied on the boys, Overdrive began replacing perfectly-fine cutter guards and sneaking the old ones back into the baler's spare parts crib. He was close enough to catch bits and pieces of what was said ... there's a hay wagon to unload ... came just in time ...

give me a second to put on my boots and gloves ... and so on. About then, the farmhouse's back door slammed, and Kathy smiled and waved as she fast-walked in Kirk's direction. After a hug, the three of them stood in a circle and chatted, smiles all around. Suggestions were made and accepted. Shortly, the three of them walked back behind the barn. Apparently, Kathy was fine with watching the boys finish unloading a wagon before having some quality time with Kirk. May wonders never cease.

* * *

Saturday just before noon, Ted's office manager called to say Overdrive and Mary were needed at Ted's office that evening for a meeting. Milking ran late, causing them to rush through a quick wash-up and change of clothes. Overdrive drove with a lead foot to Random Lake, but couldn't make up the time. When they walked into Ted's conference room, a breathless Mary said, "Sorry we're late."

Ted said, "No problem." But then betrayed his impatience, by adding hastily, "Okay, Darkwater's on speaker, and everyone's finally here on this end, so let's get going. Tonight, we'll start with Wolf's source for the two lists. Obviously, several of Peter's employees had access to the outstanding loan list and the shareholder list. However, this data is also filed annually with the banking division of the Wisconsin Department of Financial Institutions. So, the leak could've been from either the bank or in the banking division. We pursued both."

Peter jumped in, "I've got to say, the prospect of

investigating my own employees had me worried sick. We're a small shop in a small town. If something had gone wrong, it could've destroyed morale or the community's trust in us. We really tore our hair out on how to go about it."

Interest peeked, Overdrive asked, "What'd you come up with?"

Peter breathed deeply, then said, "Well, our Human Resources or HR is very informal. I mean, we don't even have job descriptions. Our plan was to have Jason pose as an HR consultant hired by me. He'd interview employees about their duties, and then write up job descriptions. This'd give him the cover to ask about shareholder and client loan lists, and what they knew about them. I'm sure Jason would've done fine, but fortunately he never had to try."

Jason picked up the thread, "As luck would have it, we found our man at the banking division before the interviews kicked off. Trust me, I'm as happy as Peter about that. I did lots of things at the FBI, but HR wasn't one of them."

A few half-laughs echoed through the room, then Mary asked, "How'd you find the guy at the banking division?"

Ted fielded that, "With Wolf in Fondy and the banking division in Madison, it seemed logical for communications to be by phone. But searching phone records is an onerous job, so we had to narrow the time window. To simplify things, we only considered the dairy farmer loan list first. Wolf became aware her first run at the farm failed on September 29th of last year. That's when we served her with Darkwater's insurance settlement offer. She wouldn't start plotting a new scam before then, so that was our begin-date. On the tail end, Bert Baker ... aka Al Stone ... needed the list before January 5th. That's when he first showed up at an NFO meeting, and right after, began recruiting new members. Jason searched for calls between those dates from Wolf's home to the banking division, or vice versa. Surprisingly, there were none."

Overdrive harrumphed, "Maybe Wolf doesn't work from home."

Jason responded, "I had the same thought. So, to test that theory, I searched her phone records for last September, when the hunt was on for Darkwater in Forest County. There'd been multiple calls, both incoming and outbound, between her home and pay phones in Wabeno and Crandon. She goes in to her bank on occasion for legit reasons, but Wolf does her dirty work from home."

Ted chimed in, "She'd be a fool to do it any other way, it'd jeopardize her regional bank."

Mary asked, "The banking division has dozens of numbers, right? Checking them all must've taken forever. You did all that, and still came up empty?"

Jason corrected her, "Actually, the entire banking division has one main number, with extensions for individual staff members. It wasn't so bad, but I did come up empty."

Ted added, "Obviously, we were very disappointed. Who knows, maybe Wolf had driven to Madison that one time. But we still believed in the underlying theory that most communications would be by phone. In fact, if somebody like Wolf had an insider at the banking division, chances are, she'd use that person on a regular basis. That's why Jason looked for later calls."

In tag-team fashion, Jason continued, "I found one on May 5th, originated from Wolf's home, to the banking division. The phone company doesn't record the extension, but the receptionists at the banking division ... wonderful civil servants that they are ... keep excellent logs, and were happy to share them. The extension belonged to a Ryan Weiser."

Ted admitted, "May 5th, by the way, lines up nicely with when Wolf would've needed the shareholder list. But at that point, we still didn't know how Wolf got the loan list before January 5th. But if Wolf and an insider worked together regularly, it's possible they'd become familiar ... perhaps familiar enough to use Weiser's home phone. From a criminal's point of view, this might even be safer. It was a long shot, but Jason looked into it anyway."

Jason continued, "The Madison area phone directories included a half dozen listings for people named Ryan Weiser or R. Weiser. The one in Sun Prairie received a call from Wolf's house on Saturday, December 4th ... bingo."

Peter chuckled, "Jason's *bingo* came the day before his interviews with my staff were to begin. I think he's actually trying to give me cardiac arrest."

Jason, in a comic tone, "No-no, that wasn't my intent. It's just that you can't rush perfection. At least, that's what the lab rats at the FBI always said."

Ted leaned toward the phone, "Darkwater, are you still on the line?"

Darkwater piped up, "I'm here, listening and learning from the masters."

Ted, dispensing unusual praise, "Speaking of

masters, why don't you tell us about the shit storm brewing up north."

Putting a little gravel in his voice, Darkwater said, "Don't mind if I do. Make Wit pulled some strings, and the group developing the alternative casino plan was expanded to include one of his most trusted men, Cedar Root. The intel coming back has been interesting. As it turns out, Wolf's idea of placing a casino on sacred lands had been distasteful to many elders, not just Make Wit. The others only went along because Long Body insisted it was the fastest route out of poverty. Now they know better. The group has already revisited land parcels with historic ties to the tribe, and picked one inside Milwaukee's city limits. Most gamblers are from Chicago and Milwaukee, and the new site is more convenient for them. The tribe needs a new developer, obviously, and we were able to provide some hot prospects. Ted, I'm a little sketchy on how that happened, can you help me out?"

Ted, in a matter-of-fact tone, "Absolutely. As you recall, approvals from two Wisconsin state agencies are required before a casino can move forward. Last year, while investigating Rachel's casino scheme, I established contacts with both. I called them, and learned some interesting news. Not a single casino proposal has come forward since the law went into effect, and they're extremely disappointed. So much so, that they've organized an educational conference for developers and tribes, to try to gin up some business. Advance registration is open, and the conference happens next week. When I told them I'm trying to pair a tribe with a developer, they offered to send me the conference brochure and advanced registrants list.

Honest to God, I didn't even need to ask! Make Wit received a copy by courier earlier today."

Darkwater jumped in, "The tribe's working group was completely blindsided. The registrants list included a few people from Wolf's outfit, Development Partners, but not a single Potawatomi. Long Body never told the other elders about the conference, and must've decided on his own to delegate the whole thing to Wolf. The working group is operating nonstop now. They've reached out to every developer on the registrants list operating in the Milwaukee area. The first face-to-face interview happened today, and the rest are scheduled over the next few days. These are all being conducted in strict secrecy, in a hotel room in Milwaukee. If all goes well, they'll be teamed with a developer in time for the conference. Then it becomes a matter of how quickly the developer can lock up land, and make a pitch to tribal council."

The room exploded in a chorus of hopeful theories, but Ted raised his voice to silence the fracas, "People … people … let's not get too carried away here. The working group needs to ink a deal with a developer, and the developer needs to acquire the land. These kinds of things can take time. In the meantime, it'd be a horrible mistake for anything to be said publicly about any of this. If Wolf finds out before it's a done deal, she'll find a way to muck it up."

Intended or not, Ted's comments sucked all the oxygen out of the room. After an awkward silence, Overdrive said tentatively, "I'm all for caution. If the tribe has a chance to drop Wolf and switch sites, I pray they don't blow it. Once the casino is targeted to another site, our farm is off the hook."

Mary countered, "Well, the farm would no-longer be needed for a casino. But with Wolf still free, who's to say she wouldn't keep coming for it anyway. The woman is crazy."

Darkwater jumped in, "I could see her doing that. She came after me that second time, just to settle a score. She might feel the same way about the farm."

Seeing an opportunity to get the conversation back on track, Ted said, "These are all good points. We won't be fully in the clear until Rachel is behind bars." Then, after a pause, "Darkwater, why don't you tell us the rest."

Peter, surprise in his voice, "There's more?"

Darkwater, in a humble tone, "Well, a little bit. After the fire, Robin and I took extreme precautions. We lived like fugitives, yet somehow Wolf found me and nearly had me killed. On the theory that the tribe may've helped, Make Wit sent Round Wind to make discrete inquiries among the tribe. Most thought I'd disappeared, with or without the insurance money, or had died. But a few heard another rumor ... that I'd continued as a guide in Eagle River, and was living nearby. This rumor was traced to an overheard conversation between several of Long Body's insiders."

Mary gasped, "You think Long Body's people found you?"

Overdrive muttered, "What an asshole."

Darkwater agreed, "Yeah, it looks that way. After Round Wind reported back, Make Wit decided to have a careful conversation directly with Long Body. When asked what'd become of me, Make Wit said the body language gave him away. Of course, Long Body claimed I hadn't been seen since the fire, at least as far as he knew.

But Make Wit walked away certain that he'd given up a member of his own tribe."

CHAPTER 4

Rachel's Short-Lived Celebration –
Wednesday; June 9, 1965; 9:00 AM

Rachel awoke to find Rose already up, probably tending to Jake. As she yawned and stretched, she turned sideways and caught a glimpse of the bedside clock. Wow, she'd slept in. Rolling to her back, she stretched once more and stilled. She felt gloriously well rested, but it was more than that. Her entire life would be back on track by the end of the day. Darkwater Flint … dearly departed. Oostburg Bank … hers. The Evans farm … back in her grasp. The Headwaters of the Milwaukee River Casino … soon to be breaking ground.

Rachel imagined herself floating in the clouds, surveying the little people below, doing her bidding whether they knew it or not. The tingles started, and her lips curled into a faint smile. She could literally feel her glands pump the happy-face chemicals into her bloodstream. Her heart quickened, and sent the elixir coursing throughout her body. Soon, the old familiar thrum began to build. Then, as if flicked on by a switch, came the other-worldly senses. Rachel caught a whiff of her mate's delicious scent, and heard the faint patter of her feet. Rose was coming. What had been a faint smile, blossomed to smolder.

Anticipation grew, as Rachel observed the knob turn and the door swing gently open. With stealth so as not to disturb, Rose peaked around the door. Seeing motion, she began to say, "Well, good morning sleepy h...", but lost audio upon registering the expression on Rachel's face. "Oh my", was all she managed before Rachel was on her.

In an instant, Rose was up against the wall, nightgown up and off. Rachel growled, "I've been waiting for you!"

Rose protested, "Rachel, stop! Jake is still in his high chair!"

As her hands went everywhere, Rachel said, "Well, then you'd better get to work on mommy, because mommy doesn't want to keep her little man waiting."

Rose blushed and giggled, "Yes ma'am. Any particular requests?"

Rachel groaned, "Just do me everywhere. Trust me, it won't take long."

Afterward, a humming Rose went off to fix breakfast. Meanwhile Rachel made a quick pit stop in the bathroom, and then stepped into the study to call Ryan Weiser at the banking division. She knew she'd put in the winning bid for Oostburg Bank, but direct verification never hurt. Ryan was away from his desk. She considered leaving a message, but thought better of it. Instead, she made a mental note to call again later.

When a disheveled Rachel walked into the kitchen, she was greeted by Jake's most brilliant smile.

But then he noticed her bed-head, and the smile dissolved into a belly-laugh, which melted her heart. As she cooed to her little man, it occurred to Rachel that today just might be the best day of her life. After breakfast, she spent the rest of the morning in domestic bliss with Jake and Rose. At midday, Rose served an exquisite lunch on the patio.

✽ ✽ ✽

After lunch, Rachel was about to enter her study when the phone rang. With a few quick steps she caught it on the second ring, "Hello."

Vince, high on adrenalin, "Rachel, it's Vince. I just got word. Darkwater Flint is a dead man!"

Rachel pounded her fist on the desk, "Y-y-y-e-e-e-s-s-s! Hallelujah baby!" She covered the receiver and let out a roar, then said in a giddy voice, "Details. Give me details."

Vince gushed, "Well, after they found him, Long Body's boys studied his routines from a safe distance. Apparently, before taking clients out fishing, he always went to the same place to collect live bait. The bait run was to a little dead-end cove. The place was remote, perfect for an ambush. Phil sent a pair of shooters north yesterday. Not goombahs, but native Wisconsin boys who knew their way around boats, outboards, and deer rifles. Today, while Flint was out with his morning clients, Long Body's boys led the shooters to the kill-spot. They planned their ambush, then spent the rest of the morning lying in wait. About 11:15 AM Flint put-putted into the cove in a small boat. The first shot put him in the water. Then they motored over, and pumped a few more into him for good measure. Afterward, they hid his boat in a cattail marsh, hung around long enough to make sure he was dead, and then got the hell out of Dodge."

Rachel savored every word, "I love it. Kudos to Phil's boys." Then, a spasm of joy overtook her, shrieks and all. When the moment passed, she said, "As you can tell, I'm in a celebratory mood. I've arranged a sitter for Jake, and booked a suite for Rose and I tonight, at the Pfister Hotel in Milwaukee. She's never been there, and I owe her big time for putting up with me through all this. But the thing is, Rose lives on toddler time. She'll probably be nodding off before we finish dinner. There's a great bar on the 23rd floor, why don't you and Phil join me there after Rose retires? I know it's short notice, but the view of the city and Lake Michigan is stunning. It'll be fun. Phil and I can gloat over our mutual good fortune, and it's all on me"

Vince, in a wolfish tone, "Hey, I've been to that place. You wouldn't believe the ladies that hang out there … they make one's imagination run wild. I'll call Phil, and get back to you."

Rachel, in a generous mood, "You do that. And if those are working girls up there, that's on me too."

Vince, pumped, "Well, that does it. Phil or no Phil, I'll be there." Within an hour after the call, Vince jingled back to say Phil would be honored to attend.

❋ ❋ ❋

The babysitter arrived early afternoon. While Rose spent an hour getting her and Jake acquainted, and showing her where everything was, Rachel went to the study to call Long Body. With glee, she jokingly introduced herself as the new controlling owner of Oostburg Bank. Then, she bragged the Evans farm would be next, and filled him in on Darkwater's demise. Afterward, she pressed Long Body on a lingering issue from their previous conversation.

Two weeks back, they'd both received notifications from the state about an upcoming conference on June 29th. Its goal was to motivate proposals for new state-authorized Indian reservations with gaming. Given the indefinite delay in Rachel's Headwaters-located casino, Long Body wanted to convene a special session of tribal council to revisit the Potawatomi tribe's path forward. He felt the conference provided an opportunity for the tribe to move forward with somebody else, and they couldn't afford to pass it up.

Rachel, of course, had blown a gasket at the suggestion. She managed to convince him to keep his mouth shut, at least until her bank-takeover venture played out. Well, it'd not only played out, but to perfection. With the Headwaters roadblocks seemingly cleared, Long Body again felt comfortable sticking with Rachel. He agreed to keep the conference to himself, and let Rachel's firm, Development Partners LLC, handle the event for both of them. With the deal back on, Rachel turned on the charm and ended the call quickly to keep it that way.

Relief washed over her, and Rachel savored it for a moment. Yes, the call had run long, but what a heavenly outcome. The reverie evaporated with a glance at her watch. Jolted into action, she hastily threw together an overnight bag, dressed, and put on her makeup. Shortly after, Jake burst into tears at the abruptness of their good-byes and hugs.

As she and Rose were running out the door to the garage, Rachel stopped and slapped her forehead. Damn it, she hadn't called Weiser back! Shoes off, she sprinted to the study and made the call, only to find him once more away from his desk. After a few choice words, Rachel eyed her watch and bit her lip. She and Rose needed to hit the road now, or they'd miss their dinner reservation. After a moment of indecision, Rachel cussed her way to the garage on the dead run. There, she found the bags already in the trunk, the garage door open, and Rose holding her shoes by the driver's side door.

They hadn't been on the road for more than a few miles before Rachel noticed something different about Rose. She was literally bouncing in her seat, prattling on about this and that, laughing, and joking. Rachel wasn't sure what to make of it. Had she been drinking, popped a pill, what? Then Rose said something that clicked, and Rachel understood. Poor Rose hadn't been away overnight since Jake came home from the hospital. She's not drunk or doped up, it's just a bad case of jail break fever. Rachel tried to observe in silent amusement, but found it contagious. Rose was always a distraction, but when like this, holy cow! Rachel had to fight off the urge to pull over and ... well, you know.

By the time they arrived at the Pfister Hotel, Rose had settled somewhat. At check-in, she was wide-eyed at the extravagant lobby and impressed when the porter grabbed their bags and led the way to the room. He opened the door and made motions to unpack, but Rachel held out a tip and motioned him to scram. Rose stood there silently, soft-warm-flushed and wearing that irresistible half-pout. After eying her watch, Rachel silently mouthed *'there's time'*. Shortly, everything they wore hit the floor, and they tumbled into bed. Afterward, they freshened up, donned their evening clothes, and made their way to the restaurant just in time.

Over dinner, Rose talked nonstop about, well, you name it ... the beauty of the setting, the ambiance, the classy people at the other tables, the wonderful waiter, the quality of the food, Rachel's perfect wine selection, the eye-popping dessert options, and how happy and grateful she was. Although they had coffee with dessert, as Rachel expected, Rose's exuberant energy began to fade shortly after the last bite went down. Rachel escorted her back to the room, and put her to bed. By the time Rachel tried to tell Rose she was meeting business associates at the bar, she'd already nodded off.

Rachel rode the elevator to the 23rd floor, and strutted into the bar as if she owned the place. There, she found Phil and Vince already seated at the prime table, tucked into a corner formed by two glass walls. Out one, they had a stunning view of Lake Michigan. Out the other, was downtown Milwaukee along the lakeshore. The men stood as Rachel approached, and Phil helped her into a luxurious chair. As pleasantries were exchanged a waiter appeared. Rachel pointed at the glasses in front of her companions, and asked, "What're you having?"

Phil did the talking, "Dewar's on the rocks. My little brother and I have always been partial to scotch."

Rachel turned to the waiter, "This table's check is on me." When Phil protested, she pointed at him and made a face, "Don't even start." With that settled, to the waiter she said, "I'll have a Maker's Mark Manhattan with a bourbon cherry and orange peel zest for garnish." As the waiter scurried off, she said to Phil, "I'm impressed you were able to get this table."

Phil waived a hand as if indicating the city below, "Rachel, this is my town. Didn't you think I had any swing around here? I'm hurt." Smiling amiably at his own joke, he leaned in and said, "You look lovely tonight."

Rachel caught Phil's eye, and said, "Thank you. Vince, you never told me what a charmer your big brother was."

Busy eying the women at the bar, Vince startled at the sound of his name, "Huh … oh yeah … sorry about that, Rachel. I thought you knew."

Rachel followed Vince's gaze, "My-my, look at all the pretty little things lined up in a row. Some of them look lonely, don't you think?"

Vince nodded, "That's what I was thinking."

Rachel swung her head as if to say go, "Well, what are you waiting for?" Vince put on a wolfish grin, picked up his drink, and headed to the bar.

Both watched, then Phil said, "Ah, to be young again."

Rachel swatted Phil's forearm, "Don't give me that. I doubt your needs are going unmet." Then she leaned in, "Actually, I was hoping we'd have some time alone. I'm anxious to know if you made out okay, … you know, as a result of our collaboration."

Phil held his tongue while the waiter set Rachel's drink on the table, then sipped his Dewar's and said, "We did alright, you know. Not a home run, but a solid base hit. Without paying a dime, we got two month's-worth of milk from three dozen dairy farmers. Then, having lost that milk, Verifine saw the wisdom in paying us a premium price to instantly restore their supply. And it was a short-haul from Town of Mitchell to Sheboygan. When you factor in the low hauling costs, we did pretty well overall. The Chicago boys were happy, so I'm happy."

A wrinkle appeared in Rachel's forehead, "Huh … it ended after two months? I thought sure you'd become Verifine's permanent hauler, at least for those three dozen farmers. Then, you could've expanded from there."

Phil took another sip, "Yeah, that was the plan. But we were only able to make part of it work. After sinking the NFO's milk diversion by closing the Papini plant, we did manage to successfully dissuade Verifine from taking the farmers back. That left the farmers nowhere to go, so they started dumping their milk. We kept Verifine going with long-hauls of milk from Chicago, figuring that within a few days, we could restore the short-haul after ABC signed up all the dumpers. For some reason, that never happened. Only a few dumpers signed, and shortly thereafter, even those dropped out. Frankly, we were shocked. We thought … shit … Verifine had been forewarned not to take the farmers back, but they must've done it anyway. But when we put eyes on the farms, Lake-to-Lake and Golden Guernsey were doing the pickups. How those bastards got in there so fast is beyond me. Then, get this, Verifine calls ABC and says they'd made other arrangements, and ABC's milk wasn't needed anymore. We still haven't figured out exactly what happened. It's a mystery. Long story short, the Chicago boys decided to declare victory and walk away from the northern expansion for now."

Rachel listened in rapt silence, and when Phil finished, she said, "You mentioned Verifine had been forewarned. What'd you mean by that?"

Phil looked side-to-side to make sure the coast was clear, then leaned in and said in a low voice, "We left a box in the president's driveway. Inside was the severed head of a Holstein cow with a note stuck on its forehead. The note read *this'll be you and your family if you take those farmers back.*"

Caught with her glass halfway to her lips, Rachel startled at the *severed head* and sloshed alcohol all over her dress, "N-o-o-o way ... oh shit, look what I've done!" She quickly dunked a napkin in her water glass, and started to rub out spots. As she worked feverishly, she said, "You're not serious, are you Phil?" Rachel glanced his way and their eyes met, "Oh my god, you are!"

Contrite, Phil said, "I'm sorry about the dress, Rachel. I'll buy you a new one. I should've waited until your glass was back on the table."

Rachel inspected her handiwork. Satisfied, she tossed the napkin down, and with a dismissive hand-gesture said, "Phil, the dress is fine. See, I've already rubbed out the spots. I will need another Manhattan, though." She got the waiter's attention, and they both placed orders. Then, she leaned in, and whispered, "Are your forewarnings always so subtle?"

Phil sat back and grinned, "Well, we do strive toward making a lasting impression. And hey, we apparently succeeded. Like I say, we watched the farms, and it wasn't Verifine doing the pickups." Phil rubbed his chin, and leaned back in, "So, tell me Rachel, what'd you get out of our mutual shenanigans?"

Rachel had expected the question. As far as she knew, Phil and the mob weren't aware of Wisconsin's new gaming opportunity on state-chartered Indian reservations. When she responded, she carefully cherry-picked the facts to keep it that way, "I've been growing my regional bank by acquiring independents over the past few years. Until now, Oostburg Bank had been a hold out. What a coincidence that most of the three dozen dairy farmers you snookered had loans at Oostburg. When they defaulted, the bank was forced to issue a public stock sale to avoid liquidation. You're looking at the new controlling owner of Oostburg Bank."

Phil whistled and shook his head, "You dirty dog, you."

* * *

The Pfister experience had been so enchanting that Rachel seriously considered extending the stay. But by morning, reality had set in. They'd only arranged the sitter for one day. And now that Oostburg Bank was hers, Rachel was eager to examine the books and determine an expeditious way to seize the Evans farm. By mid-morning, she and Rose were on their way back to Fond du Lac.

Jake played shy and hard to get when Rachel and Rose first returned, but before long was back to his usual precious self. Rachel took care of the bags, while Rose paid the sitter and got the download of what'd happened in their absence. After the sitter left, Rose came to the bedroom straight away, and said, "Rachel, a person by the name of Ryan Weiser has been trying to reach you. Yesterday afternoon, the sitter told him we'd be back today. He's called three more times this morning, so it must be urgent."

Rachel kept her expression neutral, "Thanks, Rose. I'd better give him a call. Don't worry about the unpacking, Jake needs your attention, and it can wait."

Rachel's mood darkened as she fast-walked to the study. She dialed the banking division, and asked for Ryan's extension. When he picked up, Rachel said in an accusing tone, "Ryan, it's Rachel. Where the hell were you yesterday?"

Ryan, his voice indignant, "Doing my best to save your ass, Rachel. I was part of a group pulled together in a conference room, and told to provide support to the field team of bank examiners at Oostburg Bank. We were in regular communication throughout the day. By noon it was clear things weren't going as expected. So, lunch was brought in, and they sequestered us for the rest of the day. Thank the lord, we had restrooms right across the hall."

Rachel's heart raced, and she felt a pang of queasiness in the pit of her stomach, "Okay, so what happened?"

Choosing his words carefully, Ryan said, "The examiners were shocked. Somehow, every defaulted dairy farm loan was found to be caught up, and current. They couldn't believe it, thought something was fishy, and asked for our help to find out what. We studied everything. For a while, I thought I'd found it. Oostburg went out for bids on 60 percent of their stock, and you came in as the high bidder. Usually, bank public stock sales are worded to be final at bid opening. If so, you'd have had control of the bank. But in this case, the bank retained the right to decline all offers, and that's what they did. Sounds crazy, but the examiners had no choice. They had to restore the asset values of every previously-delinquent loan. When they did, the bank was solvent."

Every word landed like a body blow, and Rachel was staggered. Struggling to comprehend, she managed to gather enough breath to say, "You mean I don't control the bank?"

Ryan tried to let her down gently, "I'm sorry, Rachel, I did everything I could. But no, the bank is solvent and remains independent."

* * *

When the mail came that afternoon, in it was a certified letter bearing the same bad news. Rachel felt whipsawed, and needed to get out of the house to clear her head. She told Rose she needed to run an errand, and went to one of Fond du Lac's parks along Lake Winnebago, to catch some air and think.

As she walked along the shore line, Rachel turned things over in her mind. She felt like such a fool, bragging to others the bank was hers before knowing so for a fact. Now what? She thought about coming clean with Long Body, but how could she? Only yesterday, she'd told him the opposite. And it's a good thing, because otherwise, he never would've agreed to delegate the state-agency conference to her. Instead, he would've gone to tribal council. Had that happened, she knew for a fact the tribe would've elected to use the conference to find a different casino partner. Who could blame them? A casino was supposed to be their ticket out of poverty. The tribe had approved her Headwaters project ten months ago, but hadn't seen any visible progress since. No, she couldn't tell Long Body the truth … at least, not until after the conference.

Thoughts of the conference further darkened Rachel's mood. She feared the conference would essentially wipe out her edge over other casino developers. She'd worked her tail off to create that advantage, and resented the use of taxpayer money to take it away. Just thinking about the time and energy she invested made her sick … maneuvering to be noticed by the Conservation Commission and named to their committee, understanding the nature of the sportsmen-tribe conflict, schmoozing with the stakeholders, drafting the statute, stewarding it into law, and so on. When it first became law, only she knew how to use the new authority to develop a casino. Post-conference, every attendee will have a pretty good idea.

Even more infuriating, the conference never would've happened had Rachel been able to submit her casino proposal when originally planned. She knew this with absolute certainty to the bottom of her hellish core. If the state had received a viable proposal to chew on, they wouldn't have needed a conference to beat one out of the bushes. In other words, this catastrophe of a conference never would've happened if not for the Evanses, Darkwater Flint, and Oostburg Bank. Her competitive advantage never would've been lost, if not for them. Rachel vowed to make the Evanses and the bank pay for what they'd done. Thankfully, she no longer needed to deal with Flint. He'd already gotten what he deserved.

Eventually, Rachel's swirling dark thoughts dissolved into laser-sharp clarity. She knew exactly what she needed to do. Rachel needed to be the first developer to submit a casino proposal to the state. If another developer beat her to the punch, word would get around, and the Potawatomi would cut her loose. To be first, all she needed was the Evans farm. All the other parts and pieces were ready to go. She'd take care of Oostburg Bank later. Feeling reassured, Rachel spent the rest of her nature walk brainstorming fast ways to seize control of that farm.

CHAPTER 5

Options for Rachel – Saturday; June 12,
1965; 8:00 AM

After spending the rest of the week pondering her options, Rachel called Vince Friday night and asked him to meet her for breakfast the next day. She picked a mom-and-pop restaurant just east of Fond du Lac off of State Hwy 23, because it had a private room with one small table. Vince was already sitting there sipping coffee, when she walked in.

After the niceties, they ordered, and Rachel told Vince the truth about Oostburg Bank. Afterword, she swore him to secrecy, including from brother Phil and especially Long Body. Vince nodded, "Of course I'll keep it to myself." Then, he hung his head, "I'm really sorry it didn't work out, Rachel. How're you doing?"

Rachel gave him a hard look, "I'm over it, Vince. Don't worry about me. We're here to discuss Plan C for gaining control of the Evans farm."

Vince studied her for a moment, then said, "Okay, I'm all ears."

Rachel swiveled her head to verify no server ears

nearby, "I want you to assemble a team and discretely monitor the farm and family, day and night. Find me a leverage point. Something I can use to force them to accept a buyout. At the same time, use what you learn during surveillance to develop some options to create leverage. I'm done dicking around with these people. They're going to be off that farm, one way or another, in a month."

Vince saw the feral shine in her eyes, and knew she meant business. He sipped his coffee as he thought about it, then said, "When you said develop some options to create leverage, what kind of things did you have in mind?"

Rachel's eyes narrowed, "Nothing is off the table. Unfortunate accidents, cattle theft, mysterious crop diseases ... you name it. But stick to things you can do without bringing the heat down on us, and provide me a budget for each one."

Vince paused while breakfast was served. Once alone again, he asked, "What's the time line on this?"

Rachel rubbed her chin and thought for a moment, "How about we meet here again ... same time ... next Tuesday morning? Come prepared to tell me my leverage options, and the costs to use them."

Vince made a face, "It's going to be a busy few-days."

Rachel smiled, but it's the type that could turn predatory, "That's why you're so generously compensated." Then, in a huskie voice, "By the way, how'd things go with that Pfister Hotel Barbie Doll you picked up the other night?"

As they ate, Vince filled her in, and they got caught up on other topics. When finished, the waiter cleared the table, except for their mugs and a fresh pot of coffee. Alone once more, Rachel and Vince got down to work. She pulled a folder out of her bag, containing several sets of documents. First, they reviewed copies of the Evans farm expansion plan. Rachel had kept hers from back when her Cascade branch bank agreed to finance the project. The expansion plan was ultimately completed as proposed, and provided an excellent overview of the farm's various owned lands, rented lands, structures, livestock, and machinery. Rachel used it to school Vince on the scope of the Evans farm operation. Next, they reviewed copies of the legal descriptions of the various parcels of owned and rented lands, as well as plat maps showing the locations of all the parcels. Rachel had gotten these from the Sheboygan County Register of Deeds office the previous day, and they gave Vince a thorough understanding of the lay of the land. By the end of the meeting, Vince had a much better idea of what to do, and how to do it.

Afterward, Vince went back to his motel room for a deep-dive study of the documents, and to plan his moves for the next day. After some thought, he decided he didn't need or want a team. In his view, the more prudent approach was to work alone. Right now, Phil and Long Body believed Rachel controlled Oostburg Bank. If that were true, to get the Evans farm she'd simply call their note due, and when they failed to pay in full, boot them off. If Phil or Long Body caught wind of his current assignment, they'd know something was wrong. They'd start asking questions Rachel wouldn't want to answer. No, better to work alone. Less risk of a leak, plus there isn't time to get somebody else up to speed anyway. There also wasn't time to look for existing leverage. Instead, he'd focus on creating some.

* * *

First thing the next morning, Vince drove to Cascade. Using the village as his base, he began driving the country roads adjacent to the lands owned and rented by the Evans family. On the passenger seat sat the documents Rachel had given him the previous day. As he surveyed the land, he made pencil scribbles on the plat maps, adding details such as topography, forests, wetlands, field entrances, and farmer's lanes. He paid special attention to the barns and other outbuildings, and how they might be approached without being detected. He also viewed where the herd at the main farm was pastured when not being milked, as well as where the young cattle at the Lemke, Adcock, and Ulbricht farms pastured.

After finishing his first drive-by reconnaissance, Vince had lunch in Cascade, then parked under a shade tree on a street overlooking Firemen's Park to plan his next move. The pencil hen-scratching he'd done while on the go was barely legible, so he improved the notes while the land-features were still fresh in his mind. Then he studied the plat maps for the main farm, looking for opportunities to create leverage.

The main farm's buildings, a cluster that included the house, sat on a hill that provided a commanding view of Bates Road. Between the parents and six kids, Vince figured someone would always be around except at night when all were asleep. He guessed a relatively safe window for shenanigans might be 11:00 PM to 5:00 AM. He thought about what could be done to force the

Evans's hand. Mentally, he tried to put himself into the shoes of a dairy farmer, and thought some more. It dawned on him that losing your milk check would be a big deal. A dairy farmer wouldn't survive long without a milk check.

Next, Vince considered the various ways to make the milk check disappear. After a while, he kept coming back to stealing the milk herd. Obviously, it'd have to be done in the dead of night. He recalled seeing a gated entrance into the herd's pasture, directly off of Bates Road at the base of the hill below the buildings. To better visualize the possibility of using it, he drove back there. It became immediately obvious the idea had a problem. The Evans's had a farm dog, some sort of German Sheppard mix. During a cattle heist, the dog would surely sound the alarm. After some more thought, it occurred to him that a dog could be put down beforehand.

As he mulled it over some more, Vince realized that even with the dog out of the way, problems remained. He'd hoped the hill would have enough crown that the Evans farmhouse would be over-the-horizon from the pasture's entrance. Instead, the house's west-facing windows had a direct line-of-sight to the pasture gate. Loading 80 bovines onto a convoy of cattle trucks would raise a ruckus. With no hillside or other obstructions to diffract the sound, the noise would surely reach the windows.

The house was too old for central air conditioning, and there're no window-bangers in sight. That meant there'd be no AC background noise, and worse yet, sleep would occur with the windows open. Someone would surely hear the commotion, and wake up to see what's going on. On a cloudy moonless night, they might not be able to see anything from a window. But in rural Wisconsin, they'd probably grab a rifle or shotgun and come investigate.

After dismissing the idea of stealing the herd through the Bates Road gate, Vince carefully examined the area, looking for another way. It caught his eye that the pasture was long and narrow, created by fencing a hillside that sloped steeply away from the buildings on top of the hill. The long dimension extended far back from the road, around a gentle bend in the hillside to the right, and out of sight. The unusual lay of the land sparked a new idea, best explored by studying the plat maps. Vince returned to his shady spot in Cascade, to do just that.

According to the maps, only a thin band of waste land separated the back end of the pasture from a large field. The field was accessible from Rock Road, which ran north-south. To the south, it ended in a tee-intersection with Bates Road, but to the north it connected to State Hwy 28. From the back end of the pasture, the Evans farmhouse would definitely be over-the-horizon. In fact, that locale, the thin band of wasteland, and the accessible-field's remote back corner were all remote from the various nearby farm houses. Further, the back corner of the field looked promising as a place to load cattle. If so, the cattle trucks could exit the field onto Rock Road going north, and in less than a mile, be on Hwy 28. From there, they could be anywhere in the state in no time, and across state lines not long after.

To ground-truth the idea, Vince took Bates Road out of Cascade, and turned left on Rock Road. The field he was interested in was immediately on the right. The field ended, when the road dipped into a swale, and came upon a cattail marsh. To take a closer look, Vince pulled over and parked just shy of the culvert. It occurred to him that the car would look out-of-place, but told himself he'd be quick. He fast-walked the edge of the field, toward the back corner. Once there, he looked in all directions, and smiled. Of the three farmhouses nearby, the Evans and Nutter places were both over-the-horizon from where he stood, and Lemke's was on the far side of a sizable wooded area. The ground was solid and well-drained, and even in a rain, the cattle trucks would be unlikely to mire down. He also noted that it wouldn't take much effort to fence a little loading area here.

Next, Vince quickly maneuvered through the narrow parcel of scrub to the back end of the pasture. Once there, he smiled again. Creating a temporary lane for the cattle through the narrow band of wasteland would be a quick and easy task. There were enough scrawny trees and shrubs to use as posts, so they wouldn't have to set any. All they needed to do was run a few lines of barbed wire on either side of the lane, tack them to the vegetation here and there, and trample the growth in-between so the cattle could see a path.

Vince played in his mind this new version of the cattle heist, start-to-finish, in an effort to uncover any flaws. On the second replay, he realized he still had a problem. For the heist to succeed, they'd need to congregate the entire herd at this end of the pasture, where they couldn't be seen or heard while being driven through the scrub-land lane, and loaded onto trucks on the other side. But unfortunately, cattle tended to spread out to eat grass and lounge when pasturing. Left to their own devices, there'd be cows on the Bates Road end of the pasture, cows here, and cows scattered everywhere in-between. How could he get them all here, without waking anyone in the Evans house?

Stumped, Vince climbed onto the nearby stonewall fence, and sat on a boulder to think. This vantage point gave him a nice view of the acreage behind the Evans barn, which was strip-cropped following the contours of the land. One of the strips appeared to be stubble, as if recently-hayed. On it laid a solitary bale of hay. Vince thought that odd, and let his mind wander, positing explanations for how it got there ... kickoff baler missed the wagon, wagon bounced over rough ground and a bale fell out, and so on.

Suddenly, Vince had an idea. You see, Vince was no goombah. He was a practical guy by nature, and had been doing Rachel's dirty-work in America's Dairyland for a long time. By now, he'd become a jack of all trades. He climbed down, jogged over to the bale, and brought it back to the pasture. Using his pocket knife, he cut it open and grabbed a pad of hay. Then, he scanned the pasture for the nearest cow, walked over, and held out the pad. She raised her head from the grass, sniffed the pad, and open her mouth to take a bite. The cow came up empty when Vince pulled back the pad, but began to follow him when he slowly walked away, holding the pad out behind. When he turned left, she turned left ... when he turned right, she turned right. When he arrived at the desired destination, he dropped the pad on the ground, and the cow contently began to eat it. Apparently, congregating the herd at the back of the pasture wouldn't be a problem after all.

Concerned over the length of time his car had been parked on Rock Road, Vince hustled back in that direction. Along the way, another remaining problem resurfaced in his mind. He'd still have to put down the dog. He found it frustrating when problems occurred to him one-by-one, instead of all at once. It made him feel uncertain whether he'd thought of them all. He decided to drive past the Evans farm on the way back to Cascade, to see if that would trigger him to think of any more problems with his cattle heist plan.

When Vince reached the car and climbed in, it felt like crawling into a blast furnace. It was hot and sunny, and like a dummy he'd forgotten to crack the windows. After cranking them down, he let the car air out for a moment, then brought the engine to life. With the steering wheel and gearshift nearly too hot to touch, he gingerly pulled out onto the road, and used the next field entrance to turn around. Then, he drove toward the Evans farm with his left arm resting on the driver's door window-opening. As he drove, he used his hand to deflect air into the car, and hopefully help cool it off.

As Vince came even with the Evans farmhouse, the Evans dog came out of nowhere and nearly took off his arm. Startled, Vince checked his arm for blood, and saw some. Meanwhile, the mutt launched a kamikaze assault on the car, barking and nipping at the front driver's-side tire. Cursing a blue streak, Vince regained control and kept driving at a steady speed. Eventually, after a hundred yards or so, the dog lost interest. After the attack ended, Vince took some slow deep breaths to relax. That's when it hit him. The Evans dog was a car chaser. If he came up road kill, it wouldn't even raise an eyebrow. Feeling smug, Vince made a mental note to find out if the neighbors had dogs.

With the drama over, Vince returned to his peaceful Cascade parking spot and took a moment to review his progress. He had a cattle heist plan, and was confident it would work. All he had to do now was price it out. If the Evanses lost their milk herd, gone with it would be their only significant income stream. If they refused to accept a buyout, stealing the herd would provide the leverage Rachel needed to make them change their minds.

Vince was pleased with himself, but he wasn't done yet. Rachel wanted a menu of leverage options. Since he's well into it already, Vince considered whether additional cattle rustling options made sense. But before long, he concluded young-cattle heists from the Lemke, Adcock, and Ulbricht farms would be a waste of time. Young cattle were female heifers being raised to produce milk in the future. Losing one, two, or even all three cohorts of young-cattle would be a financial blow, for sure. But the financial pain would roll in slowly, over the next year or year-and-a-half. In the meantime, the Evanses would still have their milk check. No, Rachel needed fast-acting leverage to force a quick decision. Stealing young-cattle just wasn't fast enough.

Vince moved on to other ideas. He found the tragic accident options lacking. Taking out James Evans, as opposed to another family member, would probably have the biggest impact. So, say we did that. That still left the wife, six kids, and grandpa to carry on. To provide what Rachel needed, there'd need to be far fewer survivors. Multiple accidents would look fishy, so that meant one big one with many fatalities.

Arranging that wouldn't be easy because they're never all together. On any given day, they're spread all over the place mowing, baling, and hauling. Also, Rachel said she didn't want any options likely to bring down the heat. Multiple fatalities would mean a very serious investigation. The kind that might notice it wasn't really an accident after all.

After systematically eliminating things like poisoning the water and stealing machinery, an idea caught Vince's fancy. Why not burn down the barn at the main farm? If done right, the fire could destroy not only the barn and cattle-fodder stored inside, but some or all of the herd. Even if they managed to save the herd, they wouldn't have the means to milk them. Dairy cows left un-milked contract mastitis. Within a week, the beasts would be sold as future hamburger to the Milwaukee stockyard, for pennies on the dollar. Oh yeah, selling out would surely have appeal after a loss like that.

After settling on barn-burning, Vince mulled over how best to do it. His criteria were simple ... cause the most loss while minimizing the chances of being caught. Greatest-loss implied setting the fire during milking, when the herd was inside. Least-risk implied setting it during the evening milking, when fading daylight would provide better cover for the firebug's ingress and egress. Evening might also lead to greater loss, since herd-salvage and firefighting efforts would start near dusk, and only become more difficult as the night wore on. If tacked on to the end of a long workday, the effectiveness of these efforts might also suffer from fatigue.

Next, Vince envisioned how the community

might respond to a large barn-fire during evening milking. This time of year, the barn would be partially full of hay and straw. Shortly after the flame was set, the barn would likely explode into a towering inferno. Sitting up on the hill like it does, the barn-fire would be visible from miles around. The magnitude of the fire would be far beyond the capacity of the Cascade Volunteer Fire Department to contain, so multiple volunteer departments would likely respond. There'd be alarms blaring in multiple nearby villages, and emergency vehicles speeding to the Evans's farm from multiple directions. In addition, people would flock there to gawk.

Vince frowned at the thought that local roads would be teeming with potential witnesses to a suspicious vehicle heading away from the fire. Concerned about how the fire-bug could make a getaway undetected, he consulted the plat maps, looking for an escape route. It caught his eye that the Evans farm backed up to the Waldo swamp, and beyond the swamp lay State Hwy 28. There appeared to be several swamp-entry points off of Hwy 28. The best of them were almost two miles as the crow flies, from the Evans barn.

Vince thought about that. Hay and straw ... hell, they're like kindling. Once a fire got a good start, there'd be no stopping it. The whole barn would probably go up in a whoosh with only one or two five-gallon cans of gas. Ingress through the swamp would be time-consuming, and tedious as hell carrying gas cans. On the other hand, he could probably stash the gas near the back end of the pasture beforehand. That's only one-fifty or two-hundred yards from the barn. That'd work.

For egress, the swamp would be even slower-going as daylight faded. But he liked the idea that the fire would essentially serve as a giant diversion all night long. A vehicle pulling onto Hwy 28 almost two miles away would go unnoticed. Vince decided to call it a day, and sleep on the idea.

* * *

Vince woke the next morning with no doubt in his mind. He knew he needed a path through the Waldo Swamp, and hurried through breakfast to get an early start on reconnaissance to find one. First, he drove to the portion of Hwy 28 that he reckoned was due-north of the Evans farm. Driving slowly on the shoulder, he investigated possible entry points to the swamp. Then he did a second pass, and looked more closely at the most promising options. He settled on what appeared to be a farmer's lane, across the highway and down somewhat from a large commercial orchard near Waldo.

Vince looked in all directions, and saw nobody. Then, after waiting for traffic to clear, he turned down the dirt lane. After several hundred yards, the farmland and lane ended, and an old logging trail continued into the woods. He followed the trail until it became impassable, and then parked. Vince spent the rest of the morning working with his compass, seeking to find and mark a way through the swamp. By luck, he eventually stumbled onto a path that felt like an actual trail from the distant past, an old Indian trail perhaps.

After traversing the swamp, the trail split. Vince followed the right leg, and recognized that it came out behind the old Lemke farm on Rock Road. Then, he backtracked to the trail junction and followed the left leg. This one eventually came out into what appeared to be hundreds of acres of cropland, divided into contour strips that flowed across a sweeping hill. He recognized it as the Evans farm. On the right he could see the back end of the side-hill pasture, where he'd been the previous day. Satisfied that he'd found a viable route, Vince backtracked the way he'd come and timed the hike back to the car.

Vince was confident he'd found two leverage-creating options that Rachel would like. He spent the afternoon calling around for prices, and developing budgets. When done he felt ready, and none too soon. The next morning, Rachel would expect to hear about them over breakfast.

* * *

The next morning, Vince filled Rachel in over pancakes, scrambled eggs, and bacon. When done, she offered rare compliments. Then, she began to explain his next assignment, "I've decided to go to the expense of having the Evans farm appraised. Farmers typically don't know the value of their own farm, and therefore don't know a good offer when they see one. There's a well-known and respected farm appraisal outfit, and I know a guy there. Every farmer in Sheboygan County would probably recognize this firm's name. My guy is willing to do the deed."

Confused by Rachel's pause, Vince asked, "Okay, sounds like a plan. What's that got to do with me?"

Rachel winked at him, "I was getting to that.

Farm appraisals are usually driven by one of two needs. Either the farm is being sold, and the buyer's bank needs an appraisal before it'll lend the money ... or, the current owner wants to borrow against his farm, but the farmer's bank needs an appraisal before it'll make the loan. In both cases, the farmer knows an appraisal is coming, wants it to be done, and willingly facilitates it. None of this is true in our case."

Vince thought a moment, then said, "Hmmm ... good point. But I still don't understand why you're telling me this."

Rachel snuck a sip of coffee, then said, "Well, it'll take a little night-time trespassing to get the job done. My guy is shady enough to do it, but he'll need a tour guide. He'll accept a lot of the data in the Evans farm expansion plan at face value, but he's going to want to get into every barn and major outbuilding to see for himself. He also needs to inventory and assess the condition of the livestock, tractor fleet, machinery, and so on. Of course, all this needs to be done without being noticed."

Vince squeezed the bridge of his nose for a moment, and muttered, "Aw, man ... is this really necessary? I'll have to kill or drug every farm dog in the Town of Lyndon."

With a touch of snark, Rachel replied, "Might appear a tad suspicious if all the dogs turned up dead."

After the table was cleared, Rachel and Vince shared ideas on how to get the appraisal rolling. Rachel had already sent the appraiser, by courier, copies of the Evans farm expansion plan and the plat maps and descriptions from the Register of Deeds office. Vince was concerned about the intrusiveness of actual site visits, and convinced Rachel they needed to persuade the guy to rely on the paperwork wherever possible. Then, after the guy was finished digesting the materials and had his absolute-minimum list, Vince needed a face meeting to walk the guy through how they'd get each item.

After breakfast, Rachel told Vince to follow her home, so they could give the appraiser a call. Rachel started out by setting the ground rules, then introduced him to Vince. Harsh words were exchanged over the time line, but the appraiser held his ground. He claimed to be swamped at work, considered this a side job on personal time, and demanded a full week to prepare for Vince's planning meeting. Having no alternative, Rachel relented, and the plans were set.

❈ ❈ ❈

Vince used the intervening time to get a head start. He already knew the safest approach to the Lemke and main Evans barns and out-buildings ... park at the end of the logging trail off of Hwy 23, and hike through the Waldo swamp. The next day he began his search for screened-from-view approaches to the Adcock and Ulbricht barns. For Ulbricht's, a long farmers lane going west off of Rock Road led up over a hill, and then zig-zagged to the left, and came out at the back of the barn. The Rock Road turnoff was out-of-sight from nearby houses, and the approach to the back of the barn was hidden from Ulbricht's farmhouse by an odd mound-like hill, compliments of the last glacier.

The Adcock place wasn't so easy. The farmhouse and barn were both up close to Bates Road, one on either side, and directly across from each other. The only protected approach to the barn was from the wooded lowlands to the rear. Vince went exploring to find out what was on the other side of those woods. From the Adcock place, he took Bates Road into Cascade, turned left on the first street, drove past the Fireman's Park, turned left again, and drove out of the village on County Rd. NN.

Around the next bend, Vince noticed a secluded mink farm on the left. He turned in, found the place deserted, and saw two rows of abandoned mink sheds heading off to the left. Between the shed rows was a dirt lane, and he took it. The lane dead-ended at the woods, but an overgrown turnaround provided a convenient hiding place for the car. There was no trail leading into the woods, at least that Vince could see. But by consulting the plat map and using his compass, he was able to find a way to the back of the Adcock barn. The path was marshy and slow-going, and crossed Nichols Creek downstream of Cascade, but Vince figured it'd do. On the way back he marked the trail, then hiked the roundtrip again for timing.

Over the course of the appraiser's prep period, Vince communicated with him daily by phone. On those calls, the appraiser dropped hints that he wouldn't need a full week before their meeting. Vince worked hard to win the appraiser's confidence, and was rewarded by being trusted to gather certain data on his own.

Meanwhile, Vince had come up with a dog-management approach, and was chomping at the bit to try it. Every farmhouse in the vicinity had an associated dog that ran free. At the Evans and Lemke places, water and food bowls were in open run-in sheds near the farmhouses. At the Nutter, Adcock, and Ulbricht places, there were actual dog houses near the farmhouses. Vince spent two to three hours on several different nights parked hidden from the road, in farmer's lanes or field entrances, listening with the car windows down. To his surprise, it was fairly common for dogs at one place or another to raise an alarm. When they did, the others often joined in, creating a chorus throughout the area. Vince considered this to be a good thing. It meant people trying to sleep were used to hearing the dogs, and probably were inclined to ignore them unless an exceptional ruckus broke out.

After considering his options, Vince decided that drugging the dogs would best serve his purpose and raise fewer suspicions. He bought cheap but thick cuts of pot roast, and cut the beef into two-inch squares. To use as a trial, he grabbed a meat-chunk, made a slit in one side, inserted a single horse-sedative pill, and sutured the slit closed. To test his handy-work, Vince motored along Rock Road at 11:30 PM one night, feigned a flat tire, and pulled over near Lemke's.

The Lemke dog was on the scene before the jack was out of the trunk. It stood off ten yards, growling and barking and bounding like a po-go stick. Vince knelt, spoke to the mutt in a soothing tone, and tossed him a laced chunk of beef. The dog went silent, sniffed the morsel, inhaled it, and looked at Vince for more. It wasn't long before Fido was out cold, and flat on his side. When the dog first raised the alarm, Vince heard the other dogs in the area join in. But when Fido fell silent, so did they. No light ever came on in the Lemke house.

By all appearances, Vince's experiment was a success. But in reality, he needed to know how long the sedative would last. To find out, he stayed the night. If anyone came along, he'd say he changed the tire, but afterward was too weary to pack up and drive home. As cover, he set his jack, tire wrench, and spare tire on the ground as props to back up the story. Then, he spent the night in his car watching Fido. The dog began to stir at sunrise, and with great difficulty managed to wobble to a sitting position. He sat there a few minutes, with an unfocused look about him. Then, he stood up, shook his head, and weaved his way back to his shed. By the time Vince packed his things and drove away, he was confident the neighborhood dogs wouldn't be a problem. Even so, during his first use of the method on an actual data gathering foray, he proceeded with great caution.

As the days clicked by, the appraiser delegated more-and-more data collection to Vince … livestock head counts at the four locations, tractor and machinery inventories, and so on. To keep up, Vince ventured onto Evans properties every night, rain or shine. The laced meat chunks worked like a charm. After the first encounters, it was as if every dog looked forward to his arrival.

To Vince's delight, the appraiser was prepared to meet with him after only five days. At the meeting, the remaining data needs were divided into several buckets, each small enough to be gathered in a single nocturnal outing. Thereafter, the two men went out nightly and had all the data the appraiser needed in no time. From that point forward, the ball was in the appraiser's court.

The appraiser's job was a little more difficult

than usual, because Rachel had given him special instructions. She knew farmers, even ones who wanted to sell, often were hesitant to do so because of the onerous task of clearing out their personal property. Dealing with livestock, machinery, fodder and everything else could be overwhelming. Rachel didn't want inertia of this sort to get in the way, so she instructed the appraiser to estimate two market values, farm-only and farm plus personal property. If the Evanses preferred to avoid the hassle, Rachel would buy it all and get rid of the personal property herself.

❋ ❋ ❋

While Vince was busy finding leverage and pushing the appraisal along, Rachel focused on how to put all her puzzle pieces together to expeditiously boot the Evanses off their farm. In broad strokes, her plan was to make the Evanses an offer and provide a copy of the appraisal as reassurance of its fairness. If they declined, Rachel envisioned raising her offer a few times. In essence, she'd make an offer they couldn't refuse. If they foolishly declined anyway, she'd create leverage with one of Vince's intervention options, and wait them out.

Rachel was unsure how high the offers could go before making the casino project no longer attractive, so she decided to find out. Unlike normal people, Rachel enjoyed conducting financial analyses. In fact, the more complicated the better. She didn't have the appraisal yet, so just for the fun of it, Rachel pushed the numbers on a scenario where she paid the Evans family her best guess of fair market value for their farm. At this price point, going forward with the casino was a no-brainer compared with starting over at a different site. She repeated the analysis multiple times, with higher and higher prices paid for the Evans farm, and estimated she could pay at least four times her guesstimated market value, and the casino project would still come up roses.

Incredulous, Rachel developed a different methodology completely independent from the one previous, and re-ran the numbers. The result was the same. Mystified, Rachel reviewed both methodologies step-by-step, rechecked both sets of calculations, and still nothing changed. Now fully immersed in the problem, Rachel finally understood that the answer to the mystery lay in the sunk costs. She'd already invested so heavily in developing a casino at the Headwaters of the Milwaukee River site, that any course of action other than seeing it through would be foolish, at least from a financial stand-point.

Now that she understood her limits on pricing, Rachel racked her brain for other details that needed to be sorted out before she could make her move. She couldn't think of any. After the Oostburg Bank stock purchase went awry, she'd put the returned cashier's checks into an interest-bearing savings account at her regional bank. This meant she had plenty of liquid assets on hand to make the farm acquisition, and could pull the trigger on these funds at any time.

Rachel's plan was locked and loaded. After receiving the two-tier appraisal, she'd finetune her good-better-best offers, and pull the trigger on a rapid-fire sequence of events. If the Evans's were foolish enough to reject her generous offers, then she'd coax them with leverage. The choice between stealing the herd or burning the barn, would be a game-time decision. Although the if-then nature of each step meant the plan could unfold in multiple ways, all paths had one thing in common. At the end, the Evans farm would be hers.

CHAPTER 6

Offense Turns to Defense – Thursday;
June 24, 1965; 9:00 AM

Rachel met the courier at the door, and tore open the package like a bear on a trash can. After days of pent-up anticipation, the appraisal finally came. At long last, she'd be able to pull the trigger on the Evans farm. To buy it, Rachel planned to use the same shell corporation, Headwaters of the Milwaukee River LLC, as previously used to acquire the Lage, Salveson, and Nitsch farms. Rachel hadn't told him yet, but Vince would reprise his role as the HMR acquisition rep. When she grabbed the phone to give Vince a call, it rang in her hand.

Surprised, Rachel put the handset to her ear, and said, "Hello."

"Rachel, this is Bert Baker. Sorry to bother you. Do you have a minute?"

Caught off guard, Rachel hesitated, then said, "Bert … yes, of course. What can I do for you?"

She picked up traces of nervous stress in Bert's voice, as he said, "Well, yesterday a private investigator by the name of Jason Binder stopped by the farm. I wasn't there, thank God, so Ernie answered the door. The guy was asking questions about Al Stone. I thought you should know."

Shocked, Rachel asked hastily, "What'd he ask? And what'd Ernie say?" Bert filled her in on the conversation, and reassured her that Ernie had stuck to the script. She thought about that, then asked, "You say Binder asked for you, right after asking about Al Stone?"

Bert, vocal-chords tight, "That's right. But Ernie told him that's none of his business, and ordered him off the property."

After a moment, Rachel muttered, "It sounds like Binder knows Al Stone might be you."

Bert, with despair, "That's what I'm afraid of, yes."

Rachel thought some more, "Refresh my memory. When did the NFO supposedly reassign Al Stone?"

As if it were yesterday, Bert spouted, "February 2nd, right after the Sheboygan County chapter approved the milk diversion. Since then, I've been laying low with Ernie, working our farm and selling seed corn on the side."

Rachel hadn't really covered her tracks from back then, and as time passed uneventfully, had assumed there'd be no need. Now, she wasn't so sure, "Is this the first time anybody came around asking questions?"

Sheepishly, Bert admitted, "Well, not exactly. The same guy talked to Ernie in early May. But back then he never asked about me, only about Al Stone."

Rachel snapped, "Early May! And you didn't think to tell me?"

Bert, sounding a little defensive, "Well … you know, you wrote the script and Ernie stuck to it, so we figured no harm done." Misjudging Rachel's silence as ascent, Bert changed the subject, "Rachel, I've been meaning to ask, we've still got a deal, don't we? I mean, right-off-the-bat you wrote off half our debt, just like you said you would, and we appreciate that. But you also promised to restructure the remaining debt in a year's time ... you know, so we could make ends meet more easily. It'll be a year in early December. That's still on, right?"

Rachel, teeth bared like a Great White snack-hunting on a Florida beach, "You morons, I said I'd restructure if things went as planned! Well, they didn't. They might've, if only you'd called me in May. If I'd known we had a snoop on our tail, maybe I could've done something about it." Rachel went on belittling him, but eventually ran out of steam. Once calmed, she told Bert she'd think about it, and call back.

Once off the phone, Rachel poured herself a glass of wine, and sat down to noodle on her predicament. She put herself in the shoes of Oostburg Bank, and let the story unfold in her mind from that point of view. The bank issued a stock-sale under duress, and she put in the high bid. The NFO's failed milk diversion had triggered the bank's problem because, oddly, most of the participating farmers banked there. This being an extremely unlikely circumstance, the bank hired someone to look into it ... hence Binder.

Rachel took another sip of wine, and put herself into Binder's shoes. No doubt, the local NFO told him Al Stone, an NFO roaming rep, was responsible for recruiting the large number of Oostburg Bank client-farmers into the NFO, just prior to the diversion. But when Binder contacted the NFO's national organization, they of course, never heard of him. Binder would then loop back to the local NFO, where he'd learn that Al Stone had been welcomed aboard on the basis of a Fond du Lac County farmer's recommendation ... Ernie Baker.

Confident she understood what led Binder to Ernie Baker, Rachel now considered what that meant for her. In early May, Binder only knew about Al Stone. But yesterday, Binder also asked about Bert. At this point, he may only suspect that Al is Bert. But if he pulls Bert's driver's license photo and shops it around, dozens of NFO members would identify him as the man they know as Al Stone. She had to assume Binder would nail that down soon, if he hadn't already.

Rachel had put in the high bid, plus had a history with Oostburg Bank, so naturally Binder would consider her a suspect. She reasoned Binder would try to connect the Bakers to her, in some kind of conspiracy to take over the bank. If the Bakers turned state's evidence, she had a problem. After some thought, her initial reaction was to kill them both. But the more she noodled, the more foolish the idea appeared. If the Bakers disappeared now, conspiracy would be the least of her problems. She'd be wanted for murder. No, she couldn't just kill them ... not right away, anyhow.

With a sigh, Rachel began to consider what else to do with them. She revisited their old deal. They believed they'd done their part, and she should do hers. She could see why they thought that way. She'd never told them her true goal, for good reason, so they weren't in a position to know their collaboration had failed. Even so, she felt no obligation to live up to the back-half of that old deal. No, things hadn't turned out, the bank wasn't hers. And if a new deal was struck, she needed to gain something from it.

Rachel put her mind to the task of clarifying what she'd want from a new deal. She believed Binder was trying to nail her for creating a criminal conspiracy to takeover Oostburg Bank. Obviously, she wanted to be shielded from legal jeopardy. How could the Bakers help in that regard? She knew criminal conspiracy cases weren't easy to prove. In her mind, she ticked through the possible defenses for such a thing, and kept coming back to the same idea. She needed reasonable doubt. In other words, there needed to be a plausible explanation for why the Baker brothers did what they did, which didn't involve her.

Try as she may, Rachel couldn't come up with a reasonable explanation. She tried putting herself into Bert and Ernie's shoes, but it didn't help. She'd never been anything close to a dairy farmer, and couldn't think like one. Frankly, she considered them fools for toiling so hard for such little gain. Rachel was about to throw in the towel, when a thought struck her like lightning. Bert was a world-class bullshitter. Why not ask him to come up with a story?

Mind made up, Rachel grabbed the phone and made the call. When Bert picked up, she said, "Bert, it's me … calling back like I said I would. Look, about our deal. You held up your end, and I can understand why you think I should hold up mine. But that deal was contingent on things turning out as planned, and well … they didn't."

Bert, his voice rising to a near whine, "Oh come on, Rachel. We did everything you asked us to. If things didn't turn out, you can't blame us. Plus, you say things didn't turn out. But how do we even know that's true? You never told us what you were up to."

Rachel, calm but unyielding, "Things didn't turn out, you'll just have to trust me on that. And I only told you what you needed to know, for your own protection. You'll have to trust me on that, too. But I'm looking for a way to be fair, so hear me out, okay? I'd like to strike a new deal. This time, no contingencies you can't verify. Are you interested?"

After a moment of dead air, Bert, in an incredulous tone, "I'm listening."

Rachel nodded to herself, "Okay, good. Now, think about everything you and Ernie did for me under our old deal. Then, take me out of the picture, and think about you and Ernie doing those very same things under your own initiative. For the new deal, all you have to do is come up with a credible story explaining why you and Ernie, independently and on your own, did those things."

Bert thought a moment, "Huh … that's it? All we've got to do is make up a good story?"

Rachel, coaxing him along, "That's right. Then, if anybody asks, stick to the story. You do that, and the new deal stands no matter what."

Bert thought some more, "Okay, that shouldn't be a problem. But say we do all that, what do we get in return?"

Rachel considered this to be the delicate part. She feared Bert would be turned-off if she only offered the old quid pro quo in return. So, she said, "Well, that's up to you. Like before, I could restructure your remaining debt … you know, so you could make ends meet. Or, if there's something you'd rather have, I'd consider that too ... you know, so long as the cost was in the same ballpark."

Bert's brow beetled, and he said, "There you go again ... so long as ... those're weasel words. How're we supposed to know what your costs are?"

Rachel sighed, "Look Bert, just try me, okay? I couldn't very well tell you to ask for anything ... sky's the limit ... cost's no object. If restructured debt no longer suits your fancy, tell me what does. I'm just trying to be fair."

As the conversation wound down, Rachel pushed Bert for a face meeting the next day, to finalize their new deal. She needed to hear their story firsthand, to judge its credibility. She was also curious what they'd ask for. Bert said he'd put his thinking cap on, and let her know later that day if tomorrow was possible.

❋ ❋ ❋

Bert called back in four hours to confirm tomorrow, and Rachel was ready. She gave him a time and place in Campbellsport, and told Bert to be there with his brother. She said her colleague, Vince, would pick them up and drive them elsewhere for the meeting. When Bert protested the cloak and dagger, Rachel reminded him they couldn't be seen together. She also shared her fear that someone might be watching the Baker farm, and perhaps even following Bert and his brother wherever they went. She meant no disrespect, but unlike them, Vince was a professional. If followed, he'd know and would call an audible to keep them all safe. Grudgingly, Bert saw the wisdom in that.

For the meeting, Rachel selected a small café in the

village of Eden. It roughly split the distance between the Baker farm and Fond du Lac, and she knew the owner. With few exceptions, the café's entire clientele were regulars. If a stranger appeared, the owner promised to let her know. Rachel took a booth in a quiet corner, and shortly thereafter Vince arrived with Bert and Ernie. He led them to her booth, locked eyes with Rachel, and used head motions to reassure her there'd been no tail. Then, he returned to his car to stand watch.

After exchanging pleasantries, Rachel lightened the mood by offering to buy lunch. Once the orders were placed, she got right down to business, and said, "So, Bert ... you've come up with a story and know what you want in return, correct?"

Bert cleared his throat, and said, "Yes ma'am."

Rachel smiled but it didn't reach her eyes, "Excellent. Let's start with the ask, first. Hypothetically, let's say I like your story and believe it'll stand up. Obviously, for inventing the tale and agreeing to stick to it, you deserve something in return. What do you want?"

Being the smooth one, Bert did the talking, "Well, Ernie and I've done a lot of soul searching on this. I'm retirement age, and he's pretty close. Frankly, we're both weary of trying to make a living on that farm. We aren't in a position to know if this is ridiculous cost-wise, but we'd like to retire. We'd like to sign over the farm to you, in exchange for enough income to live on for the rest of our lives. We plan to relocate to McAllen, Texas and live in a trailer park. The cost-of-living down there is low, so we wouldn't need all that much. We've a sister in McAllen, and our mom lives there, too. With the in-laws and nieces and nephews, it's really the only family we have left. Mom is failing, and sis could use some help, so we figure this'd be win-win for everybody."

Rachel hadn't seen that coming. She looked up, eyes focused in the distance, "Huh ... you know, that might be possible. I'd have to run some numbers to be sure, but the net value of your farm and personal property might be enough."

Bert brightened at the possibility, "Thanks for not just blowing the idea off. You considering it ... well, it means a lot. We weren't sure you would."

Rachel made herself smile again, then said, "No promises until I run the numbers, but I think I can make that happen." Then, after a pause, "Okay, now tell me the story. Pretend I'm that investigator that keeps coming around. Let's say I show up for a third time, and catch you both at the farm. The questions start coming one after the other, rat-a-tat-tat. He wants to know why you did those things with the NFO. What're you going to tell him?"

Bert pointed at Rachel, and said "Okay, you're the snoop." Then, he held her eyes, relaxed into character, and said, "You know, those're all-good questions and I'm going to tell you straight. Me and Ernie here, we've been contemplating retirement. In case you weren't aware, dairy farming in Wisconsin has gone down the shitter. It just isn't worth the effort anymore. We've got relatives in Texas begging us to join them. Every year they ask us what're we waiting for. Hell, we'd already made up our minds to sell out and go. But then the NFO caught fire in Sheboygan County ... you know, claimed they could force up the price of milk. Well, if that were true, dairy farming wouldn't be so bad. So, we decided to stick around another year, to see what happens."

"Then we got to thinking ... rather than be spectators, why not try to help? If they succeeded in getting a processor to pay more for milk ... well, maybe we'd be able to ship our milk there, too ... you know, go along for the ride. We weren't exactly sure how we could help. So, we decided to study up on the NFO, and through the grapevine, keep tabs on how the Sheboygan chapter was doing. We learned the NFO was testing a new concept where they'd send in people to help chapters move forward ... called them *roaming reps*. About then, the scuttlebutt was Sheboygan needed more members. Connecting the dots gave us an idea."

"I hate to brag, but people tell me if anybody could sell ice to an Eskimo, it'd be me. So, if more members were needed, who better to recruit them than me? I got to thinking ... what if I called Abe Van Driest, the president of the Sheboygan County chapter, and offered to do just that? Of course, Abe didn't know me from Adam, so I told him I'm a roaming rep from the NFO, and I'm here to help. I mean, that's what I intended to do, so I figured what harm could it be. Technically speaking, using the alias Al Stone probably qualified as another little white lie, but I couldn't very well use my real name. Anyway, in case Abe didn't take my word for it, I gave brother Ernie here, as a reference. Long story short, Abe invited me to his next meeting."

"Abe and I hit it off real-well, so he sent me out on the recruiting trail. I know good dairy country when I see it, so I started in the southeast corner of the county, and worked my way west, township-by-township. Then, I moved north to the next tier of townships, and went east-to-west again. My plan was to cover the whole county that way ... you know, systematically. But within a few weeks, I'd inked so many new members that Abe called to say membership was no longer the priority. Instead, he needed my help on something else."

"You see, Abe was anxious to move forward with what he called a milk diversion. The idea was to get a bunch of his members to agree to divert their milk away from their current milk processor, to somewhere else ... you know, temporarily. Then the NFO would step in and negotiate with the processor on behalf of all those farmers. Being short of milk, the processor would agree to pay a higher price. Then, all the farmers would return, mission accomplished."

"Anyway, Abe said he had all the farmers he needed, so I should stop recruiting and instead help find a temporary market for the diverted milk. At the time, I'd been recruiting in the Town of Mitchell, and as luck would have it, had run across a cheese factory about to reopen with a new owner, and in need of milk. Vito Papini was the cheesemaker's name. Anyway, I hooked Abe up with Vito, and a deal was made."

"After that, long story short, the Sheboygan County NFO pulled the trigger on their milk diversion, and it blew up in their face. Right then and there, Ernie and I decided we'd been right the first time. Dairy farming in Wisconsin had gone down the shitter, and our best move was to sell out and relocate to warm and sunny Texas. It's the best decision we ever made."

Rachel sat mesmerized, mouth agape, throughout Bert's monologue. When he finished, she took a moment to gather herself, then said, "Oh ... my ... God! Bert, that's the most amazing line of total bullshit I've ever heard. Where'd you learn to lie like that? You should've been a politician."

* * *

Rachel left the Baker meeting thrilled. If asked under oath why the brothers had done what they did, she could simply say she didn't know, you'd have to ask them. If pressed on whether she had any involvement in their actions, she could deny it. Bert's story was not only credible, but had many grains of truth embedded inside. Rachel's branch bank in Campbellsport could attest to their farm's long-standing financial difficulties. It was undeniable that Wisconsin dairy farmers were dropping like flies. If successful, efforts to elevate the price paid for raw milk could've made a difference. The Baker's did have relatives in Texas, including a mother with failing health, and a sister that needed help taking care of her. Yes, it all held together nicely.

Rachel particularly appreciated the embedded explanation ... simple geography ... for why the overwhelming majority of new NFO recruits had loans at Oostburg Bank. Bert had gone township-by-township, starting in the southeast corner of the county and going east-to-west. Then, he moved one township-tier north, and went east-to-west again before being told to stop recruiting. In the part of the county where Bert recruited, Oostburg was centrally located. Of course, most of the recruited farmers banked there. It'd just been the bank's bad luck that Bert recruited that way. It was brilliant, and would vanquish with reasonable doubt, any prosecutor's evil conspiracy theory.

Rachel also saw value in having the Bakers in Texas. It isolated them from whoever was investigating her bank takeover attempt. Instantly, it increased the expense, inconvenience, and time required to badger them. Fulfilling their retirement dream also made it less likely they'd roll over to pressure, and turn state's evidence. The state's only leverage was to grant immunity, which begs the question … immunity from what? Sure, the Bakers fibbed a little, but who doesn't? They gave the Sheboygan County NFO new members and new hope. Sure, there'd been some self-interest involved, too. But if you had a farm, wouldn't you try to save it? Where's the crime in that? No, the state had nothing on the Bakers, so long as they stuck to the story. And if they did, the state had nothing on Rachel, either. A bank issued a public stock offering, and Rachel put in a bid. So what?

Rachel spent that evening on her financial analysis, but it had nothing to do with determining the near-equivalence or not, of funding the Baker's retirement versus restructuring their debt. The Bakers were going to Texas … she'd already decided that. Instead, the mental gymnastics focused on how to do it in the way most consistent with Bert's story. Somehow, she had to take over the Baker farm and personal property ASAP, turn those assets into cash, pay off the debt to her branch bank, and set aside the remainder to fund the Bakers. She wasn't all that concerned about the size of the remaining fund. If the Bakers outlived their money … well, that was a problem easily solved.

✳ ✳ ✳

The next morning first thing, Rachel called Bert with the good news. The numbers had worked out, and retiring to Texas was doable. When she asked if they had a deal, Bert asked for a moment, and she could hear muffled discussion among the brothers in the background. When Bert got back on the line, his only question was when could they move. All parties agreed that time was of the essence.

After the call, Rachel set everything into motion. Her branch bank already had a Baker farm appraisal, so she arranged to have it updated pronto. She directed one of her shell corporations to buy everything at the appraised price. After agreeing to a timeline with the shell's manager, she called Bert and Ernie back, and told them they had until the end of June to clear out their vehicles, clothes, and anything else they planned to take to Texas. By the same date, Rachel's shell corporation would buy the Bakers out, rent the land to nearby farmers, and begin the process of clearing out the personal property. Rachel received a commitment from the shell's manager that everything would be completed within two weeks.

The Bakers jumped on the logistics of the move with great enthusiasm. Bert's sister put him in touch with several trailer parks in the McAllen area, and Bert called around to find out what was available. Sis volunteered to look at the available units. On her recommendation, Bert and Ernie signed a lease sight-unseen. Before departing, the brothers promised to call Rachel immediately, collect of course, if contacted again by Binder or anyone else. At her urging, they also left a forwarding address at the post office, and made sure their neighbors and the Campbellsport town gossips knew they'd sold out, and were moving to McAllen. To provide spending money for the relocation, Rachel gave the brothers their first check before they left. Once in McAllen, they set up a post office box, and future payments would be mailed there.

* * *

That afternoon, Rachel was feeling pretty proud of herself. In a matter of days, she and the Baker brothers had struck a new deal, and the Al Stone problem was behind her. She looked forward to spending the rest of the day finetuning her strategy to acquire the Evans farm. Anticipation was a strange thing. The simple act of pulling the Evans files sparked a tremor of excitement. Arranging them on her desk, sparked another. She was about to delve into her labor of love, when the phone rang once more. Somewhat peeved at the interruption, Rachel snapped up the receiver, and answered in a sharp tone, "Rachel Wolf here."

Phil, taken aback, "Rachel, it's Phil. Have I gotten you at a bad time?"

Mortified, Rachel backtracked, "Phil ... oh gosh no." Then, she fibbed, "Sorry about that. When the phone rang ... well, I expected it to be someone else. What can I do for you?"

Sensing she was busy, Phil jumped right in, "Well, somebody's been nosing around, and I thought you should know. Three days ago, an investigator by the name of Jason Binder paid a visit to our favorite cheesemaker, Vito Papini. It's a long story, but I only found out about it just now."

Rachel gasped, "Oh shit! Is that going to be a problem?"

Phil chose his words carefully, "No, I don't think

so. We still have Papini's daughter because ... well, in our opinion, he'd only been partially successful on his little assignment for us. As best I can tell, he parroted what he'd been told to say ... which was to say nothing, and refer inquiries to my attorney here in Milwaukee. The little shit should've called me right away, but he thought the attorney would. I only found out because I call Vito weekly ... you know, to keep him goosed about his daughter. Not hearing from the attorney pissed me off, but his story is that nobody ever contacted him. It's no secret the guy represents us, so maybe Binder didn't want to waste his time."

Rachel thought about that, then said, "So, because of the daughter, you think Papini will hold strong?"

Phil exhaled heavily, "Oh yeah ... he's solid. Plus, we wouldn't stop at the daughter, and he knows it. But these jokers snooping around ... they're pretty persistent." Phil told Rachel about the calls to ABC, and to the Chicago-area beverage milk processors. Then, he wrapped up by saying, "Don't worry about this, Rachel. As you know, we're pretty good at keeping our collective lips sealed. But what about you? Are all your ducks in a row? If we get blowback from our little milk heist, the big boys in Chicago might not be happy. We don't want them unhappy ... if you know what I mean."

Rachel understood instantly, and said with haste, "Phil, there's absolutely nothing to worry about. Everything's under control up here." Phil probed with a few more pointed questions, just to make sure Rachel fully understood the stakes were high. And not just for her, but him as well. Then, he clicked off.

Stunned and immobile, Rachel began to experience classic anxiety symptoms for the first time in her life … sweaty upper lip, racing heart, shortness of breath. Apparently, even when you're Rachel Wolf, the mob can have that effect on you. Did she truly have everything under control? Suddenly unsure, she replayed the entire bank takeover scam in her mind, looking for vulnerabilities. The Bakers had been a weak spot, but they're solid now. The mob had ABC and Papini under control. The only other vulnerability she could think of was her banking division stoolie, Ryan Weiser.

Rachel refocused her considerable mental gifts to examine in detail, her dealings with Weiser. For one, he'd been her source for the list of farmers with loans at Oostburg Bank. True, Bert Baker's story provided a plausible explanation for why so many of Oostburg's farmers got caught up in the NFO milk diversion. But that doesn't mean a thorough investigator wouldn't look for other explanations. And it's beginning to look like Binder is very thorough.

Rachel had also used Weiser as her source for the names and addresses of Oostburg Bank's stockholders. She replayed in her mind what she'd done with those, and the importance of it. The bank first tried to regain solvency, by assessing existing stockholders to raise capital. She'd scuttled that attempt by sending each shareholder an anonymous letter on the heels of the bank's request. In it, she promised greater returns to those who refused to ante up, and instead allowed the bank to sell their shares to the highest bidder. The letter implied that shareholders would get a very high price for their shares, and of course the share-buyer would also pay the assessment. After the assessment failed, the bank was forced into a public stock sale, which created Rachel's opportunity to step in.

Rachel thought about that, and concluded the stockholder list was only a problem if authorities could prove Rachel sent the anonymous letters. So, could they? When Rachel received them, the envelopes had already been stuffed, sealed, and addressed. She personally applied the postage, and wiped each envelope clean before sending them. She was certain her prints would not be found on either the envelopes or the letters.

But a short time later, Rachel's eyes widened as she realized she might've made a mistake. Fearing the bank's assessment would go out any day, she'd been focused on making sure her letters were ready to send right after. The most expedient thing to do was to use her regional bank's administrative staff to produce them, and that's what she'd done. Her bank's admins had typed-up the letters, and stuffed and sealed the envelopes. More likely than not, the letters that went out were filthy with admin finger prints.

As she thought about that some more, Rachel's eyes narrowed and her shoulders tensed. But after systematically thinking it through, she began to relax. She reasoned that even if prints were found, they'd never find a match. After all, what're the odds that a bank secretary's prints would be in the system. The paranoia surged back momentarily, at the thought that the letters might be traceable to the bank's typewriters. But in short order, she dismissed the idea as Hollywood fiction, and her fears gradually subsided. The letters had been sent some time ago. For all she knew, by now they'd met their fate in a landfill or gone up in smoke through a burn-barrel. Sure, she'd be a suspect, but Rachel doubted the authorities could prove she sent the letters. Any bidder might've done it, and all she needed was reasonable doubt.

Though somewhat reassured, it bothered Rachel that something still nagged at the back of her mind. Frustrated over not being able to pull it up, she replayed the entire scam once more in her mind. When nothing popped, she replayed the scam again, and there it was. She'd utilized for nefarious purposes information received from Ryan Weiser. That's the detail that'd been nagging at her. But the only way authorities could prove she'd used Weiser, is if Weiser talked. Rachel needed to make sure Weiser knew what to say, if they got to him.

Inspired by her experience with Bert Baker, Rachel called Weiser and gently reminded him of the dirt she had on him … specifically, that he'd been convicted of bank fraud in Pennsylvania, and relocated to Wisconsin to start over. Then, she told him to make up a plausible story that explained why he and Rachel talked on occasion. A few hours later, he called back and ran it by her. It was perfect.

In hindsight, Rachel was glad Phil had scared the living daylights out of her. If not for his call, she may never have bothered to properly circle her wagons. Now that she had, she felt impregnable. With legal jeopardy from past shenanigans no longer a concern, Rachel vowed to go back on the offensive.

CHAPTER 7

Succession Plan-A Bites the Dust –
Sunday; June 27, 1965; 7:30 AM

With the milking machines working their magic on the last six cows, Overdrive stood in the center aisle, hands on hips and over-bent in the backward direction, hoping to work out a kink. As he gently twisted left and right, his mind was busy finalizing the work plan for the day. Due to a few more rain delays than normal, the Evans family was behind on its goal of finishing second-cutting hay by the end of June. But the last of it was cut and on the ground at the Riley farm, and some of those fields would be dry enough to bale tomorrow. If all went well, they'd finish baling at Courtland's today, so Overdrive felt good about the prospects for catching up.

Unfortunately, one small hiccup needed to be resolved before today's baling could start. Old Bill and the younger boys had moved the elevator to the Ulbricht barn last night, but their attempt to set it up had been unsuccessful. Somehow, one side of the barn door at the back of the barn had fallen off the track, and they'd been unable budge it. Until the end of the elevator was inserted into the barn through that door, there'd be nowhere to unload the hay. For tasks where failure was not an option, Overdrive always threw himself and Jumbo at it. This was one of those cases. They'd tackle it right after breakfast, while the others fed the young cattle and caught up on spreading manure.

Over breakfast, Overdrive picked Old Bill's brain to determine the tools he and Jumbo would likely need to fix the barn door. Based on that, they loaded into the cow car's trunk a gravel shovel, an ice pick useful for prying, a short length of eight-by-eight post to pry against, and log chains. Then, Jumbo headed to Ulbricht's driving the slow-moving scoop tractor, and Overdrive took the cow car. The car beat the tractor to the scene, so Overdrive looked things over as he waited for Jumbo to arrive.

The back of the barn was mostly shaded during the day, which explained why the ground in front of the barn-door was still soft and muddy from the recent rains. The barn door opening was formed by heavy beams above and on both sides, and was nominally 20-feet-high and 16-feet-wide. Best-practice for covering openings this large called for two doors that joined in the middle, and slid open to either side. But Ulbricht had been a cheap sonofabitch, and used one gigantic door to save on hardware. The door had wheels attached near each end of its top-side, which were supposed to hang on a track attached directly to the horizontal beam. The horizontal beam and track spanned the barn door opening, and extended another 16-feet off to the right to accommodate opening the door. When closed, these types of doors flopped in-and-out due to wind pressure, unless secured. This particular one was secured with giant-sized hooks mounted chest-high on each side of the door, which dropped into 'eyes' screwed into the opening's side-beams.

Old Bill claimed when he and the boys arrived the previous evening, both sides of the door had been unhooked, and the left-side wheel had been off the track. Overdrive knew for a fact the door hadn't been left that way after its previous use, because he'd closed it himself. As he examined the door, he noted that mud had washed downhill against the bottom-right. The only way to open the door, was to slide it to the right. Obviously, this door couldn't be opened until that mud was dug away.

As he examined the scene, Overdrive developed a different theory about what really happened last night. Old Bill and the boys arrived, unhooked both sides of the door, and then had the strongest of them try to slide it open. That'd be Joe. The door wouldn't budge, so Joe being Joe, he heaved against it with all his might, rather than look to see what the problem was. The door was unable to slide right due to the mud, so the left-side tilted up and off the track. Once off, the door was too heavy to be lifted back on.

Overdrive smiled internally, at the thought that he'd caught his father and the boys in a little white lie. For the fun of it, he decided to verify his theory. He looked closely at the ground around the left side of the door, expecting to see Joe's boot prints, and he did. What surprised him, though, was the presence of other boot prints ... ones he didn't recognize. All the Evans men and boys wore the same brand of boot, and these weren't of that brand. They'd been partially covered-over by Joe's markings, which meant they'd been there first.

About then, Jumbo put-putted his way around the barn on the scoop tractor. Never one to be caught just standing around because of the poor example it'd set, Overdrive grabbed the shovel and began to dig out the mud-packed portion of the door. By the time Jumbo arrived, the mud had been cleared.

Working together, the two men threaded a log chain under the door's righthand-side, where the mud had formerly been. Sufficient clearance existed, because the right-side of the door was still on the track. With one man inside the door and one outside, they pulled the chain left as far as they could. Then, using the wood block and long ice pick, Jumbo levered the lefthand-side of the door upward a tad, while Overdrive again jerked the chain left as far as it'd go.

Satisfied that the chain was far enough to the left, the two men hooked one end of it to itself around the lower-left corner of the door, and the other to the scoop tractor's bucket. Using the bucket's hydraulics, they raised the over-sized door until the errant wheel was above the track. Then, with shoulders to the door, they pushed it inward until the wheel and the track were in alignment. By gently lowering the bucket, they dropped the wheel back onto the track.

Working a difficult task together, especially when successful, creates a bond among men. There's a certain kind of afterglow, almost primal, from a job well done. Jumbo used this special moment to broach a difficult subject, "Dad, I need to have a private conversation with you and Mom. The sooner the better."

Overdrive stepped back and appraised his son, "Okay, we can do that. You want to tell me what this's all about?"

Jumbo looked down and shook his head, "Not really. I'm pretty sure it'll be a difficult conversation, and I'd just as soon only have to go through it once."

Overdrive understood, and looked away. He took a moment to compose himself, then said, "Okay, how about we do this tonight, after milking?"

Jumbo nodded, "That'll work."

Overdrive thought some more, then said, "At dinner, we'll tell everybody you and I are moving the baler and empty wagons to Riley's after milking. I'll finish at Courtland's this afternoon, so it's got to be done anyway. Then, we'll say Mary is picking me up from there, to go to Harbor Lights. That'll put the three of us at Riley's for as long as we need. I'll take the baler and a wagon over, and you can bring another wagon with the Ferguson."

Without saying another word, Overdrive pulled Jumbo in for a hug. Then, Jumbo mounted the scoop tractor and headed back to the home place. While watching him go, Overdrive could see his son wipe tears from his eyes with the back of his hand. Since observing the awkwardness between Jumbo and Lizzie, Overdrive had known this was coming. Even so, a sudden tilt-a-whirl feeling forced him to step to the car for support. When his balance returned, he got inside and sat. Then, after a quick head-swivel to verify no prying eyes, he pulled the door shut to muffle the sound, and bowed his head and cried.

When the moment passed, Overdrive pulled out his handkerchief, dried his eyes, and blew his nose.

With a new sense of purpose, he stepped out of the car and stowed his tools. Back at the steering wheel, he took a deep breath, cranked the engine and drove to Courtland's to bale hay for the rest of the day. Overdrive felt grateful for having something to do. Preoccupied with Jumbo's great reveal, the boot prints he didn't recognize slipped his mind.

* * *

The rest of the day unfolded as any other during haying season on the Evans farm. With the door now functional, Old Bill and the younger boys had no trouble setting up the elevator for unloading hay. Overdrive baled, Jumbo hauled wagons, and grandpa and the rest of the boys unloaded. Mary and the girls spent the day tending to the garden. The weather held, nothing broke down, and the family settled into a productive tempo.

At noon, Mary arrived at Courtland's in the family car with lunch, and honked and waved to get Overdrive's attention. Shortly after, he shut-down his rig, hopped off, and motioned her to meet him at the cow car. He'd parked it in the shade, inside the field along a fence line. They arrived at the same time, and after a quick hug and kiss, Overdrive said, "Enjoy the shade with me for a while, I've got some news to tell you." He took a seat on the hood, and patted the area next to him.

Mary handed him a fresh jug of ice water and a sandwich, then said, "Can it be quick? You're my first delivery. Lunch for everybody else is in the car."

Overdrive patted the hood again, "Sure, it'll be quick." Overdrive took a pull from the water jug as

Mary climbed onto the hood, then said, "Jumbo wants a private conversation with us." He filled her in on the plan to meet at Riley's after the evening milking, then took a bite of his sandwich.

Mary nudged him, "Come on, James. What's this all about?"

Overdrive chewed while finding the right words, "I don't know for certain, but have a pretty good idea, and so do you. I think Jumbo's decided to enlist."

They locked eyes, then Mary looked away and shook her head in denial, "What makes you think that?" He told her about Lizzie's last visit. Still in denial, she said, "No, it can't be. They'd send him to Viet Nam for sure. Only a fool would think otherwise. We didn't raise a fool, James. We didn't. Besides, how could he do that to Lizzie? How could he do that to us?"

As tears began to roll down her cheeks, Overdrive put his arm around her, and whispered tenderly, "Like I say, I don't know for sure. But I'm telling you now so you've got the rest of the day to get used to the idea, just in case. Jumbo said it'd be a tough conversation for all of us. So, what else could it be?"

Mary wiped her cheeks with the back of her hand, then shook her head, "I don't know. I can't think of what else it might be, either." Then, she gave a defeated sigh, "You're probably right."

Overdrive gave her a squeeze, "I hope I'm not. But just in case, we've got to get ourselves together beforehand. I think our son's made a hard decision. He's doing the right thing, by telling us straight. It'll be a tough conversation, maybe toughest on him. But he's been a good son, right? A good son deserves good parents, doesn't he? So, the question is, how would good parents react? By the time we're done milking tonight, we need to have that figured out."

Overdrive and Mary spent the rest of the day contemplating that question. That evening, as they milked from one end of the barn to the other, they shared their ideas on how to react. By the time the last pail of milk finished dripping through the strainer into the cooler, they'd come to a decision. They thought back to their own life experiences. They'd faced a string of big decisions, not just one. Mistakes were inevitable but could, for the most part, be corrected down the road. Every step of the way, their parents had supported them, right or wrong. Whatever Jumbo decided, Overdrive and Mary would support.

Later that evening, Overdrive, Mary and Jumbo convened as planned at Riley's. On this rental property, the farmhouse was long gone and the barn in shambles, so the default for a conversation would be to stand in an awkward circle. Uncomfortable with that configuration, Mary arrived early to consider better options. Soon Overdrive arrived, and he liked her idea. They wanted to be sitting, relaxed, comfortably spaced, and with everyone at about the same eye-level.

Soon, Jumbo arrived on the Ferguson with a wagon in tow, and parked. When it came to rest, Mary hopped up on the Ferguson, filled Jumbo in on the plan, and gave her son a reassuring smile and peck on the cheek. Meanwhile, Overdrive nosed the car close to the Ferguson's center, so the two vehicles formed a tee. With Overdrive and Mary seated on the car's hood, and Jumbo sitting sideways in the tractor seat, the three of them had their conversation.

Mary put on an encouraging smile, and said,

"Jumbo, go ahead and tell us what you need to. We promise not to bite."

Eyes wide with anxiety, Jumbo looked from one parent to the other, and said, "I've enlisted in the Army. They're short on military police. If I work hard and keep my nose clean, that's what I'll be. Once an MP, Europe currently has the greatest need, so most likely they'll send me there. After two years, I'll have seen some of the world, and if I want more education, the GI Bill will be there to help."

Overdrive smiled and nodded, "It sounds like you've done your homework."

With traces of nervous stress in his voice, Jumbo said, "I've read and re-read everything available. Had lots of questions, but they've all been answered. For almost a month, I've been revisiting the decision daily, and always came back to the same one. Every day I sleep on it, and wake up refreshed the next morning."

Mary smiled, and asked softly, "Have you talked to Lizzie yet?"

Jumbo winced, then sighed, "She knows. I can't say she's happy about it. I hope she'll wait for me, but it wouldn't be fair to ask her to. Not without a ring, anyway, and neither of us are ready for that. I told her I'd like to write ... that I wouldn't be shopping around ... and when I get a furlough, she'd be the first to know. I hope she waits, but two years is a long time."

Mary said warmly, "You did the right thing. If it's meant to be, she'll wait."

After some empty air, Overdrive asked, "When do you have to report?"

Anticipating displeasure, Jumbo squinted and said, "Monday July 12th."

Overdrive opened his mouth to say something, but decided against it. Instead, Mary tried to lighten the mood, "About two weeks. Shit, we'd better get you some new underwear!"

They chatted comfortably for another ten minutes, then Jumbo said, "This didn't go anything like I expected. Man, I'd been sweating bullets over this for weeks. When did you guys become so reasonable?"

Overdrive, eyes a-twinkle and in a faux-tough-guy voice, "Okay, buddy. Don't push your luck."

* * *

Overdrive and Mary watched in silence, as Jumbo unhooked his wagon and drove off to fetch another. After a moment, Overdrive stepped down off the hood, and gave his wife a lift down. He could tell she was fighting back tears. Once Jumbo was out of sight, Mary let go and he pulled her into his arms. Before long, Overdrive let go, too. Their grief had to come out, and they let it. When the moment finally passed, Overdrive gently raised Mary's chin and kissed her on the lips. Both were a watery mess, but they didn't care. He squeezed her one last time, then she pulled away.

Mary hopped into the car, but squeaked at the sight of herself in the rearview mirror. After rummaging in the glove box, she came out with some napkins and they both went to work, trying to clean up. Dry but still red-eyed, they went for a walk up the lane. Calmed by the pleasant evening breeze, and the scents of drying hay and honey suckle, they returned to the car. When Mary checked in the mirror again, she felt much better about herself.

Harbor Lights, a rustic resort on Lake Ellen about a mile from the home place, was where Overdrive and Mary went when they needed to talk in private. On the drive over, they regrouped in silence. Upon arrival, they put on their game faces and walked inside. There, they greeted the bartender and other patrons as they always did. After getting caught up on the local gossip, they migrated to their favorite table in a quiet corner, each armed with an ice-cold Kingsbury beer.

They clinked bottles, and Mary said, "I think that went as well as it could've. At least we didn't dump our drama all over Jumbo. He's dealing with enough of his own right now. Thank God, he gave us time to mentally prepare. Otherwise, I'd have been a basket case."

Overdrive nodded at her, "I agree. When I enlisted, the level of anxiety I felt surprised me. It wasn't really fear, but more just not knowing exactly what came next. Jumbo may be feeling the same way." He paused to take a sip, then his brow beetled, "I sure hope he's right about ending up as an MP in Europe."

Mary looked at him, but her eyes lacked focus, "I just can't go there. Jumbo has made up his mind. He's signed on the dotted line. What happens now is anybody's guess. But like you told him at Riley's, he appears to have done his homework. Maybe it'll turn out." They chatted for ten or so minutes about running the farm without Jumbo, and concluded it wouldn't be a problem, at least in the short-term. But since Jumbo's adventure may end up being more than just a two-year sabbatical, they both agreed to pay more attention to their other children as prospects to someday run the farm.

As the Jumbo-conversation petered out, Mary's

eyebrows shot up, "Oh, I almost forgot! I followed up on the mystery."

Overdrive, not following, "Huh? What mystery?"

With arm motions like a teacher would use with her slowest student, Mary tried again, "You know, the sick dogs. Anyway, I went around to all the neighbors. Every dog on Bates and Rock Roads has caught it ... whatever it is. But up on County Rd F, none of them have. Isn't that strange? I mean, they're all running loose. If something was going around, you'd think they'd all get it."

Overdrive thought about that, and his eyes narrowed, "That's interesting. The dogs only got sick on the roads where we use the farm-buildings. Do you think it's something we did? Put out rat poison, or something?" They hadn't. After kicking around a few more theories, none of which made any sense, they shrugged and rose to leave.

On the way out, Mary said in a round-about manner, "Feels like Humpty Dumpty fell off the wall today, and splattered my emotions all over the place." Then, after a hip bump and eye-waggle, she added, "I may need to be reassembled and test-driven tonight ... you know, just to make sure everything's still in working order."

Overdrive slipped his hand around her waist, and whispered into her ear, "Being a handy man and all ... I think I can help with that."

CHAPTER 8

*The Investigation Grinds On – Tuesday;
June 29, 1965; 8:00 PM*

Overdrive and Mary were the last to arrive at Ted's office for the hastily-called meeting. Greetings were exchanged, as they entered the conference room and settled into chairs. Darkwater was in the room rather than on the line, and they nodded and smiled at him. With a circle-the-wagons gesture, Ted brought the meeting to order, "We'll start with updates from Darkwater and Jason, and then I'll weigh in."

As all heads swiveled in his direction, Darkwater said, "First off, the tribe's working group sends their regards. They also asked me, on their behalf, to say message-received regarding the need for secrecy. Some good news ... they finished the interviews and inked a deal with a new developer in time for the state-agency conference. The new guy sounds just like Ted, and wants everything kept hush-hush. The conference was today, and the new developer's firm covered it alone to avoid word getting back to Wolf that members of the tribe were there. Make Wit says the new guy is known for his ability to grease wheels in Milwaukee, and ram through real estate deal approvals. He already owns a parcel in Milwaukee that'll work, and he's cautiously optimistic it'll be rezoned and approved for casino-use in advance of the next tribal council meeting. On the presumption that this will happen, his firm and the working group are hard at work, developing the pitch materials for the July 13th."

The room started to buzz at the mention of a new developer. At the news he made it to the conference, the buzz volume dialed up. It reached a fevered pitch, when it came-out he already owned the land. The wheel-greaser remark, sparked cheers. Then, upon hearing the next tribal council meeting was possible, the room exploded in high-fives. Ted let the energy run its course, then implored, "Come on, people, let Darkwater finish or we'll be here all night."

Darkwater took that as his cue, "Anyway, there's really nothing I can do to move any of that along. That's way most of my time recently, has gone toward trying to find out who took those shots at me. I sent Robin to the Vilas County Sherriff's Department ... you know, to find out where they're at with the investigation. As it turns out, there isn't one. An election's coming up, and the Sherriff's busy hustling votes. Apparently, solving an Indian's murder between now and then, wouldn't win many."

Peter spat, "That's irresponsible. So much for being equal under the law."

Darkwater gave a head-tilt and smiled, "Maybe so, but there's plenty of people up north that don't see it that way. Anyhow, it's probably just as well that nobody else is looking into it. That gives me free reign. Me being dead and all makes it a challenge, but we've made some headway using Robin as the face of the investigation, with Round Wind in support. Cedar Root is tied up with the casino working group, but helps out when he can. The main problem is, we don't have much to go on. I know where they shot me, when they shot me, and caught a passing glance at the shooter's john boat. That's about it."

"If the john boat had any distinguishing markings, I didn't see them. I could tell it was aluminum, and one of the larger sizes ... definitely too big to stick into the bed of a pickup truck, either hanging out the back or tilted up over the cab's roof. That means it had to be trailered to a launch point, or came by water from its mooring-place. The problem is, every resort in the area rents boats like that. Plus, many of the locals own one, and some tourists tow their own in. On any given day, there's hundreds of them in and around the chain of lakes up there."

"Robin's been doing the interviews. At first, people were wondering why she's asking so many questions, so we had to come up with a sympathetic story to get past that. You know ... the poor Sherriff's so busy ... she's just trying to help ... for closure, she needs to find out what happened to her fiancée. It seems to work, because now people open right up to her. She started with the resort owner and family, his employees, and then residents of the few sparse homes in the area."

"The scene of the crime was remote enough, I felt comfortable examining that myself. But frankly, by the time I got on my feet, some of the evidence was already gone. The bent vegetation had all recovered, and any finger or boot prints had weathered away. The shooter must've picked up the brass from the first shot, taken from the opposite side of the cove, because I couldn't find it. I did find two .257 shell casings on the lake bottom, near where the shooter had taken the final kill shots. They were print-free, plus half the households in Wisconsin own a .257-caliber deer rifle, so finding the casings hasn't narrowed the problem much."

"We also conducted a widespread water-side search, led by Round Wind with the help of Cedar Root. Each manned a separate john boat with outboard. They started at the spot of the shooting, and spiraled outward in concentric circles to the extent the terrain would allow, examining the shorelines as they went. Every inter-connected lake was included in the search. When they spotted moored john boats, or spots where john boats could be launched, they marked them on a map."

"By the time they finished, they'd marked many dozens of moored john boats and potential launch sites. I took it from there, by driving the paved, gravel, dirt, or logging roads to those locations. Just to be safe, I wore disguises and kept my distance from people. At this point, I've got quite a collection of sun glasses and hats. Anyway, as I drove around, I penciled onto the map the locations of seasonal and year-round cabins and homes."

"Then, Robin followed up by visiting the cabins and homes, and interviewing the people she could find. Our hope was she'd find somebody that noticed something unusual on the day of the shooting. You know ... drivers, passengers, or vehicles they'd never seen before ... a vehicle speeding away with boat in tow

... people unusually dressed, or looking or acting out of place like city-slickers, that sort of thing."

"While Robin was busy with the interviews, Round Wind and Cedar Root spent days networking among the tribe, on and around the reservation. Our hope was they'd learn of additional rumors about what might've happened to me. They hung out at the usual places ... diners, bars, restaurants, stores ... and asked a few discrete questions, but mostly just listened, hoping to overhear something useful. You know ... so-and-so's been throwing a lot of money around lately ... knows Darkwater was shot with a deer rifle ... knows the location of the watery grave ... that sort of thing."

"Well, sad to say, none of what we did panned out. Robin did well over a hundred interviews, and couldn't find anybody that saw or heard anything unusual before, on, or after the day of the shooting. Round Wind and Cedar Root came up empty on the grapevine as well. After all that effort, we really don't know any more than when we started."

Overdrive muttered, "Well, that figures. Wolf is slick-as-shit."

Peter spat, "No kidding."

Mary, in a more encouraging tone, "Well, successful or not, the effort was herculean. Bravo Darkwater."

Ted jumped in, "Look, somebody tried to commit murder, and we had to try to find out who. We knew it was a longshot, right from the start. I agree with Mary. Given the circumstances, Darkwater and his team did a marvelous job." When nobody commented further, Ted continued, "Jason, why don't you give us the latest on your end?"

Jason cleared his throat, and said, "Sure, no problem. I've been looking a little deeper into the Baker brothers. The deed on their farm shows a mortgage lien from Campbellsport Bank, which is another of Wolf's branches under the Fond du Lac regional bank. From the looks of the farm, they were probably behind on their loan. That might be the leverage she used to draw them into her conspiracy."

"After talking with Ted, we thought the time was right to take another run at Bert and Ernie. My play was to show the glossies capturing them together in the farm yard, point to Bert, and ask why dozens of people identify him as Bert Baker, and dozens more as Al Stone. Then, after the yammering stopped, I'd lay out the theory that Wolf leveraged them into her criminal conspiracy using the loan. Next, I'd recite their misdeeds, put a number on their future stay in prison, and threaten to have them arrested. Finally, after the concept of prison sunk in, I'd tell them the good news. My boss and the authorities wanted Wolf not them, and they'd offer immunity in exchange for cooperation."

"The plan was great, but unfortunately, I never had a chance to use it. When I arrived at the Baker farm, trucks were hauling off the livestock, machinery, and everything else. I had no idea what was going on. To try to find out, I stopped at the nearest neighboring farmhouse and played dumb. The wife answered the door. After expressing my astonishment at what was happening at the Baker place, she happily filled me in. It became clear in a hurry she didn't much like the Bakers. Bernie told her he and Bert were retiring and moving to McAllen, Texas, to be near family. The lady actually scoffed out loud at this, called it nonsense, and said she knew better. According to her, they'd been behind at the bank for years, and the bank was gearing up to foreclose. If they'd finagled a deal at the end, it couldn't have been much of one."

"At first, her being so open with a stranger struck me as odd ... you know, essentially gloating over a neighbor's misfortune. But I checked out what she told me, and it seems to stand up. At the post office, the Bakers left a post office box in McAllen, Texas, as their forwarding address. Ted wants me to keep up the pressure, so I'm heading to McAllen tomorrow."

Peter rapped the table to get Ted's attention, gave him a testing look, and said in a frosty voice, "Ted, are you serious? Won't sending Jason out of state run up the expenses?"

Ted held up his hands in a placating gesture, "Come on, Peter. You want to get Wolf, don't you? Flipping the Bakers would go a long way toward making that happen. Besides, Jason's going to drive, stay in dives, and eat cheap."

Peter, with anger in his eyes, "Of course I want to get Wolf. But I also need to keep Verifine, Lake-to-Lake, and Golden Guernsey on board. The expenses are piling up, and they're getting restless. I can't foot the bill alone, you know."

Ted stood his ground, "Understood. But we need the Bakers to flip."

Overdrive, with a query in his voice, "Is our theory that Wolf took the Baker farm, in exchange for setting them up in Texas?"

Ted looked at him, "That's one theory. But here's what we know for sure ... the Bakers have been removed from the scene, period. I hope Jason can get to them while they still live and breathe in McAllen. That's why he's leaving tomorrow."

May gasped, "Are you serious?"

Darkwater held up a finger, "I wouldn't put it past her. Think about it. Think about what she tried to do to me ... twice."

The group spent a few more minutes slicing and dicing the Baker possibilities. After the buzz died down, Ted said, "Disappearing acts may become contagious among Rachel's co-conspirators. That's why I'm driving to Madison tonight. I want to confront Mr. Weiser at the banking division, before it's too late. I'll be paying him a surprise visit first thing in the morning."

❈ ❈ ❈

By showing up unannounced, Ted hoped to unsettle Weiser enough that he'd let something useful slip. If so, that'd give him a string to pull on. The Wisconsin Department of Financial Institutions was housed in a cavernous building full of hard echoing surfaces. At the main reception area, he asked for the banking division, and was directed into a corridor to the right, and told to take the second left and walk to the end.

There, Ted found the banking division receptionist. Oozing charm and male attention, he spent a moment chatting her up. After he thought he'd made enough of a connection, he floated a little white lie about running late for his appointment with Weiser, and pleaded to be walked back immediately before he missed the meeting altogether. When she hesitated, probably because calling ahead was protocol,

Ted slathered on about his long drive from Random Lake, and the wreck that'd delayed his journey through no fault of his own. In the end, Ted won her over with his most encouraging smile, and a respectful bow with hands pressed together as if praying.

A moment later, Ted was shown into Weiser's office. After giving the receptionist a genuine thank you, he quickly closed the office door before Weiser could complain, and had a seat in the visitor's chair.

Irritated by the intrusion but determined to keep this professional, Weiser said, "Excuse me, have we met? What's this all about?"

Still smiling, Ted said, "My name is Ted Ritter. You're Ryan Weiser, I presume?" Then, after Weiser's nod, he calmly slipped in the dagger, "I'm investigating a criminal conspiracy created to takeover Oostburg Bank. Fortunately for the bank, the conspiracy failed. Unfortunately for you, I've reason to believe you were part of it."

Eyes wide and cheeks bulging like a blowfish, Weiser sputtered, "Now, hold on just one minute. You can't come barging in here with all these wild accusations. I'm calling security." He grabbed the phone's handset, but Ted reached over and pushed down the button.

Still cool as a cucumber, Ted said slowly, "Now you listen to me … very, very carefully. You received a call at home on Saturday, December 4th, from our prime suspect. Within a month of that call, dozens of dairy farmers, clients of Oostburg Bank, were recruited into a scam where their milk production over a two-month period was stolen. Our prime suspect needed a source for the bank's client list, and the timing of that Saturday call suggests the source was you."

Weiser scoffed, "What? That's crazy. Why would I do that?"

Undeterred, Ted pressed on, "After two months without pay, every farmer defaulted, placing the bank in peril. Based on an anonymous tip from our prime suspect, the state's bank examiners were sent in and declared Oostburg Bank insolvent." After a pause for emphasis, he continued, "This next part gets really interesting. On Thursday, May 6th, you received a call at work from our prime suspect. Soon thereafter, Oostburg Bank assessed their shareholders to raise capital and regain solvency. On the heels of that, shareholders received an anonymous letter from our prime suspect, promising tidy profits to those who refused to ante up. The assessment failed. Our prime suspect needed a source for the bank's shareholder list, and the timing of that Thursday call suggests the source was you."

At this point Weiser raised both hands and demanded to be heard, "Look, bank executives call me all the time with their routine business. You mentioned a call to my home on a Saturday, right? Well, that must mean your prime suspect is Rachel Wolf. That woman is a pest with serious boundary issues. I made the mistake of giving her my home number, and I've regretted it ever since."

"Wolf is an odd duck. Fashions herself as a financial wonk. Almost all our conversations are about financial ratios and other banking metrics. You see, our division requires every bank in the state to submit quarterly reports. They're referred to as Call Reports. We pull data from them, and calculate a bunch of financial ratios and draw some charts. The ratios and charts are handy tools for understanding a bank's financial condition, both currently and as trends over time. We also use the information to compare each bank's performance to that of its peer group ... you know, a group of similar banks."

"Anyway, somebody got the bright idea that if these metrics were useful for regulating banks, they'd also be useful for managing them. Long story short, our oversight committee at the state legislature forced us to start sharing this information with bankers. That happened back in 1962, about the time when Wolf inherited the Fond du Lac regional bank."

Ted interrupted, "Wait ... you say Wolf inherited the bank in 1962?"

Weiser put his elbows on the table, knitted his fingers together, and said, "Yes, that's when her parents passed away. It was a tragedy, really. You might remember a private plane crash over Lake Michigan. Well, her dad was the pilot, and her mom a passenger. They both died that day."

Something clicked in the back of Ted's brain, "Huh ... I do remember that crash. But until now, I'd never drawn the connection to Rachel Wolf."

Weiser sat back, "Yeah, well, those were her parents. Anyway, she inherited the bank, and has been a major pain in my ass ever since. Always pestering me about why her bank doesn't lead its peer group in every performance category. How the hell should I know?"

Ted considered whether to drop the hammer, then he did, "Look, Mr. Weiser, I don't have time for any more of your bullshit. If what we believe is true, you're guilty of two Class 1 felonies for leaking protected information, and probably a third for being a co-conspirator on the whole shebang. But listen-up, the authorities want Wolf not you. They'll grant you immunity in exchange for your cooperation. Use your head, Mr. Weiser. Do you have a wife? Kids?"

Weiser slumped deeper into his chair, "Yes and yes."

Ted, doubling down, "Well, there you go. Take the deal for them. You ever been to the Waupun Correctional Institution?"

Weiser shook his head, and said, "No."

Ted jabbed a finger at him, "Well, trust me, you don't want to go there. If you do, you'll be watching your kids grow up from the wrong side of a plate glass window. Is that what you want?"

His voice indignant, Weiser said, "No, of course not!"

In a more conciliatory tone, Ted said, "Well, that's what the future holds for you, if you don't cooperate. Think really hard about that. Wolf isn't worth ruining your life over. Look, here's my card. When you come to your senses, give me a call." Then, he shot Weiser a cold stare, stood up, and loomed over him, "But until I get that call, we're not only going after Wolf, we're coming for you." Weiser was bug-eyed and sweaty, when Ted stomped out of the room.

* * *

Ted spent the next day stressing over the slow pace of his investigation, noodling over new avenues to pursue, and waiting for a call from Weiser that never came. The noodling concerned the new information from Weiser on how Wolf's parents died, and whether it had any significance. Knowing Wolf, and in light of her obvious motive, he was pretty sure her parent's death was no accident. Another factor also intrigued him. There was no statute of limitations on murder.

When the phone finally did ring, it was Jason from a phone booth in McAllen, Texas. In a boy-are-we-screwed tone, Jason said, "You're not going to like this."

Ted picked up on that and asked, "Oh-oh, now what?"

Jason half laughed, "Well, I got down here, and the first thing I did was find my way to the right post office branch ... you know, the one where the Bakers have their box. So, I staked it out, and a few hours later ... in walks Ernie."

Confused, Ted said, "But that's good, right?"

Jason, with pain in his voice, "Well, not exactly. When I approached him, Ernie reacted as if I were a long-lost friend. I knew something was up right away. Then, he invited me over to his place, so I played along. We caravanned to a trailer park, and pulled up in front of one of the dumpiest units I've ever seen. When we stepped inside, there sat Bert. They asked if I wanted to take a load off, and have a beer, so I said sure. The only place in that little shit-can for three people to sit was the booth in the kitchen, so we squeezed into that."

Troubled, Ted said, "I'm not sure I like where this's heading."

Jason exhaled deeply, "Trust me, you won't. Bert did the talking ... man, what a lying sonofabitch he is." Jason filled him in on the whole story.

Ted, incredulous, "You mean the Bakers claim they did all that NFO shit on their own?"

Jason, in a don't-I-know-it voice, "That's what they said."

Incensed, Ted sad, "You have got to be shitting me!" Then, after a moment of desperate thought, "They're not going to flip, are they."

After a long slow exhale, Jason said in a limp tone, "Well, the glossies were useless after their confession. I told them what Wolf had been trying to do, and their reaction was so-what, what's that got to do with us? They weren't buying that they were pawns in her scheme, either. When I suggested they're in danger ... you know, as loose ends and all, they laughed at me. No, they're not going to flip."

❊ ❊ ❊

After the call, Ted fell into a deep funk. What he had so far would be weak in court, and Ted knew it. Frustrated, he racked his brain trying to think of other avenues for strengthening his case. It dawned on him that getting out from under the previously-signed Non-Disclosure Agreements, or NDAs, might help. After Darkwater's house and car were destroyed by fire, he and others signed NDAs as part of the settlement between Wolf and Darkwater's insurance company. If he could persuade the insurance company that Wolf had violated the terms of the settlement, all the evidence from her previous run at the Evans farm became fair game now. Although circumstantial, the previous evidence established a pattern of criminal activity motivated by the desire to build a casino on the Evans farm.

Feeling it was worth a shot, Ted set up a meeting

first thing the following day with Don Schneider, the insurance company investigator that'd handled Darkwater's case. Don was based in Green Bay, and given the importance of the meeting, Ted decided to drive up and see him in person. Ted and Don had become friends, and last summer their families even spent a weekend together at a resort in Door County, Wisconsin's thumb-shaped peninsula northeast of Green Bay. Don couldn't void the NDAs. But as an insider, his support would be essential to convince the legal department in his firm to do so.

CHAPTER 9

Taking Stock – Friday; July 2, 1965; 9:00 AM

T he receptionist buzzed Don Schneider when Ted arrived at the insurance company, and he came to the lobby to greet his old friend. They got caught up, as Don led Ted to the break room for coffee, and then on to his office. Once seated, Ted filled Don in on the conspiracy and second attempt on Darkwater's life. While doing so, he was careful to draw a distinction between what he knew in his heart Wolf had done, versus how it would likely play in court given the sorry state of his evidence.

Don seemed not impressed, "Let me play devil's advocate for a moment. Somebody tried to murder Darkwater, but you can't trace it to Wolf."

Ted nodded, "Well no, I can't … at least not yet. But the shooting occurred on the same day Wolf would've gained control of Oostburg Bank, if not for the NFO's farmer-bailout. Given the history, it's hard to believe that's a coincidence."

Don, still not impressed, "Sure, but you can't prove

it … so let's move on. Next, you've got this theory that Wolf masterminded an elaborate criminal conspiracy to takeover Oostburg Bank, and thereby, the Evans farm. That's certainly one possibility. But isn't it also possible she merely kept up with the news, and put in a bid for the bank's stock when the opportunity came along?"

Ted's brow beetled and he shook his head, "That's ridiculous. Right after the milk heist, Rachel's anonymous tip alerted the state that the bank was in trouble, and in came the bank examiners. After being declared insolvent, the bank assessed existing shareholders to right-the-ship. Had that succeeded, there never would've been a public stock sale. But the assessment failed due to Wolf's anonymous letter, promising riches to those who refused to ante up."

Don put an earnest look on his face, "Again, that's one possibility. But for all we know, some other bidder tipped-off the state and sent those letters. Or maybe some disgruntled bank employee did it, hoping for new management. Can you prove it was Wolf?"

Ted stammered, "Well, no. But I'm working on it."

Don turned both palms up, and said in an even tone, "Okay, for the sake of argument, let's say you're right, and there had been a conspiracy. As I understand it, in addition to Wolf, the co-conspirators included the Baker brothers, the banking division guy, Papini, and ABC Milk Haulers. Let's say you're right again, and Papini and ABC are fronts for the mob. This begs the question … who's the true mastermind, Wolf or the mob? Wouldn't most jurors have trouble believing the mob would participate in a conspiracy not of their own design? Doesn't the mere mention of the mob create reasonable doubt?"

Ted gaped at him, "Well, I suppose it would. But ..."

Don cut him off, "And here's another possibility. What if there'd been a crime, but it had nothing to do with the bank? Isn't it possible the whole shebang was mob-led, and aimed at stealing milk? Based on what I heard you say, the hands-on doers were Papini and ABC. In both cases, the evidence leads to the mob. Maybe the bank was just accidental collateral damage."

Face twisted with anger, Ted spat, "Oh come on, Don! What're the odds that 28 out of the 36 ripped-off farmers just happened to have loans at this one bank?"

Don, hands up and with a friendly smile, "I'm just playing the devil's advocate here, Ted. No need to shoot the messenger. But think about it. By your own admission, Bert Baker's story offers a reasonable explanation for that. And Bert's an accomplished liar, right? That means Wolf's defense will put him on the stand. His tale about helping the NFO is pretty clever, too ... you know, if they really could raise milk prices, he and his brother might be able to save their farm. A Wisconsin jury might have some sympathy for that, and it'd only take one juror to swallow the bait. Hell, even if none bought it, Wolf's attorney could always say the Bakers must've been working for the mob. After all, who stole the milk?"

Ted puffed out his cheeks and exhaled in frustration, "Good grief ... you'd make a hell of a defense attorney."

Don, in a sympathetic tone, "No, not really. I just spend a lot of time with our legal department, unfortunately. Tell me, what's the name of that banking division guy again?"

Ted, still sullen, "Ryan Weiser."

Don, trying to go easy on his friend, "Well, some of what he told you had a ring of truth to it, too … you know, the financial ratios and charts. Maybe that's what he and Wolf really did talk about. Again, it only takes one juror."

Ted, with a hint of self-deprecation, "I don't have shit, do I?"

Don chuckled, "Not that I can see."

Ted, fancifully, "Nevertheless, our bedazzling oratory will surely carry the day, and convince your legal-beagles that Wolf violated the settlement, thus nullifying the NDAs."

Don laughed out loud, "Not a snowball's chance in hell. For that to happen, you'll need something concrete … the shooter traced to Rachel … the anonymous letters traced to Rachel … the Bakers, Weiser, or somebody to flip and support your theory. Without one of those, the shooting's a coincidence and the only crime is a milk heist by the mob."

Ted sat back in his chair and sighed, "I hear you."

After a beat, Don asked, "By the way, say the NDAs were nullified. What difference would it make?"

Ted took a moment to organize his thoughts, "Well, for one, it'd help us establish Wolf's motive. The evidence buried by the NDAs suggests Wolf needed the Evans farm to build a casino. We believe the conspiracy was hatched for the same reason. The history helps us prove motive for the conspiracy."

Don thought about that, then said, "Proving she wanted the farm, doesn't prove she committed a crime to get it. As I recall, Wolf sidestepped any actual crime last time around, when the Evanses voluntarily signed a loan agreement whose terms they couldn't fulfill. Being a shrewd business woman isn't a crime. And like I said before, this time around she may've simply responded to a stock-sale notice and put in a winning bid. There's no crime in that, either."

Ted, trending toward red-face, "Well, that first time around, when Wolf felt the deal slipping away, she burned Darkwater out hoping he'd die in the fire, and then launched a manhunt that would've led to his death had they caught him. Those are crimes. And if she didn't commit them, why'd she settle with the insurance company? Why did she demand we sign NDAs?"

Don didn't back down, "Technically, she settled without an admission of guilt. It happens all the time. Plus, if I'm not mistaken, all you could prove at the time was that HMR set the blaze, and Wolf owned HMR. If you took that to trial, Wolf would simply throw HMR under the bus, and claim they acted on their own. If only one juror bought it, she'd skate."

Ted, now a deeper shade of crimson, "Oh, come on, Don! You know as well as I do what really happened."

Don held up his hands in a placating gesture, "Whoa buddy, I'm on your side, remember? You told me to point out the weaknesses in what you had, and that's what I'm doing. Yes, I know what really happened. But, so what? I can't prove it either." The conversation continued like this for another ten minutes. Eventually, Ted cooled down enough to realize Don was right. He didn't have jack shit now, and even with the NDAs nullified, the case wouldn't be much stronger.

Ted spent the drive back to Random Lake reviewing where he was, and pondering what to do next. He hoped his angry response to Don's pooh-

poohing of what he had so far, wouldn't ruin their friendship. Ted felt stymied. Every avenue of the investigation tried thus far had reached a dead end. The one remaining, which they hadn't tried yet, was to connect Wolf to the anonymous letters sent to the bank's shareholders. Frankly, he wasn't very optimistic about the prospects of that panning out, either.

Since his meeting with Weiser, a long-shot possibility had been percolating in the back of Ted's mind. Halfway home, Ted came to the conclusion that his best chance to put Wolf behind bars was to go for the long-shot. So, he pulled into a gas station and called ahead to his office from a pay phone. He knew Jason would be checking in regularly, on his way back from Texas. When he got his office manager on the line, he instructed her tell Jason to come directly to the office, and to obtain an estimated time of arrival from him. Once she had Jason's ETA, she was to call Darkwater, and have him arrive at about the same time. Ted told her that having the meeting tomorrow would be best, but if Jason couldn't get there until the 4th of July, so be it. He wasn't in the mood to celebrate the nation's birthday anyway.

Ted spent the rest of the drive home working through how to handle the impromptu meeting. The desired outcome was for his team to make a fast pivot to pursue the long-shot. While Jason and Darkwater went off in the new direction, Ted would personally keep the old lines of inquiry warm, including taking a shot at connecting Wolf to the anonymous letters. To avoid headwind from Peter, Ted decided to let his team run a few days in the new direction, before reconvening with everyone in the room. The move made him solely responsible if the new direction failed, but provided precious time to prove its worth before having to defend it. If none of the above panned out, Ted had no idea what to do next.

* * *

Generally, Overdrive turned a blind eye to holidays whenever there's farm work to be done. But July 4th fell on a Sunday this year, and Mary was adamant that the kids have the day off. Although he relented to keep the peace, his consolation prize was Mary's blessing for him to get caught up on some things. He hadn't checked on the young cattle recently, so he put that at the top of his list. He started with the oldest cohort of heifers, which pastured at the Ulbricht place. Upon seeing the barn, the lost memory about the unfamiliar boot prints resurfaced. When he walked to the back of the barn, the prints were still there.

Something about those prints bothered Overdrive deeply. Renters lived in the old Ulbricht farmhouse, so on the way out he paid them a visit and asked if they'd seen any strangers nosing around the barn. They hadn't, but from the house the back of the barn was out of view. The wife commented that if anybody had come around, their dog would've sounded the alarm. Then, almost as an afterthought, she mentioned the mutt hadn't been himself lately, so maybe not.

Overdrive's next stop was the Adcock place, where the next-oldest cohort of heifers were kept. After checking on the cattle, he made a point of carefully examining the ground around all the barn entrances. There in the dried mud, he found the same unfamiliar boot prints. The people that bought the old Adcock farmhouse were home, so Overdrive stopped by and asked them the same question. They hadn't seen any strangers hanging around, either. But when asked, they also confirmed their dog had been ill on and off, of late.

Overdrive's last stop was Lemke's, where the youngest heifers were kept. The same unfamiliar boot prints were found near the backside entrance to the barn. Overdrive didn't bother to disturb old Mrs. Lemke. He already knew her dog had been sick, and when she saw unusual things she told him, although not necessarily right away.

Instead, Overdrive investigated where Mrs. Lemke said she'd seen a man trespassing on his land. He should've done it sooner, but just hadn't gotten around to it. He parked near the culvert on Rock Road, where a small stream originating from Waldo Swamp passed under the road. Then, he walked east into one of his hay fields, in the direction where Mrs. Lemke had seen the stranger. As he moved along the fence line toward the back corner of his field, Overdrive could still see impressions in his hay crop where someone had passed. When the field ended, the impressions continued in the waste land beyond, and eventually led to the backend of his side-hill pasture.

In the pasture, Overdrive bent forward at the hips, and walked slowly looking for prints. But the pasture was well-drained sod, and after a moment he realized he was wasting his time. Undeterred, he doubled-down on his search while re-crossing the narrow strip of waste land. In the scrub, some areas were low enough to be intermittently wet, resulting in clumps of vegetation surrounded by bare ground. The same boot prints were visible, here and there, in the bare spots.

Overdrive fought to keep his wits as the paranoia began to creep in. He returned to the home place, and walked the perimeter of his main barn and other outbuildings. The same boot prints were everywhere. Shaken, he hurried to the house and told Mary they needed to go for a ride. One look told Mary something was wrong, and she followed him out of the house without a fuss. They hopped into the cow car, and Overdrive drove behind the barn to the crest of the hill.

Where Overdrive parked, they had a commanding view of hundreds of acres of their land with the Waldo Swamp as a backdrop, starting at the bottom of the hill. Overdrive took a moment to gather his thoughts, then filled Mary in on what he'd discovered. Mary heard him out, then wondered out loud about the dogs … had they been sick or drugged? Together, they kicked around various theories about what was going on. Resonating the most, was one where the booted man silenced the dogs with drugs, in order to explore their property undetected. But they hadn't a clue why, and frankly didn't know what to think.

* * *

Mid-morning the next day, Overdrive was cussing a blue streak, after breaking two cutter guards and a half-dozen blades on the Owatonna. Another of those massive granite boulders, deposited compliments of the last glacier, had peeped up out of the ground just enough to snag his machine. In a fit of rage, he'd exhausted himself kicking the boulder with his steel-toed boots. He was drenched in sweat, and that, plus the fact that it was hot and unusually humid due to the previous afternoon's rain, explained why. Attracted by his sweaty stench and elevated infrared signature, a cloud of black flies was dive-bombing his face. These sorties no doubt contributed to his foul mood.

After he calmed, Overdrive pulled himself together and planned his next move. While standing next to his silenced machine, he surveyed the area looking for a more comfortable spot to make the lengthy repair. Adjacent to the hay field, was a long farm lane that provided access to the Ulbricht lands from Rock Road. His eyes were drawn to a low spot along the lane, where a small spring trickled across. At that exact spot, a shade tree towered from the fence row along the lane. Hoping the shade and cool trickle might offer some relief, Overdrive fired up the Owatonna and parked it under the tree. Then, after laying out replacement parts and tools, he sat down next to the cutter bar, and got to work.

A moment later, a large black car came bouncing down the lane from Rock Road, headed in his direction. Overdrive pulled himself to a standing position, and watched as the car approached. The look of the car clicked with Mrs. Lemke's account of the vehicle she'd seen on Rock Road. If so, there's a good chance the mysterious boot prints were made by the man behind the wheel. The thought triggered a jolt of adrenalin, and revved Overdrive's mind into action.

To put the intruder at ease, Overdrive decided to play the friendly hayseed, and smile and offer an acknowledging wave. He sensed a golden opportunity to prove the driver was the source of the boot prints, and his mind raced trying to figure out how. With a quick glance, he verified where the trickling spring crossed the lane, and what beyond it offered a place to sit in the shade. A beat later, he knew exactly how to entice his visitor to walk across that muddy ground.

Careful to appear relaxed, Overdrive maintained the smile and stepped out into the lane to control where the car must stop. He watched while it slowly nosed up to him, and came to a halt. The driver shutdown the engine, returned the smile, picked something off the passenger seat, and exited the vehicle. Overdrive was curious what the man held, and recognized it as paperwork. Continuing with his friendly-farmer act, he said, "Howdy, what can I do for you?"

Through a genuine-seeming smile, the stranger said, "Are you James Evans?"

Overdrive nodded, "That's right. And who might you be?"

Holding his smile, the stranger said, "My name is Vince Alder. If you've got a moment, I'd like to talk a little business with you."

To lighten the mood, Overdrive scrunched up his nose, and said, "I see what you're carrying. You're not selling insurance, are you?"

Vince laughed, "No, no, nothing like that. Look, I know you're busy. But if you can spare a few moments, I think you'll be interested in what I have to say."

Overdrive made a big display of eyeing him from head-to-foot, then said, "Well, come on then, let's get it over with. It's hot as hell, so let's get into the shade. There're a few places to sit over here." Without waiting for a reply, he turned, walked across the spring-softened ground, and sat down on a boulder in the shade. He motioned his visitor to the other boulder.

After walking the same path, Vince had a seat, and motioned toward the Owatonna, "I see you've had a little break down."

Overdrive patted the boulder he sat on, then said, "Yeah, over in the field there's another one of these. Like a dummy, I ran right into it."

Vince nodded, "Sorry to hear that. Looks like a nice crop of hay, though."

Overdrive bobbed his head, "That it is. Nothing but alfalfa, nice and thick."

Vince leaned in, "Look, I know you're busy, so let me get right to the point." He paused to hold up the paperwork, "What I have here are two documents. This one, is an appraisal report, documenting the value of your farm." He dropped the name of the company that did it, as he handed it over.

Incredulous, Overdrive flipped through the document. Sure enough, the firm's name appeared in the header on every page. He nodded, and said, "Sure, I've heard of them. They're supposed to be a first-rate outfit."

Vince brightened his smile, "Their specialty is dairy farms, and they're the best in the business." Then, he held out the remaining document, and said, "This one, is a cash offer to buy your farm at a 20 percent premium over the appraised value. It's a very generous offer, and I hope you'll seriously consider it."

Overdrive's eyes widened. He hadn't seen that coming. He took the document, and slowly flipped through it. When he noticed the offer was from HMR, he had to struggle to maintain a neutral expression. He looked up and studied Vince for a moment, then asked, "What makes you think we've any interest in selling?"

Vince held the eye contact, "I don't know that you do. I just know it's a very generous offer. With that kind of money, you could buy another farm." Then, he patted the boulder and said, "Maybe one not littered with these."

Overdrive groaned, "That was pretty slick, what you just did there."

Vince chuckled, "I have my moments. Not many, but a few. Anyway, think about it. Oh, and there's something else I should mention. The appraisal report documents two values, one for just the farm, the other for the farm plus personal property. The offer to buy your farm is valid either way. Basically, you decide which way you want to go, and you'll get a 20 percent premium either way. So, hypothetically, say you wanted to get out of farming altogether. Then, selling the farm plus personal property might be the easiest thing to do. On the other hand, say you'd rather buy another farm. Then, you might prefer to sell the farm only, and migrate the personal property to your new farm."

Overdrive thought about that, then said, "Hmmm, that makes sense. Sounds like you've put some thought into this."

After a humble shrug, Vince said, "We have. We're just trying to make this work out for the best, for all concerned. Anyway, there's one last thing I need to mention. The offer is time sensitive. I'll be back tomorrow to see what you think."

Overdrive gasped, "Tomorrow! You're kidding, right? That's not much time for something like this."

Vince rose to his feet with his palms up, "I know, and I'm truly sorry about that. But like I say, we're trying to make this work out for the best, for all concerned. As it turns out, the buyer needs to move fast." On his way to the car, he turned back and said, "I'll see you tomorrow."

Overdrive stood, and said, "You know where to find me."

As Vince reversed his way back down the lane, Overdrive stepped over and examined the soft ground. There in the mud, were the same boot prints he'd seen all over his farm.

Muttering to himself, Overdrive sat back down at the Owatonna's cutter bar. As he worked at replacing the broken parts, he connected the dots between what he just learned, and what he'd known before. He knew HMR was a shell corporation owned by Wolf. He knew the acronym stood for Headwaters of the Milwaukee River. Given the name, he guessed HMR was created to acquire the real estate needed to develop the Headwaters of the Milwaukee River Casino. Toward that end, HMR had previously bought nearby farms previously owned by Lage, Salveson, and Nitsch. But for some reason, instead of trying to buy his farm back then, Wolf tried to steal it instead. When that failed, Wolf built a criminal conspiracy and tried to take over Oostburg Bank, as a means of getting to his farm. That failed on June 9th, a little less than a month ago. Since then, HMR has been trespassing all over the farm, and now they offer to buy it. Which begs the question, why didn't they offer to buy the farm to begin with?

* * *

That evening, Overdrive and Mary found themselves sharing their various anxieties on the way to Ted's office in Random Lake. Jumbo's enlistment, of course, was one of their worries. The dog-drugging, trespassing, unsanctioned appraisal, and purchase offer made up another thread of angst. Then came the late-afternoon call from Ted's office, summoning them to Random Lake for what appeared to be an emergency meeting. No reason had been given, and when asked, Ted's office manager admitted she didn't know why. Recently, pop-up meetings had become routine. But previously, the notifications had always come before noon. Notice this short was out of character for Ted, and added to their concerns.

By the time they reached Ted's office, Overdrive and Mary were in agreement that they needed to bring up the latest HMR shenanigans. But they didn't want to detract from Ted's purpose in calling the emergency meeting, so they decided it could wait until the end.

Ted, Peter, Jason and Darkwater were all seated, when Overdrive and Mary walked into the conference room. Pleasantries were exchanged while they settled into their chairs. Ted started by reviewing for everyone's benefit, the litany of investigative disappointments that'd occurred since their last meeting. This included the failure to flip the Bakers or Weiser, and the stark reality-check received from Don Schneider.

Darkwater, voice thick with disappointment, "You mean my own insurance company doesn't see enough here to nullify the NDAs? Wolf put a hit on me! What … that's not good enough until I'm actually dead?"

Ted found Darkwater's eyes, "Look, everybody in this room knows Wolf violated the settlement agreement, and Don knows it too. The problem is, I can't prove it. And if I can't, neither can the insurer's attorneys. Their job is to protect their firm. Right now, they're good. Wolf's settlement payment covered your insurance claim. If they take the position that Wolf violated the settlement, and on that basis release us from the NDAs, it's a risk. Wolf would likely sue to get her payment back, plus damages for defamation of character and God knows what else, and there's a good chance she'd win."

Overdrive spat, "That's ridiculous! Whatever happened to justice for all?"

Mary gasped, "What're we supposed to do? Wolf is gunning for our farm, and she won't stop until she gets it. We can't live like this forever."

Peter fixed Ted with an icy stare, "So, what ARE we going to do, just give up? I put my reputation on the line with Verifine, Lake-to-Lake, and Golden Guernsey. At some point, they'll want to know what the hell we did with their money."

Ted's face twisted with anger, "Giving up? Hell no, we're not giving up. We're doubling down. I've expanded the investigation to include past crimes." Peter tried to protest, but Ted raised his voice, "Hear me out Peter, please. When interrogating Weiser, he dropped an interesting nugget. Wolf's parents died in a plane crash, ruled accidental at the time. That's when she inherited the Fond du Lac bank. Well, what if it wasn't an accident? There's no statute of limitations on murder, you know. We began poking around, and it turns out there's a trail of dead bodies in Wolf's wake. Odds are, she's made a mistake somewhere along the line."

Peter exploded, "Oh, come on, Ted. It sounds like

you'd be starting all over. Your sponsors, me included, would never go for that."

Ted raised both palms, "Just hear us out, okay? We've only been at this a few days, and it looks like fertile ground. Jason, tell them what we know so far."

Wide eyed as if catching a grenade, Jason said, "Umm, sure, okay. Well, Darkwater and I've completed a narrow search. We looked for suspicious deaths and unsolved murders that occurred in Wolf's proximity, and recently enough that she might've had a hand in them. We found seven possibilities."

Eyebrows up, Overdrive snorted, "What?"

Peter gasped, "You can't be serious."

Mary, white-faced, "Oh my God, you think she's a serial killer?"

Jason squinted and waggled his head, "Hold on, let me finish. We started out by establishing where Wolf spent her time over the years. Her bank is based in Fond du Lac, but Ted's father had case files that placed the Wolf family in Sheboygan. Darkwater did a search at the Fond du Lac County register of deeds office, and I did the same for Sheboygan County. Wolf's current residence is in a toney part of the City of Fond du Lac, and was acquired in August of 1958. I found a City of Sheboygan property briefly owned by her in 1962, and previously owned by a Benjamin Wolf for decades, and a Jacob Wolf before that. We've verified that Ben and Jacob are her father and grandfather."

Mary said absently, "So, Wolf's childhood home was in Sheboygan."

Jason nodded, "Exactly. When her parents died in the plane crash in May 1962, we presume she inherited not only the bank, but her childhood home. She sold the

Sheboygan property shortly thereafter. Birth records show she was born in 1932, with the same Sheboygan address listed. Say she graduated high school in 1950, that leaves an eight-year gap until 1958, when she bought the place in Fond du Lac. That's plenty of time for her to earn a degree or two, and maybe even work somewhere else before settling into the family business. To fill in the gap years, I visited Wolf's old neighborhood in Sheboygan, and knocked on some doors. I found a talkative lady in the manse next door. She told me the Wolf's were very private, but she spoke on occasion with Ruth, Ben's wife and Rachel's mother. This lady was aware that Rachel did her undergraduate studies at Lawrence University in Appleton, and then went on to UW Law School in Madison."

Overdrive observed, "That explains most of the gap."

Jason smiled, "It does, but it gets better. Once she started talking, this woman couldn't stop. Apparently, Ben and Ruth Wolf had attended her daughter's wedding, then failed to invite her to Rachel's. She's still miffed."

Mary perked up, "What? Rachel has a husband?"

Jason ticked a finger at her, "Yes, and that was news to me, too. Trust me, I peppered her with questions after that. According to the neighbor, Ruth was quite taken by Rachel's beau ... gushed on and on about his blond wavy hair. She couldn't remember his name, though, and she hadn't seen him around since the time of the wedding. She did say it struck her as odd at the time, that there hadn't been a wedding announcement in the society page of the Sheboygan Press. She thought maybe the Wolfs were publicity shy, after the loss of their son."

Peter's jaw dropped, "Rachel had a brother?"

Jason held out his palms and shrugged, "That was news to me, too. His name was Max, and he died at a family retreat in northern Wisconsin, near Iron Mountain. The neighbor lady couldn't remember how it happened, but she did recall the family referred to the retreat as Wolf's Run. Darkwater, since you ran that property down, why don't you cover that base."

Darkwater leaned into the table, "Sure, no problem. Okay, so I wasn't sure which county to look in, but tried Marinette first, and lucked out. Wolf's Run is a large tract just southeast of Iron Mountain, Michigan, on the Wisconsin side of the Menominee River. It's been owned by Rachel since 1962, when her parents died. Before that, it was owned by Ben, Jacob, and some other Wolfs before that."

Ted chimed in, "Just to summarize then, it appears Wolf's life was spent in Sheboygan through high school, then moved to Appleton for undergrad, Madison for law school, and finally Fond du Lac, where she lives now. Then, sprinkled throughout her lifetime, there would've been time spent intermittently at Wolf's Run. Jason and Darkwater limited their victim search to these environs. Time-wise, they looked starting in 1948 and after, because that's the year Wolf became old enough to drive. Within these narrow limits, it's remarkable that Jason and Darkwater found seven possibilities. Jason looked for victims in the southern part of the state, and Darkwater in the north." He paused to motion toward Jason, then said, "Go ahead and tell them what you found in the south."

Jason looked at his notes, then said, "Okay, well,

in May 1962, Rachel's parents, Ben and Ruth Wolf, died when their private plane crashed into Lake Michigan while enroute to Louisville for the Kentucky Derby. Although ruled accidental, it's on the list due to Rachel's strong motive. The plane took off from Sheboygan County Memorial Airport, so the Sheboygan County Sherriff's Department led the investigation. I spoke with the lead detective, and get this ... Ben's flight logbook listed two passengers, Ruth and Rachel. Apparently, Rachel backed out at the last minute. That and the inheritance caused the cops to take a serious look at Rachel, but her story checked out. According to Rachel, she woke up feeling poorly that morning, and being a widow and six-months pregnant, felt it prudent to stay home."

Mary blurted, "That monster has a child?"

Startled from a slouch, Overdrive cracked his knee on a table-leg, and muttered, "Ouch!" Then, through gritted teeth, "Seriously, her husband's dead?"

Jason grinned and nodded, "Yes and yes, presuming the pregnancy had a successful end. The husband is body number three. He died in January 1962, about a month after their wedding. Presumably, he died an accidental death while on business travel."

Reconsidering, Mary's brow beetled, "That must've been horrible, losing her husband and parents within a few months like that."

Peter chortled, "In her view was it horrible, or several jobs well done?" Then, he made a dusting-his-hands motion, for emphasis.

Jason waved that off, "Well, let's not jump to conclusions. That's what we're trying to find out." After a quick glance at his notes, he said, "Anyway, my fourth possibility happened in June 1956. The victim was a 24 year old female law school classmate of Rachel's. Both women were on track to graduate at the end of the semester. The morning of the last final exam, the victim's body was found hidden behind a hedgerow adjacent to the law library on the south side of Bascom Hill. The right side of the victim's head had been crushed with a blunt object, and she'd been stabbed 14 times with what might've been a nail file. The Madison Police Department led the investigation, with the assistance of campus police."

"According to the lead detective, they never found anything to go on. The body had been drenched in a heavy rain overnight, washing away physical evidence. The victim was attractive, smart, well-liked, and her record was clean. They looked everywhere for motive ... troubles with family, roommates or friends ... love triangles, drugs, and alcohol ... and never found one. They even considered infighting for class rank, because the victim was at the top of her class going into finals. Apparently, only the best-of-the-best get the really big bucks, so class rank can be hotly contested."

"Anyway, the law school coughed up the class rank listing that would've been public at the time of the murder ... you know, the first two-and-a-half of a three-year program. The detective pulled his copy out of the file while I was there, and explained that he'd used it to check out the rest of the top five. They all had alibis and nothing else clicked, so he dropped that line of investigation and moved on. Out of curiosity, I asked to see the list and noticed Rachel at number seven, the second-best woman." He paused to let that sink in.

Mary shook her head, "Oh, come on. She'd never

kill over something as petty as that, would she? I mean … holy cow."

Rhetorically, Ted said, "Oh wouldn't she, given all that we know?"

Jason shrugged, "Again, that's what we're trying to find out. Anyway, those're my four possibilities." Then, he pointed a finger at his colleague, and said, "Darkwater's got the rest."

Darkwater looked up from his notes, and said, "Well first off, Rachel's brother Max is on my list because he died up north at Wolf's Run. In December 1948, the 15-year-old Max apparently fell off a cliff into the Menominee River, and was swept away. The body was found downstream two days later, hung up on a fallen tree, almost half way to Wausaukee. Cause of death was a crushed skull and multiple other injuries, consistent with a long fall down a boulder-strewn bank, followed by a swift ride down a rocky river. Rachel was 16 at the time, and she and her brother were alone at Wolf's Run. The Marinette County Sherriff's Department led the investigation. They initially viewed Rachel as a suspect, but she claimed to be at the main house cooking dinner when the accident occurred, and her story checked out."

Overdrive, only partially in jest, "There seems to be a pattern here."

Ted, unable to stifle a laugh, "You think?"

Peter laughed, "Brother, rival, husband, parents." Then, in a sing-song voice, "… and a partridge in a pear tree."

Mary almost laughed, too, "I'm sorry, but this isn't funny."

Darkwater flashed a big smile, "Come on, people … let's get serious. I could've been on this list." While the room quieted to contemplate that, he glanced at his notes and started anew, "Okay, let's move on to my second one. In June 1963, a 24-year-old gas station operator along U.S. Hwy 41 between Neenah and Oshkosh, was stabbed 53 times until dead. It's on the list because the driving route from Fond du Lac to Wolf's Run follows this section of highway. The Winnebago County Sheriff's Department handled the investigation. The victim and his wife had been watching television at their nearby home, when a white car pulled up shortly before 9:00 P.M. He went out to pump gas and never came back. His wife found him in the back room of the station. They had a number of suspects, but cleared all of them."

Ted observed, "Proximity works for this one ... but 53 stab wounds ... I don't know, it seems a little out of character for Rachel. Her other crimes, at least the ones against us, were more intellectual and calculating ... they had plausible explanations leading anywhere but back to her. This crime feels more like the handy-work of a drug-crazed psycho, or someone with a personal axe to grind."

Darkwater nodded, "I don't disagree, but both proximity and time-frame worked, so I put it on the list. The same goes for my last possibility. The crime occurred near the driving route between Fond du Lac and Wolf's Run, and the time-frame, December 1963, also works. In this case, a 28-year-old rural Black Creek woman was found dead of stab wounds in her kitchen, with her 2-month-old son lying unharmed nearby. She was stabbed nine times and her throat was slashed. The Outagamie County Sheriff's Department handled the investigation. They had several potential suspects, including a Bible salesman working in Black Creek that morning, a college-age hitchhiker, a knife-wielding man at a Waupaca hotel, and a drunken transient man in Fond du Lac fleeing Black Creek. None of them panned out, and no arrests were ever made."

Darkwater paused a moment to allow that to sink in, then wrapped up, "Anyway, I've put some thought into what might possibly have motivated Wolf to do either of these crimes. For what it's worth, it's possible that the victims witnessed something they shouldn't have. That's the best I could came up with. Granted, it's weak. But with Wolf, anything's possible."

The group continued a lively discussion for the next five minutes. Ted could tell from the energy in the room that everybody was on board with pursuing the murder angle. Peter had done an about-face, and was now confident he could keep the money flowing in from Verifine, Lake-to-Lake, and Golden Guernsey. Ted was about to assign tasks and adjourn, when Overdrive cleared his throat, and said, "There're some things Mary and I need to bring up before we go."

All heads swiveled in their direction, and Overdrive and Mary filled them in about the parked car, boot prints, drugged dogs, trespassing, appraisal, offer, and how it all tied together. Ted thought about that, then said, "Generating an appraisal requires a lot of nitty-gritty data. I'll bet they drugged the dogs and trespassed to get it. If they'd have asked your permission to crawl all over the farm, you would've run them off with a shotgun."

Overdrive muttered, "Damn right, I would've."

Mary's brow beetled, "But isn't that a crime … drugging dogs and trespassing? Would the state's

158 PATRICK J. HUGHES

topnotch dairy farm appraisal firm really do that?"

Ted rubbed his chin, "Yes, it's a crime. But I doubt the appraisal firm had anything to do with it. Maybe Wolf found a rogue employee that relied on Alder to get the data. Or maybe Alder led the other guy around, and he just happens to wear the same boot brand as Alder or your family."

Overdrive looked at him, "Huh … I never thought of that."

Jason had a thought and his eyes widened, "I get putting the dogs down to access the farm buildings and collect data for an appraisal. That explains the boot prints around the buildings. But why did Alder, in broad daylight, walk along the fence line in the hay field, through the strip of wasteland, and into the pasture?"

The group discussed a few possibilities, but none of them held water. When the ideas dried up, Darkwater asked, "Do you plan to sell?"

Overdrive and Mary's eyes met, and she motioned for him to go first, "Over my dead body. I was born in that farmhouse. My father and grandfather worked that farm. We'll never sell."

Mary caught Darkwater's eye, and added, "And you were almost killed helping to protect that farm … twice. Of course, we'd never sell." Then, she made a motion indicating the whole room, "We're all here to put that evil woman away. We've all been threatened or harmed by her in some way. Of course, we'd never sell out to a monster like that."

Ted said solemnly, "Well, what we just learned proves nothing has changed. Wolf still really, really wants that farm. The casino remains her overarching motive. I hate to say it, but we've underestimated her in the past. Underestimated the lengths she'll go to, to get what she wants." He paused to motion toward the Evanses, "From now on, you need to be on high alert. Wolf won't be happy when she hears you've rejected her offer. She may try to force your hand in some way. We all need to put some thought into how she might try to do that. In the meantime, just be careful."

As the meeting wound down, Ted reviewed everyone's priorities. Jason and Darkwater were directed to focus exclusively on the murders known to be somehow connected to Wolf, meaning the brother, husband, and parents. Ted would lead the effort to try to link Wolf to the anonymous letters received by Peter's shareholders. As part of that, Peter promised he'd help claw back from shareholders, as many of those letters as possible. The Evanses were told to take every precaution, and call Ted immediately after every contact by HMR.

Overdrive and Mary left for home bearing a heavier burden of dread than ever before. Up until now, they knew Wolf was evil. But after tonight, they feared she may be a serial killer. Even worse, a serial killer obsessed with their farm. Ted wants them to take every precaution, but what does that even mean?

CHAPTER 10

Rachel Manages the Game – Tuesday;
June 29, 1965; 9:00 PM

Impatient by nature, waiting wasn't one of Rachel's fortes. A nightcap of brandy and Benedictine, or B&B, usually soothed her. But tonight, she's on her third, and still pacing the study in a funk. The state-agency conference should've been over hours ago, and Vince was supposed to call right after with an update. When the phone finally rang, she literally leapt to retrieve it. Handset to her ear, Rachel huffed, "Hello."

Caught off guard by the tone, Vince ventured carefully, "Rachel, it's Vince. Is this a bad time?"

With a spark of anger, Rachel said, "Bad time? You were supposed to call right after the conference. Where the hell have you been?"

Vince, after a quick mental adjustment, "I'm sorry, Rachel. I must've misunderstood. I thought you just wanted a call before bedtime. A group of conference attendees went out for dinner, so I went along thinking I might score some useful intel for you."

Rachel, somewhat mollified, "Well, that's not what

I said, but go ahead and give me the highlights."

Relieved, Vince took a breath, and said, "Well, the conference room was packed. They handed out an attendee list that showed 72 people, and that's about how many I counted. Not all the people on the attendee list included their affiliation, so I can't be sure how many tribes and developers were represented. My best guess is four tribes, and about a dozen developers. HMR had a team of four not counting me, so say all the tribes and developers had four, that comes to 64 plus me. The list included eight people from the two state agencies, so it adds up about right."

Rachel thought about that, then asked, "Which tribes were there?"

Vince tapped his forehead, "Well, the attendee list only showed Ho-Chunk and Chippewa, but while networking around I also ran into Oneida and Menominee. It was interesting, a lot of them expressed surprise that the Potawatomi weren't there. I got the impression there's a back-channel among the tribes … you know, for communications. So, word might get around."

Rachel frowned, "Shit, I never thought of that. I'd better give Long Body a heads up. He'll need to get out in front of that. He told me some among the tribe are getting restless over my lack of progress. The last thing we need is for word to get out about this conference, before they hear it first from Long Body." She paused a moment, then said, "So, tell me. Did it look like the tribes were still playing the field, or were they already partnered with developers?"

Vince's eyes narrowed, "That's a good question, Rachel. The whole thing was organized to encourage tribes and developers to get to know each other. My impression was everybody was still at that stage, and not yet partnered up. But I also sensed that people viewed this as a competition, and were being careful. So, if people were further along than that, they wouldn't necessarily have admitted it."

Rachel pulled at her lower lip for a moment, then asked, "Did our team learn anything new. You know, about how to proceed?"

Vince muttered, "Not a thing. I asked our guys that very question. They did volunteer that the training was excellent for people who walked in not knowing squat. In fact, it kind of pissed them off. Basically, this state-funded conference created competition where previously, none had existed."

Rachel spat, "That's exactly the way I see it. The state used taxpayer dollars to blow away my hard-earned competitive edge." She tossed down the rest of her B&B, then asked, "Anything else I should know about?"

Vince thought a moment, "No, that's about it. According to the team, the skids are greased in Madison for quick state approvals. As soon as you own all the land, they're ready to go."

With authority, Rachel said, "Concerning that, when do you get back from Madison? I've got the appraisal, and it's time to pull the trigger on the Evans farm acquisition." Vince had hoped to spend the rest of the week, and the 4th of July weekend, fishing for trout in the spring-fed creeks of southwestern Wisconsin's driftless region. He'd gone to Madison with his trunk packed full of waders, poles, tackle, coolers, and bug spray, and he'd already made motel reservations.

Against her better judgment, Rachel relented and let him go. But in exchange she extracted a promise. Vince would call in each morning and night, and come running if she needed him. If that was unnecessary, they agreed to meet for an early breakfast July 5th, in the one-table private room at the mom-and-pop place off of Hwy 23.

When the call ended, Rachel had mixed feelings. Part of her thought giving Vince a vacation meant he'd be fresh and at the top of his game, when the fun begins. The other part, wondered whether she'd just made a terrible mistake.

* * *

Rachel spent the next morning in her study, fine-tuning her planned moves to take over the Evans farm. She figured James Evans was probably the decision maker, so the first approach would target him directly. But she was reluctant to have Vince catch him at home. His home was his castle, and the power imbalance might put Vince at a disadvantage. Plus, if things turned ugly, Evans would only be a step or two away from the nearest loaded gun. Instead, she'd have Vince monitor his movements and flag him down while he's out working in a field. The element of surprise might be helpful. Also, once Evans shutdown whatever machine he was operating, Vince would have his full and undivided attention in a private setting.

Rachel decided the first offer would equal the appraised value plus 20 percent. Evans could choose between the land-only or land plus personal property offers, and would receive the 20 percent premium either way. As she reasoned through how Vince's first conversation with the man might go, Rachel jotted down what she considered to be the key talking points. She knew Vince would take her suggestions to heart, but make the final calls himself. As part of his preparation process, he liked to envision the conversation in advance. Then, he'd put what he planned to say into his own words, and commit it to memory.

If James Evans's answer on day two was no, on day three Vince would monitor the movements of Mary Evans, and approach her in a private situation. Granted, a strange man approaching a woman could appear threatening, but Vince had a way with women, and Rachel had no doubt he could put Evans at ease. For her, Rachel also considered how the conversation might go, and jotted down key talking points. Increasing the second offer to a 50 percent premium over the appraised value, was the main difference from the first. But in Rachel's view, in the pitch to Mary, it's important to emphasize what such a windfall could mean for her family. She wanted Vince to emotionally connect Mary to that better life.

In case the Evanses were wedded to farm life, Rachel reasoned that Vince should proactively cover that base in both offers, by pointing out they'd have plenty of money to buy another farm. And after the new farm was bought, they'd still have plenty of money left over for things like hired help, vacations, medical insurance, or whatever else they fancied. Rachel knew sellers didn't like to be pushed, but she didn't have time to dick around, so Vince needed to make clear he needed next-day answers. Issuing a threat to James would probably just rile him up and be unwise, but with Mary, Rachel believed Vince should throw in a subtle one at the end.

In Rachel's view, the subtle threat was necessary to bring things to a head. It'd force the Evanses to rise above their punch-drunk work-a-day world, and think for a change ... think about what's best for themselves and their family. If they came back with a counter offer, Rachel would probably consider it, just to get the deal done. But if they rejected the second offer outright, well, too bad for them. Rachel doubted she'd have the patience to fool around a third time. Instead, she'd create leverage and force the Evanses to sell.

Rachel considered it likely that leverage would need to be created. For over a week, she'd been ruminating over which option to choose, cattle heist or barn fire. After much thought, she'd come down on the side of the cattle heist. Financially, it made the most sense. She'd have cattle to sell for cash right away. Then, with their milk check gone, the Evanses would be forced to accept an offer, perhaps even a lower one. And once the farm was hers, there'd be other bankable assets to sell, such as hay and straw. If she burnt down the barn, things she could sell ... cattle, hay, and straw ... would instead be lost in the fire. Only a fool would do that, and Rachel was no fool.

While still noodling in this vein, the phone rang and snapped Rachel out of her reverie. After the hello, a familiar voice said, "Rachel, it's Bert Baker. Do you have a minute?"

Rachel took a moment to pivot mentally, then said, "Bert! Good to hear from you. You're calling from a pay phone, right?"

Bert said, "Yes – yes, just like you told me."

Rachel asked, "Where are you?"

Bert chuckled, "Ernie and I are sitting in our newly rented trailer in McAllen, TX, each drinking a Lone Star beer. Did you know Lone Star bills itself as the national beer of Texas? Says so right here on the label. These Texans seem to be confused. They think they're a country unto themselves."

Rachel allowed herself a half laugh, "Actually, I had no idea. But if I were you, I'd find out if these Texans are serious, before going around correcting them. Otherwise, you might end up needing dental work."

Bert laughed out loud, then said, "Dental work, my ass. Down here, everybody carries a gun. They'd probably just blow me away."

After a quick glance at her watch, Rachel said "Well, you'd better watch your step then. So, Bert, what can I do for you?" Bert filled her in about the move being complete, and their initial impressions of Texas. Then, he gave her their new phone number and post-office-box address.

* * *

Rachel had just returned to the study after lunch, when the phone rang again. Thankful that it wasn't an interruption, Rachel answered in a voice more pleasant than normal, "Hello, Rachel Wolf here."

Phil said, "Rachel, it's Phil. It appears I've caught you at a better time today, I can tell by the tone of your voice."

Though it required effort, Rachel sustained the pleasant tone, "You did indeed. Just finished lunch, and wasn't in the middle of anything. But you shouldn't worry about that, Phil, just call me anytime. So, what can I do for you?"

Phil exhaled heavily, and said, "Well, something interesting came to my attention, and I'm wondering if you know anything about it. Milwaukee's Common Council just approved rezoning a parcel to allow construction of a casino. Can you imagine? Since when can you build a casino in Wisconsin? Last I heard, you couldn't even do bingo up here. If this is somehow now legit, it might be an opportunity ... you know, something we might consider pursuing together."

Rachel was gob smacked. No-o-o, echoed from all corners of her brain. She needed to keep Phil talking, to give her time to think. She heard the interest in his voice, so asked, "When did this happen?"

"This morning."

"Who pushed the approval?"

"The parcel's owner, an outfit by the name of Vangard Partners. They're a pretty well-known commercial real estate developer down here. Legend has it, they have the Midas touch when it comes to ramrodding things through Common Council's standing committees, and Common Council itself."

"How do you know about this?"

"We've got insiders as staff for Common Council and the Mayor's Office."

"Are any more approvals needed?"

"Not by the city. This thing seemingly came out of nowhere, yet everybody's already on board. Two powerful standing committees ... Zoning, Neighborhoods and Development ... and Community and Economic Development ... brought it to Common

Council. Then, the City Treasurer and the Mayor himself came and spoke in favor. When it came to a vote, every Alderman voted yes. Our stoolies had never seen anything like it. They've done some digging and found out what really happened. Apparently, Vangard Partners sweetened the city's take on casino revenues, over and above what they'd skim from a typical business. Plus, the parcel was a total armpit in a high-crime district, so the deal also helps Milwaukee clean up some urban blight."

Rachel already knew the answer, but she asked anyway, "You say the deal cleared the city, but what about other jurisdictions?"

"Well, there's no hurdles at the county level, but our people say some state-level approvals are still required."

Again, no-o-o echoed from all corners of Rachel's brain. She jerked her grey-matter gearshift into warp speed, and considered whether to come clean with Phil, or not. Instantly, she concluded Phil and the mob were bound to find out about the state's new gaming authority sooner or later. She couldn't afford to be caught in a lie with the mob. But on the other hand, she didn't want them as a partner on her casino project, either. So, she walked a thin line, and said, "In answer to your original question, I am aware of a relatively new gaming authority in Wisconsin. In a nutshell, the state can accept donations of land, and hold those lands in trust on behalf of one of the Indian tribes, as a state-authorized Indian reservation. Then the tribe can partner with a developer and build gaming facilities on the new reservation."

Now it's Phil's turn to be gob smacked, "You've got

to be kidding me! When did that happen?"

"The law became effective on July 1st, 1964, so about a year ago. I first caught wind of it about six months before that, and have been monitoring it ever since." Then, keen to keep the mob out of her business, she said, "Well, more accurately, I've partnered with a tribe, and we're well down the road on our own casino project."

"Oh, shit! I'm toast, if the Chicago boys find out I missed something big like this. I'm supposed to be up on all the new business opportunities, here in the Badger State. Up to now, my eyes and ears are all in Milwaukee. I'd better expand that to Madison, and fast."

Seeing an opportunity to keep the mob at arm's length, Rachel lied, "I'm sorry Phil. Actually, I thought you and your bosses were probably the drivers behind the new legislative authority ... gaming being one of your core businesses, and all. You never suggested we partner and I thought it'd be presumptuous to ask, so I went another way."

❊ ❊ ❊

After the call ended, Rachel kept the handset at her ear and immediately dialed Long Body. They exchanged greetings, then she said, "I've got two things for you. First, Vince tells me the Ho-Chunk, Chippewa, Oneida and Menominee were all at the state's conference, and were surprised not to see Potawatomi there. He got the sense there were back-channel communications going on between the tribes, and word would likely get back to your people."

Long Body harrumphed, "Well, that's just great."

Then, he sighed loudly, and said, "Damn, I should've thought of that and had a few people there. Now the other elders will probably accuse me of keeping them in the dark. I can just hear that asshole Make Wit whining about it."

Rachel thought about that, then said, "Maybe it'd be better to be proactive. Call the elders together, and tell them about the conference, and how HMR dutifully served the tribe's interests there. You could drop the intel that our project is far-and-away further along than any other." They spent the next five minutes discussing Vince's observations at the conference, and his hunch that the other tribes were still playing the dating game with developers.

Initially resistant, Long Body came around, "You're right. It'll get the elders together, and get out in front of this. What's the other thing you had for me?"

In a flat voice, Rachel said, "Well, I thought you should know. Although we're ahead now, it looks like we've got some competition on the horizon." She filled him in about the City of Milwaukee approval.

Long Body spat, "Sonofabitch! Can't you do anything to stop it? That'll cut off our Chicago and Milwaukee clientele."

Rachel, in a reassuring tone, "Relax, I'm told the parcel is an armpit in a high-crime district. They'll attract the seedy gambling addicts … you know, the type with no nut to piss away unless they knock off a liquor store on the way there. Our casino development will be a vacation destination for big spenders and their families … golf, trout fishing, skeet and trap shooting, an actual hunting preserve, hiking, horseback riding, fall colors, and so on, all in beautiful rural Wisconsin."

Long Body, partially mollified, "Well, I hope you're right."

Rachel, with an air of confidence, "Of course I'm right. And if it'll make you feel better, I'll see if there's anything I can do to stop it, or at least slow it down. But in the meantime, I need you to do me a favor. Network among the tribes, and find out which one is partnered with Vangard Partners."

Long Body allowed, "I can do that." They continued the conversation for a few more minutes. Rachel would try to find dirt on Vangard Partners. Then, once Long Body found out Vangard's tribal partner, they'd use the dirt to break up the happy couple.

When Vince checked in that evening, Rachel filled him in about the Milwaukee approvals secured by Vangard Partners. The name sounded familiar, so Vince pulled out the conference attendee list. Sure enough, Vangard Partners had been there. Rachel put Vince on alert that she may need him sooner than July 5th. From now on, rather than checking-in morning and night, Rachel wanted him to call morning, noon, and night.

✳ ✳ ✳

Mid-morning the following day, Rachel was sipping a fresh cup of coffee in her study when the phone rang. From the other end came another familiar voice, "Rachel, it's Ryan Weiser. We need to talk." With the Ted Ritter conversation fresh in his mind, Weiser filled her in on what went down. Weiser had the presence of mind to call from a phone booth, since Ritter had found him using phone logs.

Rachel thought about what he told her, then said,

"Okay, so if I understand correctly, Ritter made threats and painted a dismal picture of your future, then offered immunity in exchange for your cooperation. But being a stand-up guy and all, you stuck to your story about why we occasionally talk on the phone, and Ritter went away unhappy."

Weiser took a breath, "Yeah, that about sums it up. But I'm telling you, we need to be more careful going forward. We should always be calling from a pay phone." They spent another ten minutes rehashing Ritter's surprise visit, but found nothing more to be concerned about, and Weiser vowed to stick to the story.

When the call ended, Rachel smiled inwardly at the thought that Ted Ritter was on her tail. None other than the scion of the oft-outmaneuvered lawyerly Ritter family of Random Lake. For generations the Ritters had been delusional, believing themselves capable of bringing a Wolf to justice. It never happened, and it never will. Ritter's last great foray ended with the evidentiary drivel he managed to scrape together buried under an NDA in the Flint settlement. How pathetic.

Rachel mused a moment about Ritter and Jason Binder, the PI. Her guess was Binder worked for Ritter. She knew Ritter's law office was a one-man show, so without a sponsor there wasn't much he could do. Then it dawned on her. Oostburg Bank might be on the warpath too, if they believed their public stock sale had been forced, rather than simply bad luck. Okay, so the bank probably hired Ritter, and they're looking into me because yours truly put in the high bid. After kicking that around, Rachel relaxed. She had intimate knowledge of the bank, and knew very well they didn't have the resources for much of a dust up, either.

Rachel spent the rest of the day enjoying quality time with Rose and Jake. The next morning while in her study, and engrossed in the Wall Street Journal, the phone rang once more. Her favorite Texan was on the line, calling collect from a pay phone. Rachel accepted the charges, and he said, "Rachel, it's Bert Baker again. Jason Binder found us." Bert filled her in on the conversation.

Rachel laughed, "Ernie invited him over for a beer?"

Bert, with pride, "Yes, he did. We gave him a Lone Star. Binder liked it, said he planned to buy a few cases before he left the state."

Rachel, still merry, "You actually laughed at him, when Binder claimed you were in mortal danger?"

Bert offered a friendly amendment, "Laughed? We nearly split our guts. Spasmed into curly-cues, couldn't breathe, tears pouring down, the whole shebang. I mean, here we are enjoying family in sunny Texas, with you picking up the tab. And he's telling us we're loose ends. It struck us as hilarious." After a few more minutes of picking Bert's brain over the details, Rachel lied and said she had to go.

Alone in the study, Rachel pondered her situation. The Weiser and Baker firewalls were holding. The thought of how frustrating that must be for Ritter had her grinning ear-to-ear. But the grin turned somber, when she thought of the fate of the Baker brothers once their money inevitably ran out. She really got a kick out of Bert, and would miss him when he's gone.

CHAPTER 11

New Direction – Tuesday; July 6, 1965;
10:00 AM

It was a sunny day, already hot for mid-morning but with a nice breeze, and much less humid than the day before. Unlike yesterday when he ran into the boulder, today Overdrive was making great progress cutting hay. After he turned at the end of a row, his buoyant mood dissipated. With the Owatonna now facing east, the farm lane leading from Rock Road was visible. From the dust cloud, he could tell a vehicle was motoring down the lane on the far side of the hill. When it crested, he saw that it was Alder's car. After shutting down his machine, Overdrive walked the shortest route to the lane, and waited for him.

Like the previous day, Alder was friendly. He took the rejection without skipping a beat. He expressed his disappointment with good humor, and never tried to change Overdrive's mind. He apologized for the interruption, and excused himself before turning to leave. Overdrive noticed Alder's smile never reached his eyes, and the eyes themselves were stone cold. The man's bearing as he returned to his car was almost cocky, as if in his view, this wasn't over. Overdrive made a point of memorizing the license plate number. When Mary brought lunch, Overdrive filled her in, and she promised to call Ted and pass the word along.

The next morning, Mary was cultivating corn in a field along Bates Road when a large black car parked under a shade tree on the side of the road. She noticed the car right away, but kept cultivating. She risked an occasional glance in that direction, while being careful not to swerve and dig out corn rows. The driver had gotten out, climbed over the stonewall fence, and appeared to be waving at someone. After a few quick glances all around, she concluded he must be waving at her because nobody else was around. By now Mary was pretty sure she knew who it was, so she pulled to a stop and shut down her rig. By the time she stepped down, the man had covered half the distance to the tractor, with a big sorry-to-bother-you smile on his face. She smiled back, and said, "Are you Mr. Alder?"

Alder's smile widened, "I am. And I take it you are Mary Evans?"

Mary nodded as she stepped in his direction, "That's right."

Alder waited for her, then shrugged with his palms up, "I'm so sorry to bother you, but can you spare a moment to talk?" He paused to glance at the cultivator, "I can see you're busy, and I promise it won't take long."

Mary appraised him, then said, "Well, James told me you don't bite, so I guess it'll be alright."

Alder blotted his forehead with his handkerchief, and motioned to the shade tree, "How about we sit in the shade?" She nodded her assent, and headed in that direction. He fell into stride beside her, and said, "You knew my name, so I take it you and James have discussed the offer?"

Mary nodded, "We have. We're just not interested in selling right now."

What followed was silence, as if Alder was taking that into consideration. When they reached the shade, Alder motioned for her to sit on a nice smooth stone about chair height. He purposely sat on a low-lying one, giving her a downward view of him. A document was laying on the ground, and after they settled, he pulled it onto his lap, and said, "I promised I wouldn't waste a lot of your time, so I'll get right to it." He held the document out to her, "This is an updated purchase offer for your farm. We're willing to pay the appraised value, plus an additional 50 percent. Same as before, you decide whether to sell just the farm, or the farm plus personal property. You'll get the 50 percent premium either way."

Mary took the offer in her hand, thumbed through it absently, and said, "But I just told you, we're not interested in selling right now."

Alder showed all his whites, and gave her an exaggerated comic smile, "I know. But when you said that, accepting the offer would've only made you rich, now it'll make you filthy rich."

Mary rewarded him with a giggle, then said, "Well, money isn't everything, you know."

With an index finger at his ear pointing skyward, Alder switched into his mad professor impression, and said, "I do know that. Money isn't everything, but family is." Then, he dropped back to a normal voice, and said, "You have children, don't you Mary?"

Still amused, Mary nodded, "Yes, I do. Two girls and four boys."

"Well, think about being filthy rich, and then think about what that'd mean for them. Like most farmers, you probably hope one of them will carry on when you're gone, right?"

"Yes, that's true."

"Well, what about the rest of them? If you're filthy rich, you can give them all a good start in life. Most farmers can't do that. It's so challenging to keep the farm's financial equity together while the one works his way into it, they have nothing left to support the hopes and dreams of their other children. If you accepted the offer, you wouldn't have that problem. You could help them all."

"But ... but we will help them all. They'll all have a good high school education. They'll all have a strong work ethic. They'll all have actual work experiences and skills to tout. They'll have resilience, grit and determination because they grew up on a farm where not having them wasn't an option."

"Mary, everything you say is true. If your kids have the traits mentioned ... and I'm sure they do ... they can make a living, maybe even a good one. But what if some of them aspire to something beyond that. Beyond what can be achieved with a strong work ethic, resilience, grit and determination. If you don't mind my asking, has anyone from your family ever gotten a college degree?"

Mary looked down, "No."

"If one of your kids wanted to try, how would they do it?"

"Well, I guess they could go into the service, and use the GI Bill."

"But you have to admit, that's a better idea in peace time than now, right?"

"Yes, you're right."

"So, it's possible. They could spend years in the service and then use the GI bill. Or, they could study like a fiend, or workout and practice hard, and maybe win an academic or athletic scholarship. But tell me, do your kids have the same amount of time for studying, workouts, and practice as city kids do?"

Mary looked down again, "No, I suppose they don't."

"So, it's possible they'd win a scholarship. I mean, if they're off-the-charts gifted and could be competitive even without putting a lot of time into it. But all things considered, it's pretty unlikely, wouldn't you say?"

Mary seemed about to tear up, "Yes."

"Okay, so it's still possible. They could take a gap year or two, and work and save up enough money to go to college. They could take out loans, and so on. But the fact is, if you come from a family where no one has ever made it through college before, you probably won't do that. You probably won't go off into the great unknown … you know, where there's nobody who's gone before, to guide you and maybe even pull a few strings on your behalf. Instead, what generally happens with highly capable kids coming off of farms, is they dismiss their higher aspirations as pipe dreams. They have the traits you mentioned, they're highly employable, so they go out and earn an honest living. There's nothing wrong with that. But I'm just saying, if you took the offer, your kids could settle for that if they wanted to, but they wouldn't have to. That's the key, they wouldn't have to settle. Anyway, shouldn't you and your husband at least think about that?"

Mary, in a beaten down voice, "I guess so."

Vince looked up at Mary and caught her eye. He could tell he'd made an impression. He gave her an encouraging smile, and said in a soft voice, "Like I told your husband a few days ago, the offer is time sensitive. I'll come around tomorrow to find out what you've decided. Just think about it, that's all I ask." Then, he rose to his feet, and added, "You seem like a really nice lady, and an excellent mother. I sincerely hope you accept. It pains me to think what might happen if you don't."

Mary sat in stunned silence, a tear leaking out of one eye, as Alder climbed over the stonewall fence and drove off. Too upset to continue cultivating, she finished to the end of the row and then drove the rig home. When she pulled to a stop in the yard, the girls straightened up from their weeding in the garden, and shouted ... *why back so early* ... from forty yards away. Crying and a mess, Mary kept her head turned from them, and shouted back ... *diarrhea* ... as she ran to the house with the offer.

Once in the bathroom, Mary splashed cold water on her face and toweled off. Then, she peed and flushed as cover for her story, and loitered in front of the mirror until she looked passable. On the way out of the bathroom, she flushed again for good measure. In the kitchen, she grabbed a water jug off the counter, pulled an ice tray from the freezer and dumped it in, and then filled it with water. With the jug and offer in hand, she hurried out of the house, slamming the door on the way. The girls looked up again, and Mary yelled over she's fine. Then, she held up the jug and shouted she's taking it to their father. After cranking the cow car to life, she headed to the Ulbricht farm where Overdrive was cutting hay.

Overdrive came out of a 180-degree turn facing east, and focused on aiming the Owatonna at the next swath and lowering the head to cutting height before he got there. Once cutting was again underway, he glanced up and noticed a dust cloud rising from the farm lane, on the far side of the hill. He frowned at the thought that more company was coming. Shortly, the vehicle crested the hill, and he felt relieved at the sight of the cow car. A moment later, when he recognized Mary behind the wheel, the frown returned. His first thought was she must've had a breakdown with the corn cultivator.

After shutting down his machine, Overdrive walked the shortest route to the lane, and waited for his wife to arrive. He smiled and waved as she approached, but he didn't get much of either in return. She parked and got out, carrying a water jug and a document. After a half-hearted hug, she handed him the new offer and filled him in on the Alder conversation. Outraged, Overdrive spat, "You mean he actually threatened us!"

Mary nodded, "That was certainly my interpretation."

Still angry, Overdrive scoffed, "And the nerve of that guy, trying to come across as if he gave a shit about our kids. That was really low."

Mary, introspectively, "He certainly knew how to push my buttons."

Overdrive thought about what'd transpired, then said, "Well, you'd better call Ted to let him know what happened. Tell him we need some advice on how to protect ourselves, and we'll call him this evening after milking to get it."

Determined not to let Alder ruin her day, Mary said, "I'll do that. Then, I'll get back to cultivating corn."

* * *

Mary left the water jug, took back the offer, and returned home to make the call. Ted heard her out, then said forget calling later because he needed them at his office that night in person. The rest of the work day, dinner, and the evening milking passed uneventfully. Then, Overdrive and Mary were off to Random Lake.

When they arrived, Overdrive and Mary met Peter in the parking lot, and the three of them walked in together. As they pushed into the conference room, an animated discussion between Ted, Jason, and Darkwater came to a halt. After exchanging pleasantries, the newcomers settled into their seats, and Ted kicked off the meeting, "It's been a busy two days, so there's lots of ground to cover. Jason, tell us about the parents."

Jason took a moment to consult his notes, then said, "Okay, so the detective at the Sheboygan County Sherriff's Department has been unbelievably helpful. He let me read the case file, and provided contacts so I could follow up as I saw fit. Ben Wolf kept his Cessna 172 Skyhawk at one of the fixed-base operators, or FBOs, located at the Sheboygan County Memorial Airport. At the time of the investigation, the Cessna's maintenance logbooks were under lock and key at the FBO. Everything was up to date, so basically the aircraft was deemed to be in excellent condition."

"The detective got a warrant to open Ben's personal locker at the FBO. There, he found copies of Ben's certificates to fly, his pilot rating, and his flight logbook. Ben's flight logbook indicated ample flight hours to maintain his certificates. The Cessna's a four-seater, and Ben was authorized to fly under visual flight rules with up to three passengers. When he took off Ben was legal ... one passenger, a daytime flight, and no severe weather between Sheboygan and Louisville. However, the flight logbook did indicate two passengers on the day of the crash, Ruth and Rachel."

Peter asked, "How'd the detective get square with Rachel dropping out?"

Jason made a 'let's roll' motion with his hand, "Let me finish laying out the basic facts first, then I'll cycle back to the investigation. The morning of the crash, Rachel was at the airport to see her parents off. Ben took off right on time, and followed his flight plan out over Lake Michigan on the way to Louisville. His early communications with flight control indicated all was well, and he was about to level off at cruising altitude. Shortly thereafter, Ben called in a mayday, gave his position coordinates, and then went silent."

"The U.S. Coast Guard led the search and rescue effort. After a few days of finding nothing, per protocol, they transitioned to search and recovery. A month later the wreckage and bodies were found in 490 feet of water. The feds led the investigation of the wreckage. The plane was a mess, but they concluded the crash could've caused all the damage. The Sheboygan County medical examiner looked at the bodies. After a month in the water, they were a mess, too. Given the state of his body, the examiner couldn't rule out that Ben had suffered an acute medical issue, which caused him to lose control of the plane."

Overdrive's eyes narrowed, "So, the plane might've been sabotaged but they couldn't prove it."

Jason shrugged, "That's certainly one possibility. Anyway, aside from Rachel, the investigators never seriously considered another suspect. But it wasn't for lack of trying. They just couldn't find anyone else with a credible motive. They tried following the money, but everything Ben and Ruth owned was debt-free. The Wolfs kept a low profile, and their social circle was mostly old money. These were the kind of people that already had plenty of money, and didn't really need any more. If Ben and Ruth Wolf had enemies, or were the target of jealousies or blackmail, none of the people in their circle were aware of it. Likewise, if the Wolfs had been recently depressed, or more stressed and anxious than usual, nobody noticed. In addition, the investigators turned the Wolf's Sheboygan mansion upside down, and never found anything that raised an eyebrow."

Peter held up a finger, "So, Rachel was their one and only suspect."

Jason nodded, "Exactly, and the detectives took more than just a cursory look at her. The statement from Ben's estate attorney indicated Rachel as sole heir of a significant fortune. In addition to the Sheboygan mansion and Wolf's Run, she inherited controlling interest in the Fond du Lac regional bank, and assumed Ben's role as chair of the bank's board of directors. Then, there were stocks, bonds, and bank accounts. Rachel certainly had ample motive. But the attorney's statement also noted that Ben viewed Rachel as his successor at the bank, had mentored her for the role, had no doubt she'd succeed, and bragged on her often. As far as the attorney knew, Ben and Rachel had a great relationship. The detectives also questioned the Wolf's neighbors and social circle about the father-daughter and mother-daughter relationships. If any friction existed, nobody knew about it. So, aside from motive, the only other thing that pointed to Rachel was her last-minute decision not to board the plane."

Mary frowned, "That should've been enough for them to dig deeper. You and Darkwater found seven possible murders in two days. None of us would be sitting here, if only they'd looked."

Jason cocked his head sideways and shrugged, "Well, hindsight is 20-20, but put yourself in the detective's shoes. There'd been no known conflicts between Rachel and her parents. She was already living in style, and had no pressing material reason to off Ben and Ruth. Besides, as sole heir, she knew she'd get everything eventually. Plus, at the time, she was recently widowed and had a baby on the way. Why would she kill her future child's grandparents?"

Mary thought about that, then said, "I guess I can see that."

Jason continued, "Anyway, Rachel's actions and statement also lined up pretty well with everything else that was known. The day of the crash, the lead story on the evening news was the missing plane over Lake Michigan. Rachel claims she heard the news, panicked, and called the Louisville hotel to see if her parents had arrived. They hadn't, so she called the Sheboygan County Sherriff's Department. The hotel-clerk and Sherriff's duty-officer both described her as distraught, if not hysterical. Plus, when the detective took Rachel's statement, he judged her grief and demeanor to be credible, given the circumstances."

"In her statement, Rachel told the detective the Kentucky Derby trip was an annual family tradition. She always looked forward to going, and had every intention of doing so again. The night before, she stayed over with her parents in Sheboygan. But that morning, she woke feeling ill, and felt it'd be safest for the baby to stay behind. After seeing her parents off at the airport, she drove home to Fond du Lac. All of that checked out. The Louisville hotel verified that the Wolfs always came for derby, including Rachel, and Max before he passed away. They also said the second room for Rachel had been canceled that morning. So bottom line, Rachel's statement explained her being listed as a passenger in the flight logbook, and also why she didn't go."

Overdrive squeezed the bridge of his nose, and muttered, "How convenient."

Jason nodded at him, "I hear you. But when the wreckage investigation proved inconclusive, the detective came around to the medical examiner's line of thinking. Ben must've experienced some sort of acute medical issue, and lost control of the plane. Ruth couldn't fly, and wouldn't have been much help in an emergency. Ben's personal physician said he'd been doing well for his age, but the family history included strokes and heart attacks. As for Rachel, reaping a windfall from a tragedy is only a crime if you caused the tragedy. The detective didn't think she had. And by his way of thinking, backing out of a doomed flight isn't a crime either, it's called luck."

Peter looked disappointed, "So, that's it? Rachel

didn't do it?"

Jason hunched his shoulders and leaned into the table, "Well, I'm not ready to throw in the towel just yet. Each entry in the Cessna's maintenance logbook included a mechanic's signature. For years, the same mechanic had done all the work on Ben's plane. His head was likely the last one under the hood of that plane before it went down. If the plane had been monkeyed with, my theory is he either did it himself, or should've noticed that someone else had."

"I decided to pay the mechanic a visit, and drove over to Ben's old FBO at the Sheboygan airport. I figured if I arrived unannounced and braced him, his reaction would show me something. I made up a story in advance, to get past the office manager. Basically, I claimed the mechanic and I had played sports against each other at rival high schools, and knew each other from that. Then, I claimed to be considering a career move from auto to aircraft mechanic, had heard he was one, and wanted to pick his brain about it. I knew the guy wouldn't recognize me or my name, but figured with a story like that it'd be understandable, and he might see me anyway. Plus, asking for someone's advice always appeals to their ego."

Peter teased, "Pretty devious, for being one of the good guys."

Jason winked, "I did feel a little sneaky … you know, about the misdirection. But what can I say, the FBI trained me well and it worked. Guess what I found out?" After a dramatic pause, he said, "The mechanic, Ray Knobloch, resigned less than a month after the crash, in June 1962. He gave no reason, just two-weeks-notice and moved out-of-state. Knobloch had been a long-timer and the FBO is a small outfit, so losing him had been a major blow. I could tell from her body language, the office manager is still miffed. Anyway, she knew the guy's family, and gave me sibling names, and where she thought some of them lived. I found his little sister in the phone directory, and gave her a call. After hearing my tale, she coughed up a Florida phone number and address."

Mary put two-and-two together, "You think he ran?"

Jason shrugged, "He might've."

Overdrive opined, "He'd be dead by now if he hadn't."

Peter guessed, "So, let me guess, you're going to Florida?"

Jason beamed, "Believe it or not, I've been invited. I called Knobloch, with my story tweaked to say his sister sent me, and I'm already in Florida on vacation. He invited me over for a beer. I'll have to fly out tonight to make that date."

The room exploded, with voices talking over each other. Did they finally have something on Wolf? After all the dead ends, could they dare hope? The chatter went on along those lines for five minutes or so, then Ted suggested, "Before Darkwater starts, let's take a five-minute break. I don't know about the rest of you, but I need a potty break."

* * *

When they reconvened, Darkwater said, "Okay, so I've been trying to gather information on the husband. Goal one was to get a name. My first thought was it

188 | PATRICK J. HUGHES

might be in the case file on Rachel's parents, but Jason read the whole thing and didn't recall seeing it. Just to be sure, I called the detective and he couldn't recall anything about the husband, either. But he thought Ben Wolf's estate attorney would at least have the name, so I went there next."

"The husband's name was Brad Herbick. Ben Wolf had been concerned about the sudden appearance of Herbick in his daughter's life, and had contacted his estate attorney about it. Apparently, Rachel had sprung the news about her relationship and engagement at the same time. Then, only a week later, Herbick and his parents came to visit, and the following week they were married."

Mary leaned back, "Wow, that was sudden. Was she pregnant?"

Overdrive's brow beetled, "Hmmm ... in a shotgun marriage, usually the bride's father carries the gun, not the bride."

Darkwater tilted his head and shrugged, "I'm not sure if she was pregnant when she sprung the news. Based on the child's birth date, it's certainly possible. Anyway, Ben was upset there wasn't enough time to hire a PI and conduct a proper background check on his son-in-law to be. But he didn't want to make waves, either. So, he settled for having the attorney update his and Ruth's trust documents, and craft an addendum. The latter was intended to aide a future court in identifying the correct Brad Herbick. It documented everything Ben knew about the man. The trust updates tweaked how assets would flow, when the last of Ben and Ruth passed away. If Rachel was then single, their assets would go directly to her. If married, their assets would instead be held in trust for her. Should Rachel pre-decease them, their assets would be held in trust for Rachel's then living children. If no living children, Ben and Ruth's assets would be donated to their favorite charities. In other words, the way it was set up, Herbick would never get a penny."

Peter chuckled, "Welcome to the family, Brad."

Darkwater jabbed a finger at him, "True enough, but Ben might've been on to something. As it turns out, Herbick was a ghost. Ben knew next to nothing about the man. Let me read what he had in the addendum." He took a moment to check his notes, "Born and raised in Glen Ellyn, Ill, a western suburb of Chicago. His parents, Les and Martha, still live there. He earned his bachelor's degree from the College of DuPage, also located in Glen Ellyn. He made his living selling pharmaceuticals, and traveled extensively to do so." Darkwater paused to look around the room, "See what I mean? That's all Ben knew. According to the attorney, Ben had been reluctant to offend the happy couple. In his mind, that meant he couldn't ask for things like Herbick's date of birth, social security number, or driver's license number."

"Next, I started digging into the Wolf-Herbick thing myself. The Wisconsin Vital Records Office has no record of a marriage license or certificate ever being issued to Rachel Wolf and Brad Herbick. Wolf never legally changed her name. By all accounts, he moved in with Wolf in Fond du Lac, but the neighborhood postal carrier cannot recall ever delivering a piece of mail addressed to him. Fond du Lac County has no record of him. He never updated his driver's license or registered to vote. The county also never saw a body, nor did they issue a death certificate. As far as Wisconsin is concerned, Herbick never existed."

Ted snorted a laugh, "And it gets better."

Darkwater soldiered on, "So then, I started making inquiries in Illinois. Glen Ellyn is in DuPage County. DuPage has no birth record for a Brad Herbick. Glen Ellyn schools have no record of a Brad Herbick ever attending, and neither does the College of DuPage. The U.S. Census Bureau has no record of a Les, Martha, or Brad Herbick ever living in Glen Ellyn. None of them were ever registered to vote there. According to the county property tax rolls, none of them ever owned property there. They apparently didn't rent either, because the electric, gas, water, and sewer utilities had no record of them. Like I say, Herbick is a ghost."

Ted's conference room exploded with questions. For most of them, there were no answers. The conversation chased many possibilities, but never caught one. From all appearances, Brad Herbick and his parents had never existed. Since Rachel had brought them into Ben and Ruth's life, one can only presume she created these phony people for reasons known only to her. Birth records were found for Rachel's son, Jake, but by then the husband-that-never-was had already passed away, so the only parent listed was Rachel.

❊ ❊ ❊

Ted feared the Herbick-mystery buzz would linger forever, so he rapped the table and raised his voice, "Okay people, enough already. The husband never existed. As to why Rachel created him, we haven't a clue."

Mary took a stab at the mystery, "I'll bet she got pregnant by some unsavory character, then hired actors and fabricated the whole thing to protect her place in polite society. It's plain as day."

Ted glared at her, "Maybe so, Mary, but running those details to ground won't help us. We're looking for murder victims, remember. More specifically, ones we can tie to Rachel. No husband means no victim. So going forward, I've asked Darkwater to refocus on Rachel's brother, Max. Jason, of course, heads to Florida tonight to see Ben Wolf's plane mechanic. If we're lucky, we'll claw together enough evidence to connect Rachel to the parents, the brother, or both."

Peter pulled at his lower lip for a moment, then said, "What if we're not lucky. As you know, we haven't exactly been on a lucky-streak lately."

Ted opened his mouth to say something defensive, but decided against it. Instead, he said in a confident tone, "Then we'll move on to the law school classmate. Wolf has killed before. I can feel it in my bones. When she went after Darkwater ... twice ... something about it just felt casual. You know, as if to her, killing someone was no big deal, just another day at the office. She's definitely killed before, probably multiple times. We just need to find one we can prove."

Overdrive's eyes narrowed, "I think you're right, Ted. But as we've found out, she's slippery. Like Peter says, what if we can't find a murder we can prove?"

Ted put an earnest look on his face, and said, "Look, I don't have all the answers. My hunch is, Wolf got better at her craft as time went on. The Wolf we're dealing with now is experienced, and at the top of her game. But there's a reasonable chance she made a mistake in one of these earlier cases. And by-the-way, we're not giving up on her recent crimes. In fact, we've made some progress on trying to prove the criminal conspiracy charge. With Peter's help, I've recovered dozens of those anonymous letters ... the originals. As it turns out, a lot of Peter's shareholders are packrats. They file everything."

Mary lit up at the possibility, "Well, that sounds like good news." But then her forehead beetled into a frown, "But how does that help again?"

Ted appreciated being asked a question he could answer, "We've sent the letters off to the FBI. An old colleague of Jason's there owes him a favor, and he's called it in. She agreed to dust the letters for prints, and run anything she finds through their databases. Every letter will have the shareholder's prints, of course, but we're hoping she'll find instances where the same prints appear on multiple letters. If so, the prints could be Rachel's, or from people she hired to produce the mailing. Only the multi-letter prints will be run through the databases. Of course, to get a match, prints from Rachel or the others would need to be in there."

The group chatted for another five minutes about the prospects of tracing the letters to Rachel through finger prints. When the conversation petered out, Overdrive rapped the table to get the room's attention, then motioned toward Mary. She took a deep breath, and filled them in about Alder's visit earlier that day. After some back-and-forth to clarify what really took place, Ted said, "So, Alder blatantly threatened you."

Mary nodded, "That's right."

Ted hesitated, then said, "Remember at the last meeting, we concluded most of Alder's boot prints all over your farm could be explained by the need to gather data for the appraisal. However, the tracks from Rock Road through the hay field and waste land to the back of the pasture were an exception. When the three of you walked in earlier, the PIs and I were in a heated discussion about what might explain those prints. Jason had an interesting idea."

After Ted motioned toward him, Jason said, "At the FBI, they taught us to always follow the money." He looked at Overdrive and Mary, "Just out of curiosity, when it comes to money, what's the most important thing in the life of a dairy farmer."

Without hesitation, Overdrive and Mary both said, "The milk check."

Jason nodded, "That's what I thought. Now, Alder didn't come out and say as much, but by issuing a threat it's possible he's sending the message that today's offer would be the last one, so you'd better accept it. If you don't ... I forget, Mary, ... what did he say again?"

Mary picked up the thread, "It pains me to think what might happen if you don't." Then, with a tremble in her voice, "Just like Wolf did with Darkwater, I'm afraid she'll come after us. Well, us or the kids or Old Bill."

Jason pursed his lips, and shook his head, "Well, anything's possible with Wolf, but I doubt she'll come after you. Doing so wouldn't solve her problem. Put yourselves in her shoes. She needs your farm to move forward with the casino. She wasted a lot of time trying to steal it a few times and now, literally, the natives are getting restless. Desperate, she's now trying to get you to voluntarily sell it to her. If that fails, what do you think her next move will be?"

Overdrive jumped in, "Force us to sell?"

Jason nodded, "And how would she do that?"

Mary's eyes widened, "Somehow take away our milk check?"

Jason smiled, "Bingo. Which might explain the tracks to the pasture. There wouldn't be much of a milk check if they stole the herd."

Overdrive spat, "Sonofabitch!"

The room lit up with ideas about how to prevent that from happening. Dozens of suggestions were tossed out, discussed, then discarded. Consensus was, there'd be no point in calling the Sherriff's Department. They wouldn't dedicate a cruiser to the Evans farm on the basis of a hunch. Worse yet, if the request sounded kookie enough to them, the cops might pin the Evanses up on the crank board, slowing any future response to a real emergency.

Group-think came around to the belief that an all-night watch was necessary. Darkwater reminded everyone that tribal council met the following Tuesday, and a new developer would be there, pitching a casino in Milwaukee. If Wolf was going defend her flank, she needed to be there claiming all the land for the Headwaters location was now hers, state approvals were in the works, and there's no need for the tribe to switch ponies. That meant if a cattle heist was in the offing, it'd have to happen tomorrow night after the second offer was rejected, or sometime within the four nights following that.

Eventually, the group reached consensus on a compromise plan. It'd take time to organize the theft of 80 cattle, so the group felt it unlikely Wolf could strike the first night or two. Hence, the Evanses would handle the watch on their own the first two nights. This would give Darkwater a brief window to try and make something pop on the Max Wolf murder investigation. If nothing panned out in two days, Darkwater would head south and join the watch. In the meantime, Jason would be in Florida for the foreseeable future, and Ted would keep badgering the FBI over the finger prints.

CHAPTER 12

Rachel Makes Her Move – Saturday; July 3, 1965; 10:30 AM

Rachel had just put Jake down for a nap, when the phone rang. She called out to Rose that she'd get it, and ran to the study. Breathless, she said, "Hello, Rachel Wolf here."

Long Body, in a mirthless voice, "Rachel, I'm glad I caught you. Is now a good time to talk? You sound winded."

Rachel, still huffing, "Well, I hate missing calls, so I sprinted a little to get to the phone. So anyway, what's up?"

Choosing his words carefully, Long Body said, "The morning after our last talk, I followed your advice and called the elders together ... you know, to make sure they learned about the state's gaming conference from me first. My impression was, most all of them were very unhappy at the tribe not being there. A significant number expressed skepticism that HMR could be trusted to look out for the tribe's interests. One of the more outspoken elders came right out and called it a mistake. I reassured them as best I could, but it didn't appear to do much good. As they left, I got this funny feeling … you know, as if a bunch of them knew something, but purposely left it unsaid."

Rachel's eyes narrowed as she thought about it, "Huh … so you think maybe some of them already knew about the conference."

Long Body admitted, "Well, it's certainly possible. They all can keep a pretty good stone face when they want to."

Rachel asked, "What about finding the tribe connected to Vangard Partners, and the Milwaukee project? Any luck there?"

Long Body's forehead beetled into a frown, "I just got off the phone with the last tribe before calling you. None of them would admit to being involved. Frankly, I'm a little disappointed because one of them has got to be. In the past, my counterparts and I had always been open with each other, on things like this. It'd be a shame if those days are over."

Rachel opined, "Maybe, in the special case of gaming, the tribes view each other as competitors."

Long Body exhaled heavily, "It's possible. But in the past, we've competed for fishing rights on the same lakes and rivers, and hunting rights on the same lands. Yet, we'd always been able to talk openly about these issues. Why would gaming be any different?"

Rachel had an instant bad feeling, "Damn, what if Vangard Partners has linked up with elements of your own tribe? That might explain the funny feeling you mentioned earlier."

Long Body winced and shook his head, "Well, I doubt it. But it would explain some things. I'll look into it and get back to you."

After the call, Rachel examined for the first time the possibility that Potawatomi rogues had partnered with Vangard Partners. The more she thought about it, the more uneasy she became. She put herself in the shoes of the other elders. They'd approved her casino project in September 1964, hoping it'd pull them out of poverty. Almost 10 months later, there'd been no visible progress. Say, they knew all along about the state's gaming conference. That meant they knew Long Body had deliberately kept it from them. That alone, might be motivation enough to go behind his back, and seek another partner. Vangard is recently trained by the state, already owns the land for siting their casino, and has all the necessary City of Milwaukee approvals. They could go in for state approvals tomorrow, if the tribe was on board, and they'd have Milwaukee's political pull as tailwind.

Rachel let her mind run with the thread. If all this's true, the next tribal council meeting was shaping up to be an ambush of Long Body. Rachel rifled through her calendar to find when council next met … there it was, Tuesday July 13th, or 10 days from now. Unless she's ahead of Vangard by then, the other elders will sweep Long Body aside, with her project right along with him. She vowed that'd never happen, and rolled up her sleeves and got to work.

Rachel needed Vince back pronto. After verifying they'd be open on the holiday, she moved her July 5th breakfast reservation up a day, to July 4th. When Vince checked in at noon, she ordered him home a day early, so he could meet her for breakfast the next day. Then, she spent the afternoon finalizing her first and second offers for the Evans farm, and burning two copies of those plus the appraisal so Vince would have one for himself, and one for the Evanses.

* * *

First thing the following morning, Vince was already seated and sipping coffee when Rachel was led into the private dining room. They placed their orders, then Rachel got right down to business, "You're back early because tribal council meets in nine days, and I'm screwed unless the Evans farm is mine a few days before then." She filled him in on her theory that Vangard is partnered with rogue elements of the Potawatomi tribe.

Vince scratched his forehead, then said, "Is this confirmed, or just your suspicion?"

Rachel looked at him, "Well, Long Body is looking into it. But my intuition on matters like these has never been wrong before, and I don't have time to wait."

Vince picked up on her sense of urgency, "Okay, what's the plan."

Rachel filled him in on her thinking … two polite offers then, if necessary, forced capitulation by stealing their milk herd. She also shared her suggestions for the best way to approach the Evanses and handle the conversations. Then, she paused a moment, and asked, "So, what do you think?"

Just then the waitress came with breakfast and a fresh pot of coffee. Vince waited for her to leave, then said, "Let's see if I've got this straight. Tomorrow morning, I track down James and make offer number one. The next day I return for an answer. If no, on day three I find Mary and make offer number two, and return on day four for an answer. If no again, I steal the herd on the night of day five."

Rachel shook her head, "No, you steal the herd the night of day four. That'd be Thursday July 8th. Then you go back Friday morning, and drop back to the first offer's 20 percent premium."

Vince scratched his elbow and gave her a testing look, "Look Rachel, I haven't met the Evanses yet. But they lasted this long on the farm, so I'm willing to bet they're proud people. If you want a deal done Friday morning, you'd better stick with the 50 percent premium offer. Sure, they'd probably cave and take the lower offer sooner or later, but like you say, you don't have time to piss around."

Rachel consulted her pocket calendar, then said, "Good point, we'll stick with the higher offer. That way, on Monday the 12th, I can be in Madison to deliver the submittals in person, and brief both state agencies, on my new state-authorized Indian reservation and casino. Then, on the 13th, I'll make a personal appearance at tribal council to share the good news. The tribe's HMR casino deal has been submitted to the state, and we've been given preliminary approvals."

Vince scratched his ear, waggled his eyes at her, "Preliminary approvals?"

Rachel half laughed, "Well, I may have to fib about that last part. By the way, put it on your list to pull together my security detail for the 13th."

Vince studied her for a moment, smiled and shook his head, then said, "To guarantee I'm ready to pull off the cattle heist on the night of day four, I'll need to spend some money up front to get my crew into the area, walk them through the plan, put them up nearby the night before, and pay for meals, tools, and materials. That money will be lost if we don't need to go through with it."

Rachel nodded, "Don't worry about it."

Vince scratched his neck and said, "Even with the herd gone, suppose they won't accept the offer Friday morning?"

Rachel's eyes flashed a predator's shine, "Simple. Friday night you burn down their barn, and Saturday morning you return with the offer. Come hell or high water, I need to be in Madison doing dog-and-pony shows on Monday."

Vince's smile bared all his teeth "That ought to do it."

In a teasing tone, Rachel said, "You've been doing a lot of scratching, Vince. What's up? One of those ladies of the night give you lice?"

Vince scratched his arm, "No, I've just got mosquito bites all over, from trout fishing. Either the bug spray wasn't worth a crap, or it wore off in a hurry."

Rachel laughed, "Poor baby." They chatted for a few more minutes, then Rachel pushed across the table to Vince, two copies each of offer one, offer two, and the appraisal. It was time for Vince to earn his keep.

* * *

Vince checked into a motel near Plymouth on State Hwy 57, a short distance south of its intersection with State Hwy 23. He liked the location because of the nearby truck stop, his ability to blend in there, and the fact that Plymouth had better dining options than Cascade. For his purposes, it's not too close to the Evans

202 | PATRICK J. HUGHES

farm, about eight or nine miles, but also not too far away.

Vince spent some time preparing for his conversation with James Evans the following morning. After drafting the first-offer dialogue, he rehearsed his lines repeatedly in front of the mirror, and edited the words until they flowed nicely and were easy to memorize. Generally, Vince listened to his gut when preparing for important conversations. When he felt good about it, he knew he was ready, and in this case it didn't take long. Vince doubted he'd get a signed offer on day two, but even so deferred preparing for the day three conversation with Mary Evans. In his view, night-before preparations were always best. That way they'd be informed by the latest information, and the words would be fresher in his mind when he actually needed to use them.

With tomorrow taken care of, Vince turned his attention to the cattle heist on the night of day four. He needed to make some calls and other final arrangements, and wanted to get right to it, so his team would have as much lead time as possible. For starters, he pulled his notes and cost estimates for the caper out of his brief case, and refreshed his memory by rereading them. The brief exercise made him smile at his own handiwork.

Whenever he did dirty work for Rachel involving others besides brother-Phil's boys, Vince used an alias. That way, if anything went awry, he could flee the scene and not worry about being fingered. He had a driver's license in the false name, as well as a post office box and bank account, for ease in laundering money. For this operation, Vince needed three semi-trailers and three pairs of men from outside of Phil's team, to man them. In his experience, criminals not on Phil's leash needed to be carefully controlled, or they'd make off with the loot. As a consequence, he'd taken several precautions while planning, staffing, and pricing the caper. From each of the six men, he collected phone numbers, addresses, and copies of their driver's licenses and social security cards. He also told them flat out they'd be hunted down and killed, if they stepped out of line.

As part of the staffing activity, Vince had pre-negotiated compensation and timing of disbursements. He'd pay half in cash up front, and the other half in cash after the job was done. The job was to relocate the milk herd from the Evans farm to three different out-of-state stockyards, sell the cattle for slaughter, and arrange for each stockyard to cut a check to Vince's alias and send it to the alias's post office box. The plan's weak-link was the temptation it created for his accomplices to take the cattle money and run. The cattle value far exceeded that of their last cash payment.

Being no fool, Vince had designed his caper with guard-rails to prevent the crew from stealing the cattle money. Over the next few days, he used his free time between brief interactions with James and Mary Evans, to put the guard rails in place. As part of that, he rented the three semi-trailers himself, using his alias. By doing so, he obtained all the identifying information for each rig, which he'd need for the next step. During the process, he also assigned a specific two-man team to each semi, and designated them both as potential drivers.

Third-party delivery of livestock to stockyards was common. To accommodate this, every stockyard had standard paperwork to specify things like where the payment should go, for cattle delivered by driver-X in truck-Y. Fortunately, this paperwork could be completed in advance over the phone, and the stockyard would keep it on file for when the truck arrived. Due to his forethought, Vince had all the vehicle and driver information he needed, and was able to make those arrangements. While doing so, he negotiated a side-deal with each stockyard, which was fairly common at the time. Any driver that contradicted his advance-order on file at the stockyard, say by demanding a direct payment to himself, would be detained until Vince, via his alias, could be reached for confirmation. By prior arrangements made through his brother Phil, if Vince received such a call, the detainees would be dead within the hour.

When Vince originally recruited the crew, he had specific criteria in mind. Aside from being crooked, the crew was required to possess the skills needed to perform the operation. That meant three of the six men must be experienced semi-trailer drivers, and the other three ride-along passengers must possess fence-building and cattle-poking skills. Although confident in his built-in guard-rails, Vince nevertheless decided to use one of Phil's boys, well-armed, as a body guard for the operation. He figured it wouldn't hurt for the dirtbags to see firsthand the kind of man that would relentlessly hunt them down if they did something stupid. Counting Vince and the body guard, the operation involved eight people.

Although the Evans herd was about 80-head of cattle, Vince rented three semis that each pulled 30-head capacity cattle trailers. Vince figured the slack meant loading would go faster, since they wouldn't need to waste time cramming them in. The trailers were the ground-load type, with pull-out ramps in the back. Loading them involved backing up to the pen-opening, lowering the ramp, and driving cattle on board. Each trailer came with dim interior lights, essential to make cattle more willing to load at night.

The semi-trailer rigs had been rented from outfits in Illinois, Iowa, and Minnesota, which were near the Chicago, Cedar Rapids, and Saint Paul stockyards. That meant after the stolen cattle were off-loaded, the rigs could be returned to home base quickly. After the three rigs left the Evans farm, they'd drive straight-through to their separate out-of-state destinations, and off-load their cargo the following morning when the stockyards opened. As previously arranged, the stockyards would mail their checks to the post office box of Vince's alias. After the checks cleared, Vince would call his accomplices and they'd pick up the rest of their cash at Vince's motel near Plymouth.

On days one and two, Vince paid James Evans two brief visits, to extend the first offer, and on the next day learn of its rejection. The rest of the time on those two days was spent on a flurry of phone calls to his six accomplices, the body guard, the truck-trailer rental agencies, the stockyards, and his brother Phil. On day three, Vince paid Mary Evans a brief visit, to extend the second offer. The rest of that day was spent pulling distances off of plat maps, using them to estimate quantities of fence-building materials, and purchasing those materials plus the necessary tools. While out shopping, he also swung by the nearby Farmer's Market and bought six bales of hay, which were set outside to be picked up later.

The evening of day three, Vince's team was due to converge on Plymouth. Vince would share his twin-bed room with the body guard, and had already booked three additional twin-bed rooms for the two-man teams. The body guard was to rent a pickup truck under the name of an alias, drive to Plymouth, and park outside Vince's motel room. The three two-man teams were to pick up semi-trailers pre-rented by Vince, drive to Plymouth, park overnight at the nearby truck stop, and walk the short distance to Vince's motel and check-in.

Vince had already reserved a private dining room at a nearby restaurant for dinner that evening. They'd use Vince's car and the pickup to get there. Over dinner, Vince would pass out copies of the plat map showing the scene of the crime, and use it as a prop while walking everybody through the plan. Then, he'd pass out copies of a hand-drawn enlargement of the acreage where two fenced areas must be built. One, was the loading pen in the back corner of the hay field. The other, was the fenced lane through the narrow band of wasteland, connecting the milk-herd's pasture to the loading pen.

After dinner, the group would meet briefly in Vince's room so the crew could get acquainted with the stash of barbed wire, metal posts, and tools Vince had purchased for the job. If the fence-building experts thought essential items were missing, there'd be plenty of time the next day to run out with the pickup and buy them. Also on the next day, the crew needed to take the pickup truck to the Farmer's Market, and haul the hay back to the motel.

On the morning of day four, Vince would be gone briefly for his visit with Mary Evans. If the second offer was rejected, the operation was a go. Aside from the pickup runs mentioned above, that meant the three two-man crews were to lay low and keep themselves well-fed and rested in advance of the all-nighter to come. Without being too conspicuous about it, Vince and the body guard would separate from the others for an hour or so. They needed to drop Vince's car at the entry point to the Waldo Swamp. This location had served as Vince's point of departure, for his nocturnal visits to the Evans farm during the appraisal process. If the cattle heist went awry, Vince and the body guard would escape through the swamp to the car, leaving the others to deal with it.

After that, all would be quiet until about 11:00 PM, when the body guard and Vince would leave in the pickup truck. Their first mission of the night, was to toss laced meat chunks to the farm dogs at the Lemke, Nutter, and Evans farms. Afterward, they'd return to the motel, and load the three fence-builders and their materials and tools into the bed of the pickup, along with the hay. When the time was right, they'd return to the scene of the crime, unload the hay and gear, and begin building the loading pen and lane. After this job was finished, the body guard would return to the motel, take the drivers to their rigs at the truck stop, and then lead them to the loading pen. Meanwhile, Vince and his three men would use the hay to lure the cattle, and hopefully have most of them in the loading pen by the time the semi-trailers arrived. Then, the semi-trailers would be loaded, one after the other, and be on their way.

* * *

It was almost 11:00 AM on Tuesday July 6th, when Vince returned to his motel after the quick visit with James Evans. Evans had rejected the first offer, as expected. Vince drank a glass of water, then sat down at the little desk and gave Rachel a call. After filling her in, she said, "No big surprise there. Have you set everything in motion for the cattle heist?"

Vince chuckled, "I'm getting there." Then he walked her through a detailed blow-by-blow explanation of the plan.

Rachel's eyebrows went up, "Holy cow! You really don't trust those guys, do you? Are you saying Phil actually has hitmen on stand-by in Chicago, Saint Paul, and Cedar Rapids?"

Vince added a little gravel to his voice, "Of course I don't trust them, they're crooks. Plus, 30-head of cattle are worth a lot of money. Even a saint might be tempted to steal them. As for the shooters, I'm not exactly sure what Phil's arrangement is, but he says every stockyard can be reached within an hour. I think the mob has … hmmm … affiliates I guess you'd call them, just about everywhere." They chatted for another ten minutes about the plan, then rang off. Afterward, Vince spent some time preparing for the next day's second-offer sales pitch to Mary Evans, then resumed his preparations for the cattle heist.

Two days later, Mary rejected the second offer and Vince got Rachel on the phone once more. She heard him out, then said, "Well, you know what to do."

With a feral snarl, Vince said, "Indeed, I do."

* * *

Later the same day, Rachel was in her study when Long Body called. After exchanging pleasantries, he said, "I'm afraid I have some concerning news."

Rachel was pretty sure she knew what was coming, but she played along, "Oh really, and what is that?"

Long Body took a moment to choose his words carefully, "Since we last spoke, a half dozen of my most trusted men have been making discreet inquiries among the tribe. Something is definitely afoot, but they couldn't get anyone to tell them exactly what. Then earlier today, I was summoned to a private meeting among the elders, rather than the other way around. That's never happened before, at least since I've been Chairman."

That got Rachel's attention, and she asked, "What'd they want?"

Long Body heard the interest in her voice, and muttered, "The bastards proposed to add an item entitled 'Casino Revisited' to the tribal council agenda, and devote an hour to the topic by stealing time from other agenda items."

Rachel worked that around in her head for a moment, then said, "How'd the vote turn out?"

Long Body, in a defeated tone, "I thought it prudent to abstain, to see where everyone else stood before I showed my hand. Well, the rest voted unanimously in favor, so where I stood didn't matter. After the vote, I tried to start a discussion about how the hour would be handled, but Eternal Oak basically told me not to worry about it, he had it covered. Everyone else nodded, so that was that."

Rachel thought about that, then said, "Who the hell is Eternal Oak?"

Long Body sounded disappointed, "He's the elder of the tribe's largest band. Up to now, he'd always been a reliable ally of mine."

Rachel, now grim, "Reading between the lines, it looks as though my intuition might've been correct. Elements of your own tribe have linked up with Vangard Partners."

Long Body spat, "It certainly looks that way."

Rachel, thinking out loud in an upbeat tone, "But you still control at least one agenda item that comes before 'Casino Revisited', correct?"

Long Body perked up, "Two, actually. Why?"

Rachel lied, "Because you're going to put me on first, and I'm going to announce the good news. The tribe's Headwaters casino plan has been submitted to the state, and we've received preliminary approvals to proceed." Rachel fed him a gaslit rosy version of the Evans farm takeover endgame and the certainty of a warm welcome in Madison the day before tribal council. They chatted for another few minutes to ease Long Body's anxieties, and then he agreed to her suggestion.

CHAPTER 13

Overdrive Makes His Stand – Thursday;
July 8, 1965; 2:00 AM

Restless and unable to sleep, Overdrive carefully rolled out of bed so as not to disturb Mary. Then, he put on his robe and tip-toed to the kitchen to make a pot of coffee. While waiting, he quietly rifled through the drawers, pulled out a pencil and pad of paper, and set them on the kitchen table. Soon, he was settled in front of the pad, sipping his cup of joe. Before long, the gears in his head began to move.

Overdrive set to work sketching the back end of the side-hill pasture, the very large hay field on the corner of Rock and Bates Roads, and the narrow band of wasteland in between. If Wolf planned to steal the herd, this's where she'd do it. Alder's trespass through the area, told him as much. He knew his farm and the surrounding area better than anyone, so he concentrated on how it'd likely come down. He considered the possibility that the cattle could be herded away on foot, but soon dismissed it. There weren't any vacant barns or fenced areas with loading facilities nearby, and a cattle drive to a more distant location could never be done undetected. No, they'll have to bring cattle trucks into the hay field and load there.

Overdrive thought about that. Wolf would want to minimize the chance that witnesses would see or hear the trucks on the way in and out. Clearly, coming in from the north on Rock Road was the logical choice. On that route there's only one house, Lemke's, between the hay field and State Hwy 28. Plus, the junction with Hwy 28 is in the middle of nowhere. Old Mrs. Lemke wouldn't stir in the middle of the night. Under normal circumstances, the nearby farm dogs would raise a stink, but they've been drugged before and would surely be drugged again. Overdrive didn't like the idea of standing by and letting that happen to the dogs. But if the dogs weren't out running loose like they always had been in the past, Wolf's people would be suspicious. He really had no choice.

Overdrive moved on to Wolf's next problem, which was how to move the cattle from the pasture, across the narrow strip of waste land, to the hay field. Herding cattle was a lot like herding cats. They couldn't simply make openings in his fences on either side of the waste land, and drive them across. Even with an army of men, the cows would end up all over the Waldo Swamp. No, they'd have to fence a temporary lane through the wasteland. After some thought, Overdrive concluded they'd probably tack barbed wire to trees and bushes to avoid setting posts. Even so, fencing the lane would take some time and effort.

Loading the cattle from the hay field presented yet another problem for Wolf's people. With just a few cattle, a half-dozen men carrying thin four-by-eight sheets of plywood could corner them, and coax them into a trailer. Overdrive considered the idea of cutting a small number of cows from the herd for loading, over and over again, but convinced himself it'd take too long. He knew from experience that cutting a larger number each time, in an effort to speed things up, would also fail. The beasts would push through the plywood and end up all over.

As Overdrive pondered the loading problem, he recalled one of Gib Buyer's tales. Through his firm, the Farmer's Market located near Plymouth, Buyer bought and sold cattle, hay, and pretty much anything else a farmer might need. Buyer claimed he once loaded an entire herd from a pasture onto a convoy of eight trucks, by using the trucks themselves as a temporary loading pen. Like any successful cattle trader, Buyer had the gift of gab and sometimes discerning fact from fiction could be a challenge. Nonetheless, Overdrive thought about how that might work. If Wolf's people used typical two-axle cattle trucks, they'd need about eight in total. He could see how one truck might be loaded that way. But to load the others, they'd need to rearrange the trucks. And when they did, Overdrive couldn't see how they'd prevent the cattle from scattering. Grudgingly, he discarded the idea.

Unable to come up with a better idea, Overdrive concluded Wolf's people would need to build a temporary loading pen with posts and barbed wire. Ironically, Overdrive sometimes pastured the herd in that hay field, which meant it already had a well-maintained fence. In other words, the crooks would probably tuck the pen into the back corner of the field, and save time by using the existing fence for two sides of their rectangular pen. Even so, the need to drive posts and string wire meant that pen-building would take considerable time and effort.

As he worked the heist around in his mind, Overdrive became troubled by the notion of eight trucks. The trucks would need to be backed up to the loading pen, one after the other. Each transition would waste time. Plus, with all the prodding involved, it often took more time to squeeze the last cow onto a truck than to load all the others. Eight trucks meant eight such time-wasting exercises. Further, when you add loading time to that spent building the lane and loading pen, one wonders if it's even possible to accomplish it all in one night. Overdrive typically went to bed at 11:00 PM and set the alarm for 5:30 AM. That didn't leave a lot of time. So, he noodled on, and finally convinced himself they'd have to use semi-trailers instead of two-axle trucks. That way they'd only need three instead of eight, and loading would go much faster.

Confident he understood how the cattle heist would go down, Overdrive poured himself another cup of coffee and reviewed it one last time. The exercise gave him an uneasy feeling. The heist wouldn't be as easy as it sounded when they were kicking it around at Ted's office the previous night. The difficulty of the operation hadn't really come up in that conversation. If it had, maybe everybody wouldn't have been so gung-ho on the idea that Wolf would steal the herd. It occurred to Overdrive that Alder's reconnaissance through the hay field to the pasture may've had a different purpose. Perhaps he'd just been looking for a way to reach the barn unseen … say, for the appraisal.

Overdrive replayed the conversation from Ted's office the previous night, and something jumped out at him. If Wolf intended to force them to sell, she needed to take away their milk check. Stealing the herd would do it. But if that's too complex, maybe they'd figured another way. Overdrive thought about that as he gulped more coffee, then suddenly jerked upright with a new thought, only to trigger a coughing fit as coffee went down the wrong pipe. As he wiped the coffee-spray off the table with a dish towel, he refocused on the new threat. Wolf could burn down the barn ... and doing so would be a lot easier than stealing the herd!

No longer certain what Wolf might do, he studied his sketches and selected an all-night watch position at the uphill back-corner of the side-hill pasture. From this high vantage point, he'd have a commanding view of Alder's reconnaissance route and could guard against either option. He'd arm himself with his semi-automatic .22-caliber rifle, one round in the chamber and 20 more in the tube, and his semi-automatic 16-gauge shotgun, also with one round in the chamber and five more in the stock. If they came to burn down the barn, it'd only be one or two guys carrying gas cans and a lighter. No problem, he'd apprehend them at gunpoint or shoot them down in a firefight, their choice. But if they came to steal the herd, he'd hear fence-building and trucks, and then what?

Overdrive considered the question. A cattle heist crew would have to be sizable, to accomplish all that work in a short period of time. They'd also be spread out over a considerable area. Hell, they might even post armed-guards. Clearly, he couldn't handle a cattle heist on his own. After some thought, he convinced himself the best bet would be to somehow trap them until the authorities arrived. He studied his sketches looking for an idea, and before long he had one.

The hay field had three culverted field entrances/exits. One, off of Rock Road near where the road crosses a cattail marsh swale. Another, at the junction of Rock and Bates Roads, and a third, off of Bates Road at the corner of the field nearest to Overdrive's farmhouse. The preferred escape route would be onto Rock Road going north to State Hwy 28. If that were blocked, the only other option was to take Bates Road. Once on Bates Road, they could go west and pick up Hwy 28 in Cascade, or east past Overdrive's house to County Rd F, and left on F to State Hwy 57. If all three routes were blocked, they'd be trapped. Overdrive visualized how it could be done, and before long was grinning ear-to-ear.

About then, Mary stepped into the kitchen, and said, "Well, well, look who's up in the middle of the night, grinning like the village idiot naked in a snowstorm."

Overdrive feigned taking great offense, then said, "I'm not naked, but say the word and I can be."

Mary rolled her eyes, "Seriously? You wake me up while stumbling out of the bedroom, keep me awake with the aroma of coffee and a coughing fit, and then think you deserve to get laid? Well, think again. And what're you doing up?"

Overdrive put on a smug look, and said, "I just finished planning the all-night watch. Well, almost." He looked up at the wall clock, then said, "To put the last piece in the puzzle, I need to talk to Scully. He'll be up by now, but I need to catch him before he leaves for work." Overdrive and Scully have been best friends since school days. They even enlisted together for WWII. Scully works for the Sheboygan County Highway Department as the supervisor of their Town of Lyndon County Shed. He and his crew maintain the roads in the township.

Mary, as she poured herself a cup of coffee, "Knock yourself out. Then, fill me in on the grand plan."

When he got off the phone, Overdrive said, "Scully will have a crew burning bumps just up the hill on County Rd F first thing. He says he needs to check on their progress sometime during the morning, so he'll time it to be done about when we finish milking. Then, he'll swing by here."

Mary decoded what he said, "In other words, Scully just invited himself to breakfast and you, being a non-contributor in its preparation, agreed."

Overdrive thought about that, then said, "Well, that's an unneighborly way of putting it. But yeah, that about sums it up. Trust me though, we'll get our money's worth out of Scully this time. I'm going to talk him into coughing up the last puzzle-piece to complete my grand plan."

Mary smirked, "Oh yes, the grand plan." She made quote marks with both hands, then said, "Do tell me about it." Overdrive filled her in on his dual fears, and how he'd handle it either way. When finished, Mary asked, "Why don't we just use some of our idle farm equipment ... you know, things like the plow, spring tooth, and disc."

Overdrive shook his head, "A semi-trailer would run that shit right over."

Mary seemed impressed, "Well, I have to say, not bad for a shit-kicking farm boy." She looked at the wall

218 | PATRICK J. HUGHES

clock and, after a beat, put on her impish grin, "You still up for getting naked? Wouldn't want to start milking early ... you know, milk production might slip if the cows get knocked off their schedule."

Being a frugal and horny man, Overdrive concurred, "We definitely can't have production slip." Then, he took Mary's hand and led her back to the bedroom.

✻ ✻ ✻

Later, after the morning milking was finished, the family cleaned up and settled at the kitchen table. Scully joined them soon after, and over breakfast regaled them with the latest Cascade gossip. Afterward, Overdrive and Jumbo joined Scully in his highway department pickup truck, and the three of them scouted the best spots for road blocks on Rock Road north of the hay field, and on Bates Road east and west of the Rock Road intersection. As they worked, Overdrive filled them in on his plan.

On Rock Road, the best place for a road block was the hill just north of the cattail marsh. In that location, the shoulders on both sides dropped off steeply to gullies, then rose just as abruptly to stonewall fences on either side. So long as the obstruction was longer than the road's width, the passage of even a small vehicle would be impossible. The men measured the width of the road, and marked the spot with small rocks on the shoulder. Then, they drove the short distance north to Lemke's, and found a spot behind the barn where the mobile obstruction under consideration could be parked out of sight from the road. On the way out,

Overdrive went to the house to ask a favor of Mrs. Lemke. She was thrilled to help.

Next, they went east of the Rock and Bates Road intersection, and repeated the exercise of finding and marking the best place for a road block. When finished, they determined the logical place to park the mobile obstruction was behind Overdrive's main barn. Finally, west of the intersection, they repeated the exercise once more, and determined the mobile obstruction could be parked at the back of the long driveway at the Adcock place. Before they left, Overdrive went to the house and gave the renter's wife a heads up on what would be parked there, and to reassure her there'd be nothing to be concerned about if they heard it being moved in the middle of the night.

From Adcock's, Scully drove Overdrive and Jumbo to the county shed on the far side of Cascade, to acquaint them with the obstructions. By now, Overdrive had explained to Scully his need to mount a five-night watch, starting tonight, which would only be effective if observed intruders could be trapped. Once he understood the need, Scully volunteered the use of his three largest county-owned dump trucks. He said it wasn't a big deal, the road-repair projects scheduled for the coming week didn't require them, anyway.

Once at the county shed, measurements confirmed the dump trucks had ample length. Later today, Scully would have his crew fill them with gravel and drop them at their hiding spots. If a semi-trailer loaded with cattle rammed into one of these gravel-loaded big boys at highway speed ... well, the semi-trailer would have a rude-awakening. Scully spent a few minutes showing Overdrive and Jumbo how to drive the dump trucks, and use their broadband radios. After a few more minutes for practice, Overdrive and Jumbo were all set.

Overdrive would take the night-watch tonight, followed by Jumbo on night two. Darkwater would arrive in time for night three, and take it from there. Scully would be on-call, all five nights, and if called, would set and guard the road block at the top of Adcock's hill on Bates Raod. Every other night, either Jumbo or Overdrive, whoever wasn't on the night-watch, would sleepover at Lemke's on a cot next to the only phone. Whoever was at Lemke's was on-call, and if called, would set and guard the road block on Rock Road.

If the person on the night-watch observed or heard preparations for a cattle heist, he'd hold tight and monitor progress. Once he heard or saw semi-trailers enter the hay field, the watchman would roust the other two road-blockers with phone calls. Then, he'd set the third road block, the one on Bates Road near the Evans farm, himself.

The watchman's first call would always go to Scully. Scully's first action would be to call the Sheboygan County Sherriff's Department. Due to his highway department role, and the fact that traffic accidents were a large part of the Sherriff's Department work load, Scully was on a first-name basis with the night duty-officer, as well as the deputies that worked this part of the county. As a result of his relationships, when Scully called for three cruisers, one for each road block, he'd get them pronto. Scully would also request that the cruiser responding to the Evans farm, include a ride-along deputy. After scrambling the police, Scully would head to Adcock's.

The hope was that police would arrive before semi-trailers tried to breach a road block. Once they arrived, the police's plan of action was totally up to them. However, the watchman would return to the night-watch position, for fear that once the fun started, thieves might try to flee on foot back to the pasture, and into the swamp. Overdrive hoped the ride-along deputy would accompany the watchman, but that wasn't his call.

Just to be sure all were clear, Overdrive, Jumbo and Scully talked through the plan one last time. Jumbo feared the thieves might hear them position the dump trucks. But after discussion, this was considered unlikely. The diesel semi-trailers would be idling in the hay field, amidst the sounds of cattle mooing, clomping up ramps, kicking trailer sidewalls, shitting, pissing, and so forth. The thieves would be so immersed in nearby sounds, they wouldn't hear anything that far away. When the conversation died, Scully dropped Overdrive and Jumbo back at the farm, and everyone got on with their day.

* * *

Mary was on the phone with Ted Ritter when Overdrive and Jumbo walked into the kitchen. She mouthed 'it's about Ray Knobloch' to her husband, and shooed Jumbo back outside.

Ray Knobloch was the aircraft mechanic that serviced Ben Wolf's plane at Chapman's Airpark, and later at the Sheboygan County Memorial Airport. As it turns out, he serviced more than just the plane. Ben

Wolf's hobby brought Rachel to the airpark during her precocious early high school years. With idle time to kill in the hanger waiting for her father to land, Rachel came into contact with Ray, who took a shine to her. She fantasized about cockpit sex with oily callused hands all over her body, and he'd been more than happy to oblige. Flattered by the attentions of a full-grown man, Rachel began paying him more regular visits once licensed to drive. She soon tired of Knobloch, and threatened to break it off. But he pleaded with her, so she agreed to continue with the understanding that someday she'd need a very big favor in return. In May of 1962, Rachel called in her chit. She provided a small device, and Knobloch spliced it into the fuel line of Ben's plane, no questions asked. The ingenious little contraption was designed to cause a fuel leak, ignite the fuel, and then melt in the fire and fall away.

Mary motioned her husband to pick up the extension. Ted was so excited he could barely speak. In Florida, Jason had no sooner finished introducing himself when Ray Knobloch came out with ... *this isn't about aircraft mechanic career advice, is it*? Although he didn't say it directly, Jason thinks Knobloch had been expecting a visit like his since Ben Wolf's plane went down. Seizing the opportunity, Jason explained he's investigating a series of crimes by a prime suspect, and had reason to believe Knobloch had information concerning one of those crimes. Jason made it clear he'd no interest in Knobloch, other than for help making a case against the prime suspect. That's when Knobloch called an attorney he apparently already had on board and up to speed. Then, Knobloch told Jason to come back in two hours, because he couldn't talk without counsel present.

After hearing Ted out, Overdrive and Mary had lunch, then Overdrive went down for a nap ahead of his all-night watch. Late afternoon, Mary shook him awake, saying Ted was on the line once more. When Overdrive entered the kitchen, Mary appeared to be leading Ted through deep-breathing exercises over the phone. By the time the extension was to his ear, Ted had calmed enough to speak intelligibly, although still in staccato bursts. Jason had met with Knobloch and his attorney. At the meeting, he was told to identify the prime suspect, and provide an overview of the alleged crimes. Their reaction to Wolf's name told Jason they'd been expecting to hear it. As he ticked off the long list of crimes, the lawyer became increasingly more relaxed and friendly. It was as if he judged his client's crime to be insignificant in comparison with Wolf's numerous offenses.

Reassured about his negotiating position, the attorney then asked which crime Jason thought his client could help with, and specifically what information Jason hoped his client might have. Jason responded with the theory that Wolf sabotaged her father's plane, and said he hoped Knobloch could help prove it. Instantly, they were eager to demonstrate just how helpful they could be.

Knobloch's attorney had obviously done his homework. He knew Ben Wolf's plane had gone down in federal waters, and hence the feds had a dog in the fight. He claimed to have worked many cases with the local FBI field office in the past, and said he knew those people well. In fact, he'd called them in advance of his meeting with Jason, to arrange the next step. That's how confident he was about Wolf and sabotage being the reason for Jason's visit. It came out that Knobloch's attorney felt his client would never be safe until Wolf was behind bars. Consequently, he wanted the next step, and all subsequent steps, to come quickly.

As part of that, Knobloch's attorney had talked the local FBI into arranging a meeting with a federal assistant district attorney, for first thing tomorrow. The assistant DA to attend, had already been designated with the authority to grant federal immunity. The problem is, Knobloch's attorney forbids him from cooperating with the investigation, until full transactional immunity from both federal and state prosecution has been granted. In fact, Knobloch's attorney also demands his client be relocated under the federal witness protection program, until such time as Rachel Wolf no longer lives and breathes.

This meant tomorrow morning's meeting is a golden opportunity to move forward quickly, but only if Ted and Jason can arrange to have the Sheboygan County DA, or a designated assistant DA, in Florida and present. Since they became aware of the issue, Ted and Jason have been working the problem from both ends. Moments ago, Ted learned the Sheboygan County DA, as well as the lead detective on the plane-crash case, would be there. Jason booked rooms for them where he's staying, and will pick them up at the airport this evening. Tomorrow morning, he'll provide transportation to the meeting, and participate in-person. Ted will be dialed in from the conference room. If all goes well, by tomorrow afternoon the Sheboygan County Sherriff's Department will be in judge's chambers, seeking an arrest warrant for Rachel

Wolf on two counts of first-degree murder.

When Ted finished, Mary burst into tears. Before long, the men joined in, although in a more restrained manner. How could they not? It had been such a very long slog, but finally … finally … they'd caught a break. When the moment passed, they awkwardly asked each other's forgiveness. But for what, they really didn't know. After regaining his composure, Overdrive filled Ted in on the night-watch preparations. Impressed, Ted dropped a few rare compliments, then rushed off to prepare Jason for the next day.

❈ ❈ ❈

After the evening milking, Mary herded the family out of the kitchen and into the TV room. That is, all except for Overdrive and Jumbo. They stayed behind and made one last call to Scully, to make sure everything was set for the night watch. Scully confirmed the dump trucks were filled with gravel and parked where planned. Overdrive emphasized once more that should the cattle heist come down, Scully must send the first cruiser on scene to Jumbo on Bates Road, where the semi-trailers would go first. The thieves might be armed, and Overdrive didn't want his son in a firefight before the police arrived.

Next, they kicked around who should take which weapons. Overdrive only owned the 16-guage shotgun and .22-caliber rifle, both semi-automatics. Scully only owned two bolt-action single-shots, one a 12-guage shotgun and the other a .257-caliber deer rifle. After discussion, they decided Scully would be fine with the two single-shots. Since Jumbo's roadblock was the most likely to be contested, he got the 16-guage six-shot semi-automatic shotgun. Six buckshot blasts at close range could drop a lot of timber. Even so, they decided he'd better wear a hunting vest full of shells in case he needed to reload in a hurry. When and if the shooting broke out, Overdrive would likely be at the night-watch position. On that high ground, there's a need for range, which made the rifle his best choice anyway.

After the call, Jumbo joined his siblings in the TV room, and Overdrive and Mary huddled in the kitchen. They decided Overdrive would wake Mary if anything happened. They feared the thieves might scatter on foot, and try to break into the farmhouse to swipe car keys, make a call, or take hostages. With the guns already spoken for, Mary would try to defend the place with a baseball bat.

At 10:00 PM, the younger kids and Mary went to bed. Jumbo lingered in the kitchen until his siblings were upstairs, then drove the cow car to Lemke's. Overdrive walked Jumbo to the car, gave him a slap on the back, and then hiked past the barn and down the farm lane to the night-watch position. The family farm dog, Duke, tagged along with Overdrive.

Overdrive and Duke assumed their positions at the back end of the side-hill pasture, near the up-hill side corner. Any cattle heist would involve the back end of the pasture, the narrow band of waste land between it and the hay field beyond, and the hay-field's back corner. In daylight, the watch position had a commanding view, not only of these locations, but also of the Nutter place at the intersection of Rock and Bates Roads, Rock Road on the far side of the hay field, and most of Bates Road from Overdrive's farm all the way to

Adcock's hill on the way to Cascade. Of course, on this cloudy moonless night, Overdrive couldn't see a thing. He'd brought a flash light, but he didn't dare use it. Even so, scanning the terrain for vehicle lights or flashlight beams played a part in Overdrive's watch.

More important however, was listening for sounds. Wherever there's an unobstructed line of sight, there's also an unobstructed path for sound to carry. That meant Overdrive could hear noises as far away as the Nutter place, Rock Road, and the hay field. As he sat in silence with Duke, Overdrive paid special attention to the ambient night sounds. By immersing himself in those, anything that sounded out of place would jump out at him.

Duke's ears perked up at 11:35 PM. Overdrive strained to hear what it was, and after a moment realized a vehicle was moving slowly along Rock Road with no lights on. Soon, Duke stood with ears on alert, and slightly adjusted his direction to point more toward where Overdrive guessed the Nutter place to be. A beat later, Overdrive detected a sound, maybe a car door but he wasn't sure. That's when Duke gave a little woof, turned, and trotted back toward the barn. Still straining to hear, a moment later Overdrive picked up the sound of the slowly moving vehicle once more, now coming his way on Bates Road.

Before long, Overdrive connected the dots. The Nutter dog had just been drugged, and Duke would be next. The Lemke dog had probably been the first to go down. Still listening carefully, a minute later Overdrive again picked up the sound of the slow-moving vehicle, now headed back toward Nutter's. As time passed, he could track the vehicle as it turned right onto Rock

Road, and headed north. As expected, Duke never returned.

All was silent until 12:15 AM, when Overdrive again heard a slow-moving vehicle on Rock Road with no lights. This time the sound idled for a moment, then changed in a subtle way. Overdrive guessed the vehicle had turned off of Rock Road into the hay field. It wasn't long before his guess was confirmed. He heard heavy things being tossed to the ground, as if materials were being unloaded out of a pickup truck. Before long, he saw brief splashes of flashlight beams here and there. Next, came the sounds of people thrashing through the waste land, and the occasional tap-tap-tap. Overdrive recognized these as the sounds of barbed wire being unrolled and stretched, then U Nailed to trees and bushes. About 45 minutes in, came the occasional chop-chop-chop, and stomping sounds. He guessed they were clearing the new lane, making it more visible for the cattle.

About 90 minutes in, the original light-beams and sounds died away, but were replaced by more distant ones. The clink-clink-clink told Overdrive they were driving metal T-Posts into the ground in his hay field. Once more, he heard the sounds of barbed wire being unrolled and stretched. Then, came the squeaks, which meant they're installing T-Post clips to attach the barbed wire to the posts. The snippets of flash light beams told him they're building two sides of the loading pen, and using his existing fence for the rest.

About 2:15 AM the pickup truck fired up, and without lights rolled across the hay field to Rock Road, then turned north. The commotion in the hay field continued for another 15 minutes or so, then light beams popped up in the lane. He could tell they're headed in his direction, toward the pasture. A moment later, beams began to flash over the pasture. Fearing he'd be seen, Overdrive shimmied down flat on his stomach, and crawled behind the pasture's thick corner-post. At intervals, he risked a peek to keep track of what was going on. He counted four men, and one seemed to be in charge. Surprisingly, they brought hay bales.

Suddenly, one of the men rolled under the lane's fence, and the others handed him bales over the top, which he stacked a few steps back. Overdrive guessed they didn't want the cattle to get at the hay. A beat later, the man on the far side cut open a bale, tossed half of it over the fence, and rolled back under himself. After a moment, flashlight beams began to search the pasture, so Overdrive ducked back behind the post. When he peeked again, the leader was standing in front of the nearest cow, holding out a pad of hay. What the hell! Now he's walking back to the lane, and the lummox of a cow is trailing along behind like some sort of zombie. You've got to be shitting me! How stupid can they be? Oh great, now all four men are leading the zombies to the lane.

Over the next 45 minutes, Overdrive watched in agony as his cows were led into the lane, and then driven ahead to the loading pen in the corner of the hay field beyond. At first it was one-by-one. But after a while, the cattle just joined right in. It was as if the beasts were in fear of missing out, or misinterpreted the situation as a longed-for jail break. By the time Overdrive heard vehicles entering the hay field about 3:00 AM, nearly the entire herd was already in the loading pen.

Compared with the one before, these vehicles gave off distinctly-different sounds. Overdrive recognized the low rumbles as coming from diesel engines. He guessed that multiple semi-trailers were in the process of entering the hay field. That was his cue to get to the phone. He grabbed his rifle and flashlight, and backed away slowly in a belly crawl. Then, he turned and continued to crawl to a safe distance before breaking into a fast-walk through the darkness.

Scully picked up on the first ring. His reaction was basically hot diggity dog! Overdrive reminded him that Jumbo was to get the first cruiser. Jumbo also answered on the first ring. His reaction ... *if I have to shoot, should I go for the legs or the kill* ... was even more concerning. Overdrive advised he go for the legs unless they were armed, numerous, or right on top of him. When he woke Mary, he reminded her to grab a baseball bat, keep the lights out, and lock all the doors.

With everyone else in motion, Overdrive grabbed his flashlight and rifle, and hurried to the dump truck in back of the barn. When it roared to life, Overdrive feared it'd wake the dead. With great concentration, he was able to rumble the great behemoth down the driveway at a low purr, and without any lights. At the road, he turned right toward his road block destination. He risked waving his flashlight beam over the front yard, and saw Duke lying flat on his side halfway to the house. A short while later, he risked a few more quick shots of light until he saw the small rocks on shoulder marking his spot. Then, came the hard part. It took a half dozen back-and-forth shimmies to plant the beast of a truck across the road. Since he couldn't see, Overdrive got out and verified he was centered, before shutting down the truck.

A beat later, the broadband radio crackled. It was Scully reporting his road block was set, and three cruisers were speeding their way, lights and flashers but no sirens. They'd cut their lights and flashers too, before turning onto Rock or Bates Roads. Scully suggested they all stand outside their road blocks, listen hard, and light up the dump trucks with their flashlights as the cruisers approached. If one of them rammed a truck, Scully said he'd be buried in paperwork for the rest of his life. After Scully finished, Overdrive and Jumbo both remembered enough about how to work the radio, to report that their road blocks were also set.

Nothing happened for what felt like an eternity. Then he caught a glimpse of flashers and lights up on County Rd F, just before they went out. He could hear the cruiser's approach on Bates Road, and at about 100 yards out, he began to flash his beam intermittently onto the dump truck. As the cruiser eased to a stop, Overdrive stepped to the driver's window, showed his ID, and thanked them for coming.

To Overdrive's surprise, the officers wanted their car on the inside of the road block. After explaining what he'd have to do to let them pass, they backed up to give him room. Once they passed, Overdrive repositioned the truck across the road and at their request, got into the back of the cruiser to talk through the situation. Overdrive filled them in on everything he knew. Afterward, the officers spent a few minutes probing Overdrive for details on the lay of the land.

After some radio time between the three police cars to finalize their plan, the officers with Overdrive gave him a summary minus all the jargon and code words. Basically, they wanted to catch the thieves red-handed, which meant after the cattle had been loaded. For the safety of the cattle, their preference was the semi-trailers never left the hay field. Hence, their plan was for all three cruisers to quietly roll forward to the hay field, and block the three culverted field exits. Then, when ready, they'd all blast the silent darkness with sirens, lights, and flashers. A beat later, over the handheld loudspeaker would come ... *This is the Sheboygan County Sherriff's Department. You are surrounded. Come out with your hands up.* What came next would be up to the cattle thieves.

* * *

With the plans set and word passed, Overdrive and one of the deputies jogged back behind the barn to the night-watch position. It wouldn't be long now. Overdrive and the deputy were seated just outside the pasture fence on either side of the thick corner post. From the distant hay field, they heard the idling hum of the diesel semi-trailers, and the occasional clomp-clomp of a cow ascending a ramp. At one point, they heard what sounded like one semi pulling away from the loading pen, and another backing up in its place.

Other than these sounds, there was total silence until there wasn't. Suddenly flashers, lights, and sirens erupted simultaneously from three points around the hay field. A beat later, came the authoritative voice over the loudspeaker, issuing crystal-clear commands audible even to Overdrive. Instantly, everything in the hay field changed. There were urgent shouts. One semi-trailer after the other put on its lights and began to move. The leader went straight for the culverted exit onto Rock Road. Overdrive could hear it gear up on its way. As it approached shots rang out, but it didn't seem to matter. In a mid-range gear at full throttle, the semi-trailer T-boned the cruiser and drove it forward across the road and far-side ditch, then through the stone wall fence and out into the corn field on the other side.

With the culverted exit now open, the second semi-trailer shot through the gap, and turned north onto Rock Road headed in Jumbo's direction. A beat later, the first semi attempted to reverse itself back onto the road, but from the chilling screeches Overdrive guessed the trailer carriage had hung up on the stone wall fence, stranding it with its butt hanging out over the road. With the path north on Rock Road now blocked, the third semi-trailer shot the gap and wheeled left toward the T-intersection with Bates Road. It drew heavy fire from the deputies at the corner field-exit, but to no avail. The semi-trailer wheeled right onto Bates Road, and began to gear up on its way toward Scully.

Just then, a tap on his shoulder brought Overdrive's attention back to the deputy at his side, who was pointing toward the lane. Bouncing flashlight beams were coming in their direction, and moving fast. It looked like two of them. The deputy stood and pointed his shotgun into the air. Caught off guard, Overdrive's military training kicked in, and he threw himself flat on his stomach, with eye at the gunsight, safety off, and rifle pointed toward the end of the lane. When the runners burst into the pasture, the deputy barked ... *halt, or I'll shoot* ... and fired a warning shot to show he meant business. One runner took off, but the other saw the muzzle flash, and returned fire with a two-handed barrage. The deputy went down. The shooter stormed forward and kept firing away.

Overdrive let him come. Using the muzzle flashes as a crude guide to the shooter's whereabouts, Overdrive put three quick rounds into what he estimated to be center mass, when the guy was 10 yards out. The shooter went down. Instantly, decades-old military training kicked in, and Overdrive rolled under the fence with rifle and flashlight in-hand, and was on him in an instant. His beam shined up two handguns, which he snatched and tossed up toward the deputy. When he turned back to him, the shooter was pulling another, so Overdrive kicked it away and landed a savage blow with his rifle butt, to knock him out cold. Seeing bloody drool, Overdrive knelt to pull up the man's shirt, revealing three chest wounds. During a quick pat-down, he took two knives off the man. Then, he scrambled to his feet, retrieved the third handgun, and ran to the deputy.

The downed deputy was awake and lucid. He'd taken a slug to the right thigh. How bad, the deputy wasn't sure. Although in extreme pain, he'd managed to rip up his shirt, and use the rags to apply pressure to his wounds. Overdrive placed all the handguns and knives within the deputy's reach, and filled him in on the status of the shooter. The deputy said he'd seen flashlight flickers in the swamp, so the other runner had fled. The deputy thought his best chance was for Overdrive to go for help. He claimed if the shooter came to, he'd be able to defend himself. Overdrive wasn't so sure, but he picked up his rifle and flashlight and sprinted for the house anyway.

* * *

Jumbo was wide awake and on high alert, sitting in his dump truck. He had the windows open to hear the night sounds, and was peering down Rock Road in the direction of the hay field. It was pitch-black and he couldn't see a thing, but the distant low-rumble of the diesel semi-trailers was unmistakable.

Suddenly Rock Road burst into lights, flashers, and sirens, and the loudspeakers rang out, clear as a bell. A beat later, the truck's radio crackled. It was Scully exhorting him to turn on the dump truck lights, including the flasher up top. Jumbo complied. In a breathless rant, Scully said the time for stealth was over. Now make the truck a beacon, he exhorted. Let the immovable behemoth be seen for what it is. Do what you can to discourage the dumbasses from trying to ram through, which'd whiplash the cattle and cause serious injuries.

With Scully still mid-rant, the sound of gunshots and a colossal crash snapped Jumbo's attention back to Rock Road. Up ahead he saw a semi-trailer pancake a police cruiser, as if it were bug-splatter on the bumper. The whole shebang went left to right, and out of sight into the field across the road. A beat later, a second semi-trailer came roaring out of the hay field and turned in his direction. Oh-oh, that can't be good.

Jumbo grabbed his flash light and shotgun, and jumped out of the truck. He ran ahead 20 yards, and stood in the middle of the road. A quick glance back, told him the dump truck was lit up like a Christmas tree, just like Scully wanted. He could hear the semi gearing

236 | PATRICK J. HUGHES

up, as it trundled in his direction. Unsure what to do, he turned on his flash light, aimed the beam at the semi, and waved his arms. The semi kept gearing up, and flicked its headlights between low and high beams a few times, as if to warn him to get out of the way.

Jumbo muttered *'fuck that'* to himself, and sprinted forward. The semi just kept bearing down on him, high beams on, as if to blind him. Jumbo pulled to a halt about 50 yards out in front of his road block. To get the headlights out of his eyes, he stepped to the right shoulder. Then, he clicked off the safety, and waited.

When the semi was 40 yards out from his position, Jumbo opened fire at the driver's-side windshield … pop, pop, pop, pop. Each shot shattered more safety glass, and the semi began to gear down. The driver yelled *'don't shoot I'm stopping'* through his open window, as the semi-trailer's momentum carried it abreast, and then past, Jumbo.

Jumbo ran back to catch up, and once abreast of the semi-cab, slowed his pace to stay there. The semi-trailer stopped maybe five yards short of the dump truck. In one smooth movement, the driver put his left hand up and out the window as if to give up, then came around with a handgun in his right. Jumbo was ready, and shot off his right hand. Then, he clambered up the side-steps to the driver's window. The driver was rolling around in agony in the foot well, so Jumbo leveled his barrel at the passenger's center mass, and waited in silence. After a beat, the passenger put his hands in the air.

About then, a police cruiser screeched to a halt behind the semi-trailer. Jumbo shouted, both to identify himself and provide status. A beat later, the passenger was cuffed, and first aid was administered to the driver. Jumbo watched and thought to himself ... *I can do this. This is just like being in the military police.* He paid particular attention, as they applied a tourniquet to the driver's right forearm, to stop the bleeding.

Shortly, backup arrived and Jumbo was asked to move the dump truck permanently, because the road block was no longer needed. A beat later, there came an ambulance, and then another. Before long, a wrecker rumbled through. One officer after another stopped by and slapped Jumbo on the back, as if to say job well done. Eventually, a detective came to take his statement.

❄ ❄ ❄

Overdrive was huffing and puffing, by the time he reached the farm buildings. He rounded the barn to see house lights on, and flashers spinning on the road out front. Initially confused, because the patrol car was outside the road block, Overdrive quickly realized the police must've called for backup when all hell broke loose. Relieved, he ran toward the cruiser. Ten yards out, a warning shot rang out, followed by ... *halt, and put your hands in the air.* Overdrive complied. Then came ... *lay your weapon on the ground, walk five paces onto the lawn, and lay down spread-eagled.* Overdrive complied again. After a beat, an armed officer approached, and asked for ID. Without moving, Overdrive told him to look for the wallet in the back pocket. After backing away to click on his light and inspect the driver's license, the deputy apologized and helped him to his feet. Overdrive gave him a rapid dump on the wounded deputy behind the barn, and the officer hustled off to get help on the way.

Overdrive's glance down Bates Road brought shock and awe. Flashing lights were everywhere. As he stood there and gaped, he felt a little hip bump, then Mary snuggled in for a hug. Arm-in-arm, they continued to stare down the road. A beat later, the officer peeked up over the roof of his cruiser, and shouted for Overdrive to move the dump truck so an ambulance could get through. As he ran past, the officer told him the road block was no longer needed, so park the truck out of the way, and stand-by to ride with the ambulance.

A moment later, Overdrive roared into the driveway and parked the dump truck in the orchard. While he waited for the ambulance, Overdrive got on the truck's radio, and Scully gave him a quick update of what went down. Six men were arrested. Three cattle-filled semi-trailers recovered. And get your sorry ass down here if you want your cattle back.

In a beat, the ambulance arrived and Overdrive got in. When they got there, the downed deputy was still doing fine, and the downed shooter still hadn't moved. Overdrive left the rest to the EMTs, and jogged back to the house.

❋ ❋ ❋

Mary wanted to come along to the hay field, so they drove down in the family car. Upon arrival, they were greeted by none other than the Sheboygan County Sherriff. He told them he decided to join the party, after learning his entire force was already here.

The Sheriff gave them a brief summary of where things stood. Among the good guys, only the deputy with Overdrive had been seriously injured. Among the bad guys, three were down ... one by Overdrive ... one by the officer with the pancaked cruiser ... and one by the civilian guarding the road block on Rock Road. Overdrive and Mary's eyes widened, and they looked at each other and mouthed 'Jumbo'. The Sheriff was aware of eight suspects. Three were being transported to the hospital, four were being held onsite, and one escaped into the Waldo Swamp and is still at large. The Sheriff's team had called in a wrecker, which managed to yank the crashed semi-trailer back onto the road. Hence, the three semi-trailers were all functional, more or less. As far as he knew, the cattle were fine.

With an eye-twinkle that shouted vote-for-me next election, the Sheriff offered to put to together a work detail using the remaining four suspects, under armed guard of course. Their objective would be to restore the Evanses property to the way it'd been before all this happened. Under phase one, which could start immediately, the work detail would unload the cattle from the trailers, drive them from the loading pen back to the pasture through the lane, and then repair the pasture fence. According to the Sheriff, one healthy semi-trailer driver remained among the four suspects, so the work detail had all the skillsets it needed.

Phase two would need to wait until after the photographers finished documenting the crime scene. But once given the all-clear, the work detail would tear back down all the temporary lane and loading pen fencing they'd built overnight. When the Sheriff finished explaining his work detail idea, Overdrive and

Mary looked at each other, shrugged, and called it a deal. But to avoid a hay field littered with holes, Overdrive added the proviso that his scoop tractor be used to pull the T-Posts straight up out of the ground.

With the deal struck, the Sherriff whistled up his detective. After making introductions, the detective led Overdrive away to take his statement, and the Sherriff excused himself to get the work detail going. Suddenly alone, Mary looked around and saw Scully and Jumbo coming her way. She hugged them both, then filled them in about the deal with the Sherriff. They'd both already given their statements, so Mary asked Jumbo to go home and bring back the scoop tractor.

When the Sherriff, detective, and Overdrive returned, the conversation turned to the fourth vehicle in the hay field, the pickup truck. Overdrive filled everybody in about hearing a vehicle make the rounds to drug the dogs, and then a half-hour later returning with the fence-building crew and materials, only to leave once more. He couldn't see so he wasn't sure, but Overdrive guessed the pickup truck had been used on both occasions. Since it's here again, Overdrive also presumed it must've returned a half-hour later with the semi-trailers, although he couldn't hear it over the noise of the semis.

The Sherriff and detective both jumped on the detail of the half-hour, as if it had some importance. They believed it must be the round-trip drive-time between the hay field, and wherever the thieves parked their semi-trailers and hung out. Most likely, that meant a truck stop and motel about 15 minutes away. Both men knew of only one, so the detective sprinted off to dispatch two cruisers in that direction. A beat later, they were racing north on Rock Road, with lights, flashers and sirens. As they all watched them go, the Sherriff explained that the suspect at large might run there, and he wanted his guys there first. The only truck stop that close was on State Hwy 57, a little south of its intersection with State Hwy 23.

A moment later, Jumbo returned with the scoop tractor. The Sherriff excused himself to light a fire under the photographers, and kickoff phase two of the work detail. As part of that, he asked the nearest deputy to have Jumbo show one of the suspects how to operate the tractor. Before long, Jumbo re-joined his parents and Scully. All too wired to go home, they decided to compare notes. Overdrive regaled them with his exploits, followed by Jumbo doing the same. When it came his turn, Scully whined about never getting off a shot, because the guys in the semi-trailer that ran his way gave up. Mary continued to lay in wait in the dark farmhouse, baseball bat in hand, even after she heard the sirens and loudspeaker. But when the backup cruiser showed up out front, she turned on the house lights, and ventured outside to introduce herself. While doing so, she saw Duke lying comatose in the yard, and carried him to the shed where he normally slept.

Before long, the T-Posts had all been pulled and the scoop tractor was free to go. As ordered by the Sherriff, the work detail had stacked the posts in the tractor's bucket, along with the fence-building tools, and the unused spool of barbed wire and T-Post clips. Apparently, the Sherriff thought Overdrive might have a use for them some day. The jumble of used wire and clips had been stuffed into the bed of the pickup truck, which was in the process of being loaded onto a flatbed wrecker, for transport to the Sherriff's impound lot in Sheboygan.

Before long, dawn was breaking and the normal milking time was almost upon them. But in order to be milked, cows needed to be relaxed enough to let their milk down. To give the herd a little more time to chill out in the pasture, Mary suggested they eat breakfast before milking, rather than the normal vice-versa routine. Overdrive and Mary led the way home, followed by Scully in his highway department pickup, with Jumbo trailing behind on the scoop tractor. Over breakfast is when the rest of the Evans family learned about last night's drama. Afterward, the family changed into their barn clothes, while Scully called in sick. When they all walked out together, only one was going home to bed.

CHAPTER 14

Rachel Doubles Down – Friday; July 9, 1965; 4:00 AM

S welling with admiration for the crew he'd picked for the cattle heist, Vince watched in awe as the last of the semi-trailers was being loaded. These guys really knew their stuff. His thoughts changed instantly, when the hay field erupted into the sensory overload of lights, flashers, and loudspeakers.

With a sweep of his flashlight beam, Vince located the body guard and ran in his direction. A beat later, they both took off running, tripping, and stumbling through the lane. When they burst into the pasture, barked orders and a shotgun blast rang out. Vince hesitated, when the body guard returned fire toward the muzzle flash. But when he charged up the hill like a mad man, Vince fled alone into the Waldo Swamp. Using his flashlight as sparingly as possible, he soon found the trail. He'd been down it so often for the appraisal that it was well-worn.

Vince made good time, and reached his car at the far side of the swamp about 4:45 AM. Within fifteen

244 | PATRICK J. HUGHES

minutes, he was in his motel room furiously packing. A smidge after 5:00 AM, he checked out. As he pulled onto State Hwy 57 going north, he saw police-car flashers at the nearby truck stop. He went on past, and saw there were two police cars. A moment later, with his eyes on the rearview mirror, he watched them cross the highway and turn into the motel.

Somewhat relieved, Vince focused on his next move. He knew of a small mom-and-pop motel on the quiet side of Sheboygan Falls. In his experience, the sheets were always clean, and no matter the time of day or night, check-in was possible, no questions asked. When he reached State Hwy 23, he turned right toward Sheboygan Falls.

Check-in was uneventful. Vince used a different alias, and paid in cash. Once in the room, he called his brother, Phil, and told him the bad news about the body guard. Phil expressed concern at the fate of one of his best men, but was thrilled that Vince had made it out alive. Generally, when he got calls at that hour, word of death came over the line. Phil reassured Vince that the body guard was solid, and if he survived, he wouldn't rat him out. The pickup, rented under an alias, was of no concern either

After the call, Vince felt a little better. He considered calling Rachel immediately, but looked at his watch and dismissed the idea. The conversation with her would be a difficult one, and he needed to be at the top of his game. That meant a shower, change of clothes, and breakfast with coffee. Lots of coffee. Over breakfast, he prepped for the call. As part of that, he decided he'd wait until 8:30 AM to call. In his experience, Rachel was far less likely to go unhinged after her own shower and breakfast.

Back in his room in plenty of time, Vince relaxed and let nature call. After finishing his business, he steeled himself for the call one last time, then dialed Rachel. She answered in a chirpy voice, so he waded right in, "Rachel, I'm afraid I have some bad news." He filled her in with crisp language, and left nothing out.

Rachel asked in a professional tone, "Can they trace any of this to you?"

Relieved at her demeanor, Vince said, "Not a chance. The HMR car was dropped north of the swamp and used for my getaway. The crew only knew me by my alias. Same goes for the semi-trailer rental places, stockyards, and motel. Plus, everything for the whole caper was paid in cash."

Rachel thought a moment, then said, "They've got the body guard and his vehicle. Is that a concern?"

Vince, confident, "If he's alive, Phil says he's solid and there's nothing to worry about. The pickup truck was rented under another alias."

Rachel harrumphed as she came to terms with what happened, then said, "How in the hell did the cops get there so fast?"

Vince confessed, "I don't know, Rachel. We were really careful. We drugged all the neighborhood dogs, drove slowly with lights out, and didn't bring in the semi-trailers until 3:00 AM when the cattle were ready to load. You name it, we did it, yet somehow the cops got tipped off."

Rachel took a moment to process that, then said, "Well, you know what to do next, right?"

Vince, confused, "Not exactly, no. What do you mean?"

Rachel, in a condescending tone, as if he were slow, "Find Mary Evans tomorrow morning, and tell her the last offer has been extended."

Vince gasped, "You're kidding, right?"

Rachel spat, with a little anger this time, "No, I'm not kidding. Think about it. All you need to do is play dumb about what happened. You weren't involved, remember? The cops caught the cattle thieves red-handed, and you weren't among them. Your coming back is completely unrelated to last night's events. Instead, you came to share the joyous news that our previous extraordinarily generous offer had been extended. Who knows, maybe the Evanses have better insight after last night ... you know, about the wisdom of staying on that farm."

Vince rolled his eyes on his end of the line, "Boy oh boy, Rachel. That's a stretch, don't you think? Yesterday, I made a threat, and last night somebody tried to steal their herd. Arrested or not, even a fool would know those two events were related. These people are no fools."

Rachel exploded with anger, "Look Vince, I don't give a shit what you tell her, okay! If you have a better play, be my guest. But I need to own that farm by Sunday night, do you hear me? Do your job. First thing Monday, I'm in Madison to pitch the casino to two state agencies. Tuesday evening, I'm with the tribe, to tell them we have preliminary approvals. If I don't, they'll throw me over for Vangard Partners. That's not going to happen, am I clear?"

Vince opened his mouth to protest, but decided against it. Instead, he said, "Crystal. But just so I'm clear on subsequent steps, what happens if they reject the offer tomorrow morning?"

Face twisted with anger, Rachel shouted, "Then tomorrow night, you burn down the barn. And the following morning, you return with the offer. And this time, don't leave until they sign it!"

* * *

Later that morning, Mary was cultivating corn in the field across Bates Road from where Vince had spoken with her previously. He parked on the shoulder, and ambled across the corn field in her direction. Mary caught something in her peripheral vision, risked a quick glance, and immediately came to a dead stop for a double-take. She couldn't believe her own eyes.

Vince Alder smiled and waved as he approached, then said cheerily, "How are you this morning, Mary?"

Mary spat, "You have a lot of nerve coming here after what you did last night. I should call the Sherriff and have you arrested."

Taking on the appearance of a puppy with a thorn in its paw, Alder said, "Excuse me. What're you talking about?"

Mary, not buying it, "Oh come on. How stupid do you think I am?"

Alder held up his hands in a placating gesture, "I'm sorry if I've offended you in some way, but I have no idea what you're talking about."

Mary snapped, not bothering to hide her anger, "Bullshit! Last night you tried to steal our milk herd."

Faux dumbstruck, Alder said, "W-what? Somebody tried to steal your herd? Did they get away with any? Are you okay, is your family okay?"

Still not buying it, Mary just looked at him, "What do you want?" Then, she gestured at the field, "Can't you see I'm busy?"

Alder, contrite, "Of course, I know you're busy. Look, I just wanted to stop by and share some wonderful news. HMR's last offer is still good. Now that you've had a little more time to consider it, I thought you might see the wisdom in accepting the offer. It's extremely generous, you know. I've been in real estate a long time, and have never seen anything like it."

Mary looked at him as if he had three heads, "How can you stand there and lie like that, and still keep a straight face. Have you no shame?"

Eyes hard with a feral shine, Vince lied, "Mary, listen to me. I'm just the messenger here. I come, make an offer, and report back. What happens from there is not my purview. According to you, something serious happened here last night after you rejected the last offer. Do you really want to risk rejecting it again?"

Mary, red-faced with anger, "Look Mr. Alder, we'll never sell our farm to HMR, no matter what the price." Then, she restarted her tractor, and shouted as she pulled away, "And you can take that to the bank."

Alder stood and watched for a moment, as Mary cultivated her way down the corn rows. She didn't notice of course, because she never looked back, but Alder had about him the aura of genuine sadness. He detested what he had to do next. These were hardworking innocent people, caught up in his boss's obsession through no fault of their own.

* * *

Back at his motel room in Sheboygan Falls, Vince reviewed his original plan for burning the barn. It called for setting the fire during the evening milking, so the herd would be in the barn. Back then, he'd planned to stash the gasoline near the backend of the pasture in advance, to avoid lugging it through Waldo Swamp. Unfortunately, the short route for the gasoline was now a crime scene, so that was no longer an option. When he'd driven past on his roundtrip to see Mary, the police had still been crawling all over the area. He didn't know how long they'd be there, and thought it unwise to hang around to find out. Instead, he resigned himself to carrying the gas through the swamp. That meant he'd need to get an early start, to allow for a slower pace and periodic rests along the way.

From his previous appraisal reconnaissance, Vince knew the Evans family finished dinner and went out to the barn between 6:00 and 6:30 PM. Milking would be finished about 8:00 to 8:30 PM. He figured it would take 15 minutes to spread the gasoline, and another 15 to light the fire and make sure it was going strong. If he wanted a half-hour margin for error coming and going, that meant he'd better arrive at the back of the barn about 7:00 PM, and be out of there by 7:30 PM. That'd leave plenty of time to return to the car before nightfall.

Vince decided to go out for an early lunch, and on the way back buy the five-gallon cans, and fill them at a gas station. Along the way, he pondered when to leave the motel to get the job done. He pegged the drive from the motel to the entry point to Waldo Swamp at 30 minutes. Unencumbered by a heavy burden, he routinely crossed the swamp on foot in 30 minutes. Just to be safe, he tripled that to 90 to account for carrying the gasoline. That meant if he wanted to be at the barn by 7:00 PM, he'd better leave the motel about 5:00 PM.

Vince hadn't slept the previous night, so when he returned to the motel, he set the alarm for 4:30 PM and laid down. Sleep never came. There were so many misgivings floating around in his brain that try as he may, he just couldn't stop thinking about them. Mary Evans had told it to him straight. The Evanses would never sell their farm to HMR. Steal the cattle, burn the barn, it didn't matter. They weren't going to sell, period. He knew Rachel didn't want to hear it, but what she'd ordered him to do was futile. He resented being put in that position, and needed to talk to somebody about it.

Lacking a better alternative, Vince decided to give his brother, Phil, a call. They chatted for a while to get caught up, but soon Vince vented what was on his mind. By the time he'd finished, Phil had the whole story.

Phil sucked air, "You mean Rachel doesn't control Oostburg Bank anymore?"

Vince shook his head, "She never did. Somehow, the bank regained solvency the day before the stock sale was to close. She didn't really want the bank anyway. That was just her means to get at the Evans farm. If she controlled the bank, she could take the farm."

Confused, Phil asked, "Why would somebody like Rachel give a shit about some farm?" Vince filled him in about the casino, and why she needed the Evans farm. It was the last parcel needed for the Headwaters of the Milwaukee River Casino. Phil sparked directly to anger, "What? You mean that bitch lied to me about that too? Rachel told me her casino deal was way down the road. Now, come to find out, she doesn't even own all the land."

Sheepish, Vince admitted, "Yes, and I knew about it and didn't tell you. Look, I know it's no excuse, but she's got something on me. She ordered me not to say anything, or else."

Phil, in a mirthless tone, "What does she have on you, little brother?"

Vince exhaled heavily, "Somehow, she knew the Chicago boys wanted me dead. She told me if I ever crossed her, she'd feed me to the Chicago mob."

Phil thought about that, then said, "Well, there was a time when that was true. Back in the day, three of the Chicago big shots each got a serious stiffy every time your name came up. But now two of them are dead, and the other's been transferred to Las Vegas. Vince, if you want back in, I can protect you. In fact, coming back might be your best bet. From what you tell me, a few of Rachel's screws have shaken loose, and it's only a matter of time before she implodes."

The news and suggestion caught Vince completely off guard. After a moment of empty air, he blurted, "Phil, that's the best news I've heard in a long time. I appreciate the offer, I really do. Let me think about it and get back to you."

Phil, in a jovial tone, "No problem, Vince. What are brothers for? In the meantime, though, don't do anything stupid for that bitch. She's not worth it."

✳ ✳ ✳

After the call, sleep remained elusive. Vince used the remaining time before he had to leave, to review his predicament. The more he thought about it, the more torn he became. In many ways, Rachel had been good to him over the years. He'd been well compensated. Most of his assignments provided the adrenalin jolt that's in his nature to crave. She'd even invited him into her bed on occasion. Of course, she'd just been using him to meet her needs, but so what?

On the other hand, Vince really did believe Rachel had recently lost her way. Her obsession with the Evans farm had become irrational. The Potawatomi have strong historical connections with dozens of sites all over Wisconsin. When the Evans problem arose, all she had to do was work with the tribe, pick another site, and move on. She had ample time to do so. It's her own damn fault that the tribe lost patience, looked for another option, and found one. In his view, what she's doing now smelled of desperation. He'd never seen her like that before.

When 5:00 PM rolled around, Vince was still undecided, but he left for the farm anyway. He vowed to sort it out before setting the blaze. Whether or not he'd do the deed would be a game-time decision. As planned, he arrived at the end of the old logging road, aka the Waldo Swamp entry point, at 5:30 PM. Over his T-shirt, he strapped on a double shoulder-holster with locked and loaded handguns under each arm. Then, he pulled on a lightweight camo-colored windbreaker, to hide the holster and help with the mosquitoes. Just to be safe, he dropped two cigarette lighters and a box of wooden matches into the windbreaker's pockets. Finally, he grabbed the two five-gallon cans of gasoline, and hit the trail.

Vince made better time than expected, reaching the edge of the swamp behind the Evans farm at 6:15

PM. During the trek, it dawned on him that the police might still be working the cattle heist crime scene. If so, that meant he'd need to rethink ingress and egress for setting the fire. To find out, he hid the gas cans and crept in the direction of the pasture, and the newly-built lane from there to the hay field. A beat later, he ducked for cover at the sight of an Evans boy in the back of the pasture. Watching from the underbrush, he relaxed when it became clear the boy was merely rounding up the cattle for milking. After he was out of sight, Vince continued toward the lane.

When he got there, Vince was shocked that the lane fencing had already been taken down. Very carefully, he followed the lane through the scrub land toward the hay field. Every ten paces or so, he stopped to listen closely for activity up ahead. He never heard any. When he made it to the hay field, he found the loading pen fencing also gone, and the crime scene deserted.

Relieved, Vince returned to the swamp for the gasoline. His plan was to walk right up the farm lane to the back of the Evans barn. The acreage between here and there was strip-cropped with alternating hay and thigh-high corn, so he'd be exposed the whole way. But fortunately, the strip at the top of the hill, the one adjacent to the barn, was corn. If he needed to duck for cover, he'd be better off in the corn than hay. He judged the walk-time to be 15-minutes, so he waited until 6:45 PM and then set out.

Before long, Vince was far enough up over the crest of the hill to see the barn all the way to the ground. From that point onward, he slowed his pace and changed his walking posture to a crouch, with arms bent at the elbows to prevent the gas cans from dragging. A beat later he froze, when he saw a man behind the barn. Thinking fast, he abandoned the lane, and used the corn for cover. The man was off to the right, so he duck-walked several paces down a corn row in that direction, and set down the gas cans. Then, he continued down the same row, crawling on hands and knees, until he guessed the man would be right in front of him. He took a quick peek and judged the edge of the corn to be 20 yards ahead, with the man another 10 beyond that.

After a pause to consider his next move, Vince decided to go in for a closer look. He belly-crawled across the corn rows, doing his best not to shake stalks or make sounds. When an arm's length from the edge of the corn, he hunkered down and reached forward to push the stalks to either side, opening a clear line of sight. There sat an elderly man on a hay bale, leaning back against a higher stack of bales, which he used as a backrest. The man's chin rested on his chest, as if asleep. Vince wasn't sure, but he guessed this was the father of James Evans. The old guy looked harmless enough, until Vince noticed the shotgun stock and barrel coming up between his legs and resting on his shoulder.

A beat later, Vince risked elevating himself for a better view of the entire area. Nobody else was in sight. He glanced at his watch, and saw he's due to set the fire in five minutes. As he lay there, Vince felt the old familiar thrum of an adrenalin rush coming on. When that happened, his instincts literally took over. There's no point in resisting, it's in his nature.

Without hesitation, Vince crawled forward into the open and toward the old man. Halfway there, he could hear the snoring. A beat later, he was at his side.

In one smooth motion, Vince pulled out a handgun, spun it butt-forward, and used it to administer a savage blow to the back of the old man's head. When he tilted forward, Vince caught him with an arm and propped him back up. Next, he grabbed the shotgun, ejected the shells, and placed it back where it'd been. Then, he collected the shells and ran for the gasoline, tossing shells here and there in the corn field as he went.

When Vince returned, the old man was still out cold. By then, the thrill of the moment had passed and his blood-instincts were no longer in control. He set the cans down, and thought one last time about what he's about to do. He envisioned how it would play out, and didn't like what he saw. In minutes, the barn would explode into a raging inferno. This helpless old man, only a few yards away, would burn to a crisp. There's a good chance other Evans family members would perish in the fire. Some or all of the herd would likely be lost.

And for what? Presuming they even survived, Vince already knew James and Mary Evans would never sign over their farm to HMR. This was crazy, all of it. Somewhere along the line, Rachel had lost her mind and become delusional. Was doing the bidding of a mad-woman the best he could do? Commit arson and murder, perhaps more than one? Why? If the heat came after Rachel, he knew she'd throw him under the bus in a heartbeat.

Vince glanced again at his watch. If he's going to do this, he needed to do it now. Had Rachel really gone crazy? If so, there's no future with her anyway. Could Phil really protect him? If not, he'd be dead in a week. Sonofabitch!

CHAPTER 15

Justice is Served – Friday; July 9, 1965;
8:45 AM

Old Bill arrived at the farm, parked under the box elder tree like he always did, and ambled toward the house hoping to catch the tail end of breakfast. Half way there, Kathy came out the back door with a basket of laundry to hang on the line. After the greetings, Old Bill commented on the early hour for laundry, and she filled him in about the early breakfast and late milking. Perplexed, the old man turned and walked to the barn. When he reached the milk house, Mary had just finished pouring a pail of milk through the strainer atop the bulk tank. He fell into step beside her, as she walked the center aisle to where Overdrive was milking.

With all three in a circle, Old Bill said, "Pretty late to be milking, isn't it? Kathy told me you switched things up this morning. Won't that knock the cattle off their schedule?" When Overdrive filled him in about what went down last night, and why the switch, Old Bill's jaw dropped to his chest. After taking a moment to process, he asked, "Did anybody get hurt?"

Mary piped up, "Well, a deputy got shot. Then, John Wayne here returned fire and put down the shooter. And when the semi-trailers made a run for it, two out of three drivers had to be shot to stop them. Jumbo got one of those. So, at last count, three thieves and one deputy are in the hospital."

Eyebrows up, Old Bill turned to his son, "You shot a man?"

Overdrive, somewhat defensively, "Well, he'd just shot the deputy and was charging up the hill to finish him off. It's not like I had much of a choice."

Old Bill seemed surprised, "What'd you shoot him with?"

Overdrive pulled a milking machine out from under a cow, and stepped toward a pail, "The Remington .22-caliber rifle."

Old Bill, impressed, "Shot him on the run in the dark, eh?"

Overdrive emptied the milking machine, "Yeah, he was moving, but it was short range. What, you didn't think I had it in me? I earned a sharpshooter badge in the Army, you know. They only put me in a Sherman Tank because I had experience driving heavy equipment, unlike most of those city kids."

Old Bill considered that, then changed the subject, "Jumbo shot a man?"

Overdrive rolled his eyes, "Well, sort of. The guy tried to pull a gun on him, so Jumbo shot him with the 16-guage at a range of about three feet. Blew the guy's right hand clear off."

They bantered about that gruesome episode for a moment, then the three of them discussed how to handle the morning's work. Mary insisted that Overdrive and Jumbo take a nap after the milking was done, since one had been up all night, and the other most of it. As for herself, Mary claimed to still be wired, and wanted to finish cultivating the corn field she started yesterday before lunch. Old Bill volunteered to keep the younger boys busy. They'd double-check the pasture fence, haul manure, and de-horn calves. Between the laundry and garden, the girls had plenty to do. They deferred planning the afternoon's work until lunchtime.

* * *

Mid-morning, Marie tip-toed into her parent's bedroom and shook Overdrive awake. Her mom was cultivating corn, Ted Ritter was on the phone and said it's urgent, and she didn't know what else to do. Pulled from a deep-sleep and still groggy, Overdrive stumbled to the kitchen, and said, "Ted, what is it?"

Ted, at a rat-a-tat-tat pace, "They got the warrant! Double homicide, first degree. As soon as everybody gets back from Florida, the Sheboygan County Sherriff is sending an arrest team to Fond du Lac to pick up Wolf. Jason just called from Billy Mitchell Field. He, the detective, and the assistant DA just landed in Milwaukee, and should be in Sheboygan in about an hour. If all goes well, Wolf will be in cuffs sometime this afternoon."

Overdrive slapped himself to wake up, then said, "That's great news, Ted! Hold on a second." Just then, Marie set a mug of coffee in front of him, and he mouthed 'thank you'. After slurping a quick gulp, he continued, "Sorry for the subdued response. Up all night and a little groggy is all, but I'll snap out of it. But holy cow, I don't know what to say. It's been a long time coming, that's for sure."

Ted, still buzzing, "It gets even better. The FBI got a hit on finger prints that appeared on multiple letters to Oostburg Bank shareholders. Her name is Joyce Dekker. She spent five years in Taycheedah ... you know, the women's state pen, for attempting to poison her abusive alcoholic husband. She's out on parole. Guess where her parole officer says she works?"

Overdrive, after another gulp of coffee, "No idea."

Ted laughed merrily, "The Fond du Lac regional bank. Dekker works as a secretary at Wolf's bank."

The mug midway to Overdrive's lips jerked to a stop, and hot coffee sloshed onto his T-shirt, "Damn, hot coffee all over me! I'm awake now." Then, to Ted, "Are you kidding me?"

Out of breath, Ted paused to suck air, "It's the God's honest truth. And get this, I called Darkwater's insurance company as soon as I heard ... you know, Dan Schneider. Anyway, within an hour he called back. Based on the fingerprints, his legal department ruled that Wolf violated the settlement agreement. Those NDAs we signed are no longer binding. Given the prints plus that old evidence, now even our criminal conspiracy case is looking mighty strong. In fact, Oostburg Bank and the National Farmers Organization are both thinking about suing Wolf for damages resulting from the conspiracy."

Overdrive, now wide awake, "Ted, I'm speechless. It's like the tide has turned. All of a sudden, everything seems to be breaking our way."

Ted said wisely, "Well, enjoy this moment. They don't come often." Then, he changed the subject, "So, tell me about you and your son's heroics last night."

Eyebrows up, Overdrive said, "Heroics? I don't recall any heroics. But we did manage to set a nice trap, and catch some cattle thieves. How'd you find out?"

Ted tut-tutted, "It's all over the news. Came across as pretty heroic to me. They're saying you saved a law man's life, and Jumbo beat a scumbag to the draw." Overdrive spent the next 15 minutes filling Ted in on how it really went down. After a moment to process, Ted said, "Look, after Wolf gets arrested, she's entitled to a phone call. I'm afraid she'll use it to order a minion to lash out at you and Mary one last time. Yesterday, Darkwater said he's pretty much at a dead end on the Max Wolf case. When he checks in shortly, I'll send him your way to help defend the farm. Stay vigilant until we're sure this is over."

* * *

A little after the normal lunch time, Mary returned home with the corn cultivator. She was still hopping mad that Alder had the nerve to come see her again. Overdrive met her in the yard, and they exchanged information about Alder's visit and Ted's call. So much was happening, it's hard to keep up. They felt the need for a private conversation to work through it all, and wanted Old Bill included. So, they settled on taking him out to lunch at Harbor Lights.

While Mary spun up the girls to feed lunch to the rest of the family, Overdrive rousted Jumbo from his nap, and got the boys together to talk through the afternoon's work. Just before they left for the lake, Darkwater called to say he's enroute south, and his estimated time of arrival was 3:00 PM.

The Harbor Lights lunch-time crowd was thinning, when Overdrive, Mary, and Old Bill walked in. They all ordered burgers and fries at the bar, then took their ice-cold Kingsbury beers to a table to wait for their food. While doing so, Overdrive and Mary filled Old Bill in about Alder's visit and Ted's call.

Old Bill shot Mary with a look of concern, "Alder threatened you again?"

Mary nodded, "He sure did. That man is a piece of work."

Old Bill, as if to himself, "With Wolf getting arrested, will that go away?"

Overdrive jumped in, "Maybe, maybe not. Ted said we'd better stay vigilant until we're sure this is over."

About then the orders came, and everybody dug in. Mary swallowed a bite of her burger, then asked, "So, what do we do?"

Overdrive swallowed and washed it down, then said, "Well, last night's watch was designed to ward off a cattle heist or a barn fire. After what happened, I can't imagine they'd try another cattle heist. So, at a minimum, we probably need to set up a watch to guard against somebody setting the barn on fire."

Old Bill eyed his son and asked, "What do you mean, at a minimum?"

Overdrive finished chewing a fry, then said, "We think Wolf is trying to force us to sell, by somehow taking away our milk check. Stealing the herd and torching the barn are two ways to do it, but there're probably others." They kicked around other ideas, but came up empty.

Mary swallowed another bite of her burger, then said, "Okay, so the barn fire appears to be their best option. How do we stop it?"

Overdrive's eyes narrowed as he thought it through, "Back when they were crawling all over our buildings for the appraisal, did you ever wonder how they got in? My theory is they came through the Waldo Swamp. They must've broken a trail or something. That'd explain how the runner got away last night. The police supposedly tried to pick up the runner's trail, but nothing came of it. I'll bet Darkwater could find it in his sleep. Say, when Darkwater arrives, we have him look for the trail, and say he finds it. If he followed it through the swamp, we'd know their entry point. Then, as part of tonight's watch, Darkwater could monitor the entry point, while I sit behind the barn with the 16-guage shotgun."

Mary groaned, "Oh, come on, James. You got what, maybe one hour of sleep before Ted called? You can't go two nights in a row without any sleep."

Old Bill jumped in, "I can handle a gun. We can divvy up the night-watch." They chatted another half-hour about the details. The trail through the swamp was repeatedly used during the time of the appraisal. By now, it'd be well-worn and easily found by Darkwater, who'd then trace it to the entry point. Everybody liked the two-tier night-watch approach, with Darkwater monitoring the swamp entry point. For behind-the-barn duty, they came up with a compromise. Old Bill would go first, followed by Jumbo, and then Overdrive. Just to be safe, Old Bill would start his watch when the family began the evening milking.

* * *

Traffic was light and Darkwater arrived at 2:30 PM. At his insistence, greetings were kept to a minimum. He was concerned Wolf would lash out when cornered, and wanted to hear the plan and get to work. By 3:00 PM, Overdrive and Darkwater were at the back of the pasture, from where the runner had fled. Darkwater had no doubt he'd be able to pick up the trail, and follow it to the entry point. When he emerged from the swamp, Darkwater would walk to the nearest house and call the Evans farm, and somebody would pick him up.

The call from Darkwater came a little after 4:00 PM, from the commercial apple orchard across State Hwy 28 from the swamp. Old Bill went to pick him up. Afterward, the two of them, Overdrive, and Mary huddled in the kitchen, while the girls were preparing dinner. By the time dinner was served at 5:45 PM, everybody was fully caught up and on the same page.

About 6:15 PM the family went out to milk, and Old Bill and Darkwater walked behind the barn with a flashlight and shotgun. He didn't say as much, but Darkwater went along to make sure Old Bill set up the watch properly. He foresaw long and tedious watches for his old friend, Jumbo, and Overdrive. They needed a comfortable roost with a clear view of all angles of approach. After surveying the area, Darkwater picked the spot. Then, he and Old Bill retrieved a few hay bales from the barn, and made a comfortable place for the night-watchers to sit.

With Old Bill in place, Darkwater found Overdrive

in the barn to discuss his concerns. The corn was thigh-high, and would provide cover for an intruder. Plus, there wasn't much open space between it and the barn. This shouldn't be a problem now, in broad daylight, but after dark it could be. Darkwater feared an intruder could make it to the barn undetected. Once there, it wouldn't take long to set a fire, and once started there'd be no stopping it. Overdrive understood, but couldn't see what to do about it. There's no yard light behind the barn, and he didn't have the means to Gerry rig temporary lighting. He promised to explain the concern to Jumbo, and have him relieve Old Bill before dark.

After the conversation, Darkwater drove to the swamp entry. Just short of the turnoff, he doused his headlights and pulled to a stop as far over on the shoulder as possible. Anticipating that later he may need mobility without illumination, he grabbed a needle-nose pliers and a flash light. Then, he hunkered down into the footwell, reached up under the dash, and pulled the fuses for all lights, interior and exterior. In a beat, he was back behind the wheel. A beat later, he turned right onto the farmer's lane, and slowly bounced along. Soon, the lane transitioned to the old logging trail, and he reduced his speed even more.

As he rounded the last turn, Darkwater froze to a stop. There, at the very end, a car was already parked. He glanced at his watch ... 6:40 PM. Seeing no movement, he reached under the seat for his handgun, flicked off the safety, and quietly slipped from the vehicle. He darted from one tree to the next, until he reached the parked car. Finding it empty, he surveyed the area but nothing popped except the stench of gasoline. GASOLINE! How long ago had they left?

Mind racing, Darkwater was uncertain what to do. If he followed, could he catch them? If he raced to a phone, would his call get there in time? … Shit, shit, shit! … Instinct came down on the side of getting to a phone, so that's what he did. With the safety back on, he plunged his handgun under his belt in the lumbar area, and sprinted for his car. He noticed a turnaround along the way, and used it to make an abrupt about-face with his car. A beat later, he was speeding back the way he'd come, shock absorbers and suspension be damned. Upon approach to the fence-line transition from logging trail to farmer's lane, the narrowness of the opening and the tall stonewall fences on either side sparked an idea. He could easily block the gap through the fence-line with his car. After taking a moment to do so, he sprinted toward the orchard where he'd used the phone earlier.

When Darkwater arrived, the buildings at the orchard were closed for the day, and everything was locked up tight as a drum … Shit, shit, shit! … He sprinted back to the highway, jerked his head both ways, spied the nearest house, and took off in that direction at a desperate pace. In his fifties, Darkwater was remarkably fit for his age when fully healthy. But only a month ago, he'd been shot once in the right bicep and twice in the torso with a .257-caliber deer rifle, and was still on the mend. By the time he reached the house, he was dragging.

There at last, Darkwater's jackhammer of a knock alarmed even himself. The man who answered kept the chain in place, and peered apprehensively through the crack. What he saw was a disheveled threatening stranger, completely out of breath. After his first urgent plea to be let in failed, Darkwater took a few deep breaths to calm himself. Then, he slid his driver's license through the crack, and identified himself as a relative of the nearby Flint farming family, and an Evans family friend. In a concise manner, he explained he'd reason to believe someone was enroute to set the Evans barn on fire, and it's urgent that he call them and the police. The chain came off, the door swung open, and Darkwater made the calls.

Kathy answered at the Evans house, and promised to run the message to her parents in the barn. A beat later, he explained the situation to the duty officer at the Sherriff's department, and asked for two cruisers ASAP but with no sirens to avoid spooking the suspects. He directed one to the Evans farm, and the other to meet him on State Hwy 28 near the large orchard west of Waldo. After a hasty thank you to the man who let him in, Darkwater was back on the shoulder of the highway fast-walking toward the orchard.

Although it felt like much longer, within 15 minutes Darkwater saw flashers coming from the east. He flagged the cruiser down, and the officer pulled over. Darkwater identified himself through the passenger window, and was asked to hop in. As the officer waited for traffic to clear, Darkwater directed him to pull out when possible, and turn left into the next farmer's lane. As they bounced along slowly, Darkwater explained what he'd done with his car, and described the general lay of the land. When Darkwater's car came into view, the officer pulled to a stop 50 yards out. From there, they proceeded on foot, firearms drawn. The officer was concerned the suspects may've discovered the car, and taken up positions behind it.

The car was clear, so the officer jogged back for the cruiser. When he returned, he nosed it up tight to the side of Darkwater's car, to prevent the suspects from ramming through the road block. Before committing to his next move, the officer asked Darkwater for a detailed description of the terrain ahead, the path of the logging trail through it, and the position of the suspect's car. After discussion, they both agreed it'd be best to lie in wait near the suspect's vehicle. That way, when the bad guys returned, they'd have the element of surprise on their side.

The officer geared up with his sidearm, flashlight in case the stakeout lasted past dark, and every pair of cuffs he could find in the car. Then, he opened his trunk and pulled out a 12-guage semi-automatic shotgun and filled it with shells. Seeing the shotgun, Darkwater made a compelling case for why he needed one too. Initially reluctant, the officer came around to Darkwater's way of thinking. The number of suspects was unknown, and if a firefight broke out, they wanted to win.

When they reached the suspect's vehicle, the officer selected his own position, as well as Darkwater's. Then, he explained how he envisioned the arrests going down. To keep the suspects separated from their vehicle, at 10-yards out the officer would bark his commands ... halt, drop your weapons, put your hands in the air, step back five paces, drop to your bellies, and spread-eagle. If they complied, Darkwater would cover them while the officer applied handcuffs, one-by-one. If they fled, the officer and Darkwater would pepper their lower extremities with buckshot. If they drew their weapons, the officer and Darkwater would aim for center mass, and shoot to kill.

* * *

It was 7:05 PM, and Vince Alder was standing behind the Evans barn with a decision to make. He could do as Rachel told him and burn down the barn, or re-join the mob and trust that his brother, Phil, could protect him.

His disillusionment with Rachel was long-standing, but over the past week had reached a new high. But during their last phone conversation, it literally shot off the charts. Over the years, he'd done many things for her that were against his better judgment. But none more so, than these relentless attacks on the Evans family. He'd stuck with her this long, because he didn't think he had a choice. But, today's call with Phil had opened his eyes. He did have a choice. He could go back to the mob.

Had Rachel become unhinged? Could Phil protect him? Vince didn't have the answer to either of those questions with 100 percent certainty. It was a toss-up. But the deciding factor had been the Evans family. He'd gotten to know James and Mary a little on a personal level, while making the purchase offers. He'd gained an appreciation for the entire family's work ethic while surveilling the farm. He knew what the family had built from the appraisal, and how they recently added to it from the expansion plan. Frankly, he admired the Evans family, and couldn't bring himself to set a fire that would cost the family their livelihood, if not lives.

It was a hard decision to make, but once made, Vince knew instantly he'd made the right choice. To avoid slogging back through the swamp with the gasoline, he pulled out his handkerchief, knelt, and wiped the gasoline cans for prints. After looking around for what else he might've touched, he also wiped the shotgun. Then, he examined the head of the old man he'd walloped. Still in the upright position, his wound was clotting well, blood loss was modest, and his breathing was stable. Though no doctor, Vince believed he'd be fine. So, he trotted back down the lane to the Waldo Swamp.

* * *

Nothing happened until about 7:30 PM, when Darkwater heard distant sounds that didn't fit with the background din of the swamp. He tossed a pebble at the deputy, then silently cupped his ear and pointed down the trail when the officer turned his way. The officer's nod told Darkwater he understood. Both men verified that shells were chambered in all their weapons. Handguns were holstered with safeties on, shotguns were held with safeties off.

A few minutes later, a lone man came into view about 50 yards out, walking down the trail at a brisk pace, but seemingly relaxed and unhurried. He was tall, dark, and moved like an athlete. There were no look-backs or pauses to wait for others, so apparently, he was alone. The man was dressed in a camo windbreaker and jeans. The windbreaker bulked out oddly under the arms, perhaps concealing holstered weapons. His hands were empty.

At 10 yards out, the officer barked his orders. The man froze as if evaluating his options, but didn't immediately comply. To help with the decision making, the officer revealed himself, leaving the man staring down the barrel of a shotgun. Seeing the wisdom of the move, Darkwater also stepped into the clear, giving him two barrels to consider.

Alder nodded to himself and slowly raised his hands, then said, "I'm holstered up under the windbreaker. Not to be picky, but disarming myself might give you an excuse to shoot."

Insistent, the officer said, "I can live with that. Throw down your weapons. If my colleague was to disarm you, he might end up as a human shield."

Alder smiled knowingly. Then, he slowly lowered his right hand. After unzipping the windbreaker, he pulled a handgun out from under his left arm and tossed it to the ground. Next, he raised his right hand, slowly lowered his left, and pulled the weapon from under his right arm, and tossed it. With both hands again high, he backed off five paces, and said, "Okay, I'm disarmed."

The officer gave him a make-my-day look, and said, "Drop onto your belly, then spread-eagle." After Alder complied, the officer said to Darkwater, "Okay, you cover while I go in to cuff him. If he makes a move, shoot to kill. But do me a favor, and switch to your handgun. Less chance I'll get peppered if he does something stupid."

Darkwater said, "I can do that." Then he leaned his shotgun against a tree, pulled out his handgun, and clicked off the safety.

After Alder was cuffed, the officer patted him down, and found no other weapons. Then, he read him his Miranda rights. When the officer finished, Alder said, "I take it I'm under arrest."

The officer nodded, "That's right."

Alder scoffed, "On what charges, taking a nature walk?"

The officer looked up and pursed his lips, "Trespassing for now, but shortly I'll be radioing in to find out what else we have on you." They marched Alder to the cruiser, and chained him to the floor in the back seat. After the call-in the officer said, "Looks like we've got you for assault with a deadly weapon, too."

Darkwater's eyebrows shot up, "Who got assaulted?"

The officer, now grim, "Bill Evans, father of James. He's on his way to the hospital."

Darkwater looked into the back seat, and spat, "You beat up an old man?"

Alder stared back, and his eyes widened with recognition. After a moment, he said, "I saved his life, would be a more accurate way of putting it. Do I know you from somewhere? You look vaguely familiar."

In return, Darkwater studied the man's face, and his eyes widened as well, "I go by Darkwater."

Alder, gob smacked as if seeing a ghost, "Darkwater Flint?"

Darkwater nodded, "That would be me." For a moment he couldn't place the suspect, but then Darkwater remembered him as the head of Rachel Wolf's security detail, the night she made her casino pitch to the Potawatomi tribal council. A beat later, Darkwater put two-and-two together, and realized this must also be the HMR rep who's been pestering Overdrive and Mary to sell their farm. Just to make sure, he said, "And let me guess, you must be Vince Alder."

Alder nodded, "That's right." Then, he leaned toward Darkwater as if to tell him a secret, "Just between us, I'm not really the one you want."

Darkwater smiled, "Oh really. Then, who is?"

Alder, coy, "Rachel Wolf, and I'm in a position to help."

* * *

Kathy burst into the barn, and headed down the center aisle at a dead run. Overdrive looked up from emptying the contents of a milking machine into a pail. Mary, standing-by to carry the pail to the milk house, followed his line of sight. They both did double-takes when they saw her face. Once told the message, Overdrive set down the emptied machine and raced for the door. On his way through it, he grabbed the .22-caliber rifle leaning against the doorjamb. A moment later, he was rounding the end of the barn toward the back.

Uncertain what to expect, Overdrive chambered a shell and clicked off the safety as he ran. After huffing up the small incline at the end of the barn, he broke into the flat behind the barn and scanned the area in a panic. Old Bill was still sitting at his watch position, there're no intruders in sight, and no flames or smoke. Confused, Overdrive slowed to a jog and looked around once more.

Satisfied there's no imminent danger, Overdrive continued in the direction of his father. That's when he noticed the five-gallon cans of gasoline. Incredulous, he asked his father where they came from, and quickly stepped over to them, and recognized they weren't his.

Irritated his father didn't answer, he turned toward Old Bill. That's when he noticed the blood, and that his father was unconscious.

Overdrive dropped his rifle, bent to a knee, and took a closer look at his father's head. What he saw made him panic even more. Just then, Mary rounded the barn and called out if everything was okay. He jumped up and shouted for her to call an ambulance. He tried to remember his Army first-aid training, but drew a blank. He guessed keeping him upright like he was, might be best.

Overdrive carefully removed the shotgun from between Old Bill's legs, verified the safety was on, and did the same with his rifle. Then, he lifted the gas cans to verify they were full, and spun off their caps to verify it was gasoline. It made no sense. Somebody had carried gasoline cans to the back of the barn, set them down, knocked out his father, and then … what, just walked away? Had they gone back for more gas, forgotten a lighter, hidden in the barn, what?

Overdrive was eying the barn doors and puzzling over the situation when a police cruiser nearly spun out, as it raced around the end of the barn. His first thought was '*impossible*', but then he remembered Darkwater had called the police. The cruiser slid to a stop nearby, and the officer asked questions and barked orders. Overdrive felt great relief at being told what to do. Even more so, as he observed skilled hands working on his father. Shortly, a breathless Mary arrived to say she'd called the ambulance. The officer confirmed he'd heard her request broadcast over police radio, and also that a unit was on the way. Then, she told her husband that Jumbo and John had stepped in to milk, and Joe to carry the pails.

Minutes later, the ambulance arrived. Old Bill was still unconscious when they put him on a stretcher, loaded him, and took off. Overdrive needed to give a statement, so Mary rode in the ambulance. He'd come to the hospital later, after the milking was done. In his statement, Overdrive covered the previous night's cattle heist, the reasons they feared a firebug tonight, the planned watch here and at the swamp entry-point, the mystery gas cans, and how he found his father.

After a moment, the cruiser's radio crackled and the officer stepped away. Overdrive knew something was up, when he returned with a big smile on his face. A man by the name of Vince Alder had been arrested, while emerging from the far side of the swamp. For starters, he'll be booked and held on charges of trespassing and assault with a deadly weapon. When Overdrive returned to the barn to finish milking, he was grinning ear-to-ear.

* * *

Earlier that day, Rachel Wolf had an inkling something wasn't right. When Vince called to say Mary Evans had rejected the 50 percent premium offer a second time, she thought maybe that was it. But the feeling didn't go away. Vince had his orders to set the barn on fire that night. He'd never failed her before, so she didn't think that was it, either.

State bureaucracies were accidents waiting to happen, so she thought maybe they'd somehow screwed up the scheduling of her Monday morning meetings. But when she called, the Conservation

Department's Real Estate Program and the Department of Administration's Office of Gaming Compliance had both said the meetings were still on, and they're looking forward to them.

She sensed Long Body was losing his grip as Potawatomi chairman, and wondered if the coup had already happened. If so, the new regime would likely cancel her speaking engagement next Tuesday evening at tribal council. But when she called Long Body, her appearance ahead of Vangard Partners was still a go.

What could it be? Rachel's Spidey-sense on these things had never been wrong before. She got to thinking that maybe the firewall insulating her from criminal conspiracy prosecution had given way. Surely Phil and the mob still had their ducks in a row, but what about her favorite phony NFO roaming rep, Bert Baker, and his brother. Or for that matter, what about Ryan Weiser, her stoolie at the banking division of the Wisconsin Department of Financial Institutions. But when she called Bert and Ryan, both claimed no further contact by investigators since they last spoke.

Rachel couldn't think of anything else it might be. But her intuition had never been wrong before, so she decided to mobilize her escape plan. She'd always known the time might come when she needed to get away in a hurry. That's why, when she bought the mansion in Fond du Lac, she also bought the vacant lot next door. Since then, she'd built a 10-foot field-stone wall around the vacant lot and established an elaborate botanical garden inside, complete with trails, a maze, and a small single-story mausoleum-like building in the center. An underground tunnel was built between Rachel's mansion and the building. The tunnel was accessible from Rachel's study, and led to a vault beneath the garden's building, with a stairway up into it.

Rachel's mansion property includes ample acreage for grounds befitting an heiress, and the lot next door was equally-ample. In fact, between the two corner lots, they occupy half a city block. The block is square, so Rachel's properties include the entire length of the block fronting one street, and block half-lengths on the two cross-streets. The walled garden has gated entrances from both streets, and from a leg of Rachel's driveway. Rachel's mansion property is neither walled nor gated, but has driveway entrances from both streets.

Due to the design of the botanical garden, with its thick vegetation and curvy drives, the garden's building and it's five-space parking lot couldn't be seen from any of the three wrought-iron gated-entrances. Mobilizing the escape plan meant the parking lot would be filled with five identical black Dodge 880's with dark-tinted glass. For the duration of the mobilization, the heavily-armed drivers would bunk, eat, and play cards in the fully-equipped garden-building. The 880's had 413 cubic-inch 4-barrel V-8 engines, capable of 125 mph on the straightaway.

Code red meant the escape plan went into action. Rachel would flee from her study to the garden building. The five drivers would start their engines. The three wrought-iron gates would open. Rachel would hop into the back of the car with Brian, her lead driver, at the wheel. The four decoys would peel out.

Two decoys would depart directly to different streets. The other two would go through the gate to

Rachel's driveway, and then depart to different streets. The routes of the four decoys were pre-planned, and all five cars were in radio communication. The decoys would report back any resistance encountered, and then use their muscle cars to lead any pursuit in pre-planned directions. Based on how all that turned out, the fifth car with Rachel would depart for Wolf's Run along the clearest route. Decoys able to lose their pursuit, or without any, would flock to the Wolf's Run route and provide a protective convoy for Rachel's car. Presuming all decoys were successful, Rachel would have two decoys ahead and two behind, for the rest of the drive to Wolf's Run.

Once at Wolf's Run, the team would assume a defensive posture. If heavy pursuit or a shortage of successful decoys made Wolf's Run indefensible, Rachel and her driver, Brian, would fall back across the Menominee River to Michigan using one of several pre-developed crossings. Transport to the Iron Mountain airport would be waiting. If further fall back were necessary, a private plane on stand-by would take them to Toronto. From there, Rachel could be anywhere in the world by the next day, if necessary.

* * *

The use of highway department dump trucks as road blocks had impressed the Sheboygan County Sherriff. In fact, his adrenalin was pumping so hard, he drove straight from the Evans farm to his office as dawn broke. Pending the outcome of a meeting that'd soon start in Florida, he had an arrest team to organize, and by God he wasn't going to let Rachel Wolf get away.

278 | PATRICK J. HUGHES

Not on his watch, no sirree. If he brought her in and the prosecutor did his job, that'd clear up two murders. Why, between that and catching those cattle thieves, the Sherriff figured all he'd need to do between now and election day was run victory laps.

By the time he reached Sheboygan, the Sherriff was flying so high, and the ideas were popping out of his brain at such a rapid pace, that he didn't dare have any coffee. Yesterday, some lawyer he'd never heard of out of Random Lake had called. It was a fellow by the name of Ted Ritter. The guy claimed to be leading the Wolf investigation that turned up Ray Knobloch, in Florida. Anyway, his message was don't underestimate Wolf. Ritter said her compound in Fond du Lac covered half a city block, and if every way out of that compound wasn't covered, she'd get away. Ritter even sent him a sketch of the compound over the phone, if you can believe it. Before then, the Sherriff didn't even know his department owned one of those new-fangled Long Distance Xerography machines.

Once in his office, the Sherriff put out his do-not-disturb sign and shut the door. Then, he got to work on his arrest team plan. The gravel-filled dump trucks had worked brilliantly, so his intention was to use them lavishly. The walled and gated lot had two exits directly to the street. Those could be blocked with one dump truck each. But the lot with the mansion was more difficult. Blocking the two driveway exits would be useless, because they'd just drive over the lawn. Plus, those in the house would know something was up, if big equipment moved in.

Try as he may, the Sherriff couldn't come up with a solution. About then, he got a call saying a deal had been struck in Florida, and the DA was on his way to the judge's chambers to get a warrant for Wolf's arrest. Incredulous, the Sherriff looked at the wall clock and said that's impossible, only to be reminded that Florida was an hour ahead. Now the Sherriff really felt the pressure. There's no maybe anymore, he needed an arrest plan.

Frustrated, the Sherriff waited until normal starting time, and then called his good buddy, the Fond du Lac County Sherriff. After being told what was coming down, the Fondy Sherriff also smelled votes in the air, and cleared his schedule to help figure things out. He knew the area around Wolf's mansion well, and the intel he provided was discouraging. It sat on a corner lot with exits onto both streets, which meant four directions to run. All four go through neighborhoods with broad-vista front lawns. By the time those streets reach areas where a road block at a choke-point would be viable, there'd be dozens of secondary ways to escape through the street grid. It'd be like water running through a sieve.

After going around and around without finding a good solution, the two Sherriff's decided to think about it on their own, and get back on the horn about noon. After hanging up, the Sherriff said a prayer, and continued to ponder his problem. About 11:30 AM, the Sherriff's secretary knocked on his door. Then, she peeked in to say the folks from Florida were back, and they'd come right in if he wanted to see them. He said of course, and after she backed out the Sherriff looked up as if to God, and winked.

Shortly, one of his detectives, the assistant DA, and a civilian he didn't know were led into the room. The civilian, Jason Binder, introduced himself as the PI that found Ray Knobloch, while under the employ of Ted Ritter, an attorney out of Random Lake. The Sherriff looked up and winked once more.

It came out in discussion that the Sherriff had been on the line with the Fond du Lac County Sherriff earlier, concerning the arrest team plan, and would need to do so again shortly. He admitted they both were stumped, and could use some fresh thinking. Then, he filled them in on what they had so far, and the remaining problem. Binder said he had some familiarity with the Wolf compound, and asked to see the sketch.

Being careful to stroke the Sherriff's ego, Binder said he agreed totally with using dump trucks to block the walled lot's two street-side gates. His only friendly amendment to the Sherriff's plan, would be to block the third gate the same way. Like the Sherriff said, the other choke points for road blocks were too far away. If vehicles existed inside the walled lot, the only way to prevent escape was to block all gates through the wall. As for the mansion, more traditional means could be used. Simultaneously with the arrest team's knock on the door, cruisers can stream in to block the garage doors and any vehicles parked in the driveway. Binder also felt the possibility of runners on foot should be taken seriously. That meant plenty of well-armed deputies around the perimeter of the mansion's lot. The walled perimeter should also be guarded, though maybe not as heavily.

More discussion covered the number of men and cruisers needed, the gear each man should have, from where to source the dump trucks, and so on. They were still talking, when the Fond du Lac County Sherriff called back. Shortly, both departments were on the same page about the plan, and who would provide what. The Fondy Sherriff agreed to arm-twist his highway department into providing the dump trucks. Binder remained an active part of the discussion, until it turned to things like who'd be allowed to preen in front of the microphones and TV cameras.

Most of the afternoon was spent getting teams and equipment from two Sherriff's departments and one highway department integrated, organized, briefed, and positioned. At 4:00 PM the Sheboygan County Sherriff, arrest warrant in hand, stood outside the front door of Wolf's mansion with the entry team. There they stayed, until the last dump truck to be positioned rumbled its way across Wolf's lawn to block the last gate.

A beat later, a series of heavy knocks rang out at the front door, followed by another series, and another. Simultaneously, four cruisers streamed onto the property and blocked the garage doors to prevent escape. No vehicles were parked in the driveway, so any escape could only be on foot.

Eventually, a woman came to the door, and opened it a crack with the chain left in place. The Sherriff identified himself, held paper up to the crack, and said in a loud and authoritative voice, "I have a warrant for the arrest of Rachel Wolf on two counts of first-degree murder, in the deaths of Ben and Ruth Wolf. Step aside, and let us in." When nothing happened, the Sherriff barked, "Open the door, or we'll break it down." In response, the woman re-closed the door to unhook the chain, then opened it wide. There stood a young woman as wide-eyed as the toddler she held. The Sherriff asked, "Are you Rachel Wolf?"

Mortified, the woman said, "No, my name is Rose, I'm the nanny." Then, she hitched the child up on her hip, and said, "And this is Jake."

The Sherriff handed her the warrant, and she verified what he said was true. Then, in a softer tone, the Sherriff asked, "Is Rachel Wolf on the premises?"

Rose looked up at him, and said earnestly, "As far as I know. I was in the play room with Jake. You might check the garage to see if all the cars are there." Rose stepped back meekly, and the Sherriff and the entry team filed in, firearms drawn. Then, with her free hand, she reached behind herself and pushed the button hidden in the elaborate woodwork in the entry way. Rachel had instructed her to do so, if a circumstance like this ever arose. It was code red.

* * *

Rachel slammed her coffee mug to the desk, and in one smooth movement knelt and reached underneath for a purse. In it, was a paddle-holster, a Smith & Wesson Model 39 with one 9 mm Parabellum round in the chamber and 8 more in the magazine, and a half-dozen spare magazines. In an instant, she slipped the holster down over her waistband at the right hip, planted the weapon in it, and put her left arm and head through the long purse-strap so it hung to her left. A beat later, she flipped a latch, rolled away the bookcase exposing the stairs to the tunnel, stepped through, flicked on the light, and rolled the bookcase back. Then, she clattered down the stairs, and sprinted down the tunnel toward the vault.

When she reached the vault, Rachel took the stairs up to the garden-building two-steps at a time. After clearing the stairwell, she raced through the door to the parking lot. There, waited five idling Dodge 880's ready to roar. As she hopped into the back of Brian's car, the other four peeled out. Shortly after screeches could be heard, and the radio crackled to life. Rachel leaned forward, "Brian, what is it?"

Brian, with traces of nervous stress in his voice, "Hold on … oh shit! The gates are blocked! All three of them!"

Rachel, hand to mouth, "W-what?"

Brian, over his shoulder, "They're all blocked, and the cars can't get out."

Rachel, incredulous, "By what?"

Brian, "Hold on." He talked into the radio, it crackled back, "Dump trucks. Tight to the walls, a body can't shimmy through. But maybe over or under."

Rachel rolled her eyes, "Dump trucks! What's with the dump trucks all of a sudden. Sonofabitch!"

The radio crackled again, and Brian said, "They're all awaiting orders. What do you want to do?"

Grey matter already at warp speed, Rachel spent a moment, then said, "There's no point fighting our way to the street, only to have no wheels. Our best chance is to get to the garage. Have the guys at the driveway gate lay down and look under the truck, toward the garage. Find out if the garage doors are blocked."

Brian, "Will do." He radioed, and you could hear the urgency in his voice. After a moment, he relayed the response, "They're saying squad cars have the garage blocked in."

Rachel gasped, "Well, we can't stay here. We'll have to pick one of the street-gates, roll under the truck and come up firing. Once we break through their line, we'll make a run for it until we find a car to swipe. Have the guys at the street gates lay down. Have a look-see on what we'd be up against."

Brian gave her a testing look, but did as he's told. When he radioed, there was a tinge of futility in his voice. What came back was discouraging, "Each gate is covered by four squad cars. Two blocking the street on each side. Behind each car, are two deputies toting shotguns." He turned to look at her straight on, "Eight shotguns at each gate. It'd be suicide."

Rachel got out of the car, and slammed the door. She bent deeply at the waist, and expelled all her air. Then, in one continuous motion, she reloaded her lungs, shot upright, and let out what sounded like the death-cry of a cornered predator. She held that feral otherworldly note for an eternity … hands bawled into fists, neck veins and tendons bulging, and mouth and eyes wide open. The blood-curdling sound echoed throughout the botanical garden, and commanded silence from everything within earshot.

For several minutes, absolute silence followed. Then, a loudspeaker came to life from the gate nearest the mansion, "This is the Sheboygan County Sherriff speaking. I have a warrant for the arrest of Rachel Wolf on two counts of first-degree murder, in the deaths of Ben and Ruth Wolf."

Rachel's eyebrows shot up, and she gasped, "W-what?"

The Sherriff continued, "You are surrounded by overwhelming force. There is no escape. Lay down your weapons. We need Rachel Wolf to come to the gate where I am, and turn herself in. After she's in custody, everyone else will be processed and released. I repeat, everyone else will be processed and released. Be smart, and live."

Rachel muttered, "Go to hell." Then she drew her Smith and Wesson, clicked off the safety, and started marching toward the Sherriff's gate.

Half-way there, a different voice came over the loudspeaker. In a voice full of emotion, Rose said, "Rachel, this is Rose. Please come out. Jake needs his mommy. Trust me, it'll all work. This is just a terrible misunderstanding."

At the sound of Rose's voice, Rachel stopped dead in her tracks. Suddenly filled with conflicting impulses, she whipped her pistol up under her chin. But at the thought of Jake, she couldn't pull the trigger, and her arm feathered back to her side. Reflexively, she looked all around, hoping to see a place to run or hide. But there was none. She spun the grey matter once more, but nothing ingenious emerged. Then, she brightened as if visited by an epiphany. With renewed confidence, she tossed her gun to the ground, and swaggered to the gate. Then, she wiped the smug smile off her face, rolled under the truck, and turned herself in.

* * *

In addition to Ray Knobloch the aircraft mechanic, Vince Alder turned state's evidence in exchange for full transactional immunity. Max Wolf and Rachel's law school classmate were before Alder's time, so he couldn't help there. But his testimony concerning crimes committed since becoming Wolf's director of special projects was so extensive, a state-wide task force had to be created.

Since that time, the various investigations of Wolf have snowballed. In addition to the two counts of first-degree murder for Ben and Ruth Wolf, the Sheboygan County Sherriff's Department is pursuing Wolf for criminal conspiracy in the attempted takeover of Oostburg Bank, and attempted cattle theft and arson at the Evans farm. Forest County is pursuing Wolf for attempted murder of Darkwater Flint, and arson of his properties. Vilas County is pursuing Wolf for the attempted murder of Darkwater Flint on a separate occasion. Winnebago County is pursuing Wolf for first-degree murder in the stabbing death of the gas-station operator on U.S. Hwy 41. Outagamie County is pursuing Wolf for first-degree murder in the stabbing death of a rural Black Creek woman. The list of criminal charges goes on and on, and involves almost every county in central and northern Wisconsin. Following close behind, are the civil suits against Wolf, which appear to be multiplying like rabbits.

CHAPTER 16

Life Slowly Returns to Normal – Friday;
July 9, 1965; 9:30 PM

Overdrive and Mary were huddled at the kitchen table, speaking in whispered tones. Slumped forward with elbows on the table, Overdrive held his head in his hands. With a hand on his shoulder, Mary was comforting him. After milking, Overdrive had rushed to Plymouth Hospital, intending to join Mary at the bed of his father. But by the time he arrived, they'd already transported Old Bill to Froedtert, a teaching hospital for the University of Wisconsin-Milwaukee Medical School. At Plymouth, they'd managed to stabilize Old Bill, but he remained in critical condition with a coma and serious head trauma. Froedtert Hospital had the area's best neurology expertise.

Overdrive blamed himself. Deep down he knew it'd been a mistake to include Old Bill in the watch, but like a fool he'd allowed himself to be talked into it. Now his father's life was hanging by a thread. Through the gloom, he heard Mary say, in soft voice, "It's not your fault, James. Your father wanted to help. Plus, you gave him the daylight watch … the easiest one. Who knew they'd try to set the blaze in broad daylight?"

Overdrive, despairing, "I should've known! Think about it. That's when the herd's in the barn. The time of maximum loss. How could I miss that?"

Mary shook her head, "We all missed that. We'd no way of knowing."

Overdrive, blinking back tears, "It's a mystery to me how he didn't see Alder coming."

Mary patted his shoulder, "I'll bet Old Bill dozed off, which by the way, is his fault not yours. But look James, your father's a tough old bird. He'll be fine."

Overdrive lifted his head and caught her eye, "The doc at Plymouth didn't seem so sure." He took a moment to organize his dark thoughts, then said, "What'll I do without him? He knew everything about this farm. All the advice he gave, and the ancestors." Overdrive stopped short, and his eyes widened. Then, he pounded the table, "What've I done! What a fool I am!"

Mary's eyes narrowed, "James, what're you talking about?"

Overdrive, beside himself, "The ancestors, I never learned how to contact them! With Dad gone, we've lost them forever. Worse yet, because of me, we've lost Dad forever. Don't you see? Should Dad pass, I'd always told myself he'd still be among the ancestors, and we'd be able to reach him that way. Now I've ruined that, too. All those years, I just couldn't be bothered with such nonsense. Now it's all gone, all because I'm so pigheaded!"

Mary took his hands in hers, and said softly, "Stop

beating yourself up, James. Your Dad's going to recover. And when he does, we'll learn together."

One sob escaped, but Overdrive held off the others. He looked at her with tear-filled eyes, and said, "What I wouldn't give, to bridge to the ancestors now. If Dad wasn't among them, at least we'd know he's alive."

Just then, Marie slipped into the kitchen from the TV room, and closed the door behind herself. After listening at the door since the fist-pound, she shook off her fear, and said, "I know how to open the bridge. Grandpa taught me."

Eyes wide, Overdrive looked up at Marie in astonishment. He motioned for her to come, then pulled her in for a hug, and said, "I hope you do. But are you sure, honey? It requires a speaking knowledge of Welsh."

Marie nodded, "I know enough Welsh to get by. I've opened the bridge by myself once before. I can do it again." Mary came around, and wrapped an arm around them both. As bed time approached, Mary pulled Marie aside for a private conversation. Soon, all the kids were taking their turns in the bathroom, getting ready for bed. But when the rest of the kids went upstairs to bed, Marie hung back.

Darkwater bunked at Old Bill's shack when in the area, so Mary gave him a call and ran her idea past him. Darkwater was all for it, so Overdrive, Mary and Marie hopped into the family car and headed to Cascade. Once there, Marie went right to work. She locked the door, pulled all the shades down, and lit candles. Then, she asked the adults to move the two stuffed chairs closer together, bring two chairs from the kitchen into the small living area, and set small tables between each pair of chairs. Soon, two cocktail glasses arrived at each table, and Marie came around with a bottle of *Drysien Gwyllt*, a Welsh liquor, and poured a jigger into each glass.

With everything set, Marie asked the adults to be seated, and then turned off the lights and took the last seat for herself. The adults stared back in wonderment, as Marie told them in an instructional tone, "We alternately sip this, and whisper a Welsh phrase that I'll tell you next. Understand?" They all nodded, so Marie continued, "We say the Welsh phrase '*a fo ben, bid bont*', which means *if you want to be a leader, be a bridge*. We'll need to practice the Welsh pronunciation, until you get it right. Otherwise, the ritual won't work. Is everybody ready?" They all nodded, again.

At Marie's prompting, they all whispered '*a fo ben, bid bont*' over and over. Marie didn't like what she heard, so they kept going. Finally, she stopped in frustration, and said, "Come on Dad, everybody's got it but you. Pay attention!" Overdrive recoiled like a wounded puppy, which set Mary to giggling, but Marie stifled her with a scowl. All serious once more, they resumed their whispered chants until Marie figured it was close enough. Then, they all began sipping *Drysien Gwyllt* and whispering '*a fo ben, bid bont*', over and over, and within a minute the bridge to the ancestors was opened.

What happened next left Overdrive, Mary, and Darkwater awestruck. Just like when Old Bill handled the ritual, they felt the vague presence of the ancestors, and noticed a change in the candles, as if they'd somehow gotten brighter. Then, Marie began speaking in Welsh, and remarkably, they began hearing the by-now familiar chatter of the ancestors in return. The adults were amazed at how fluent Marie appeared to be. Overdrive and Mary were swelling with pride.

A short while later, tears welled up in Marie's eyes. Concerned, Mary asked, "Marie, what's the matter?"

When Marie seemed unable to speak, Overdrive gasped, "Oh God, is grandpa there? Has he died?"

Stricken, Darkwater jumped in, "Has he?"

With tears now streaming down her cheeks, Marie shook her head, and said, "He's not there. They say he must still be alive."

* * *

Three days later, on Monday July 12th, Jumbo was due to report for duty with the Army, in Milwaukee. Overdrive and Mary drove him, and Lizzie Flint came along to help see him off. Although Old Bill was still in a coma, Jumbo wanted to see him, so they got an early start and stopped by Froedtert Hospital on the way. To their surprise, Old Bill had regained consciousness overnight, and was alert when they arrived. According to the nurse, on doctor's orders visitors weren't allowed. But by chance, while they're standing at the nursing station, the doc came past. He was gracious enough to give them a quick update on Old Bill's condition, and after hearing the report-for-duty sob story, conceded that a short visit should be okay.

Upon seeing them enter the room, Old Bill used one of his favorite lines, "To what do I owe this great honor?"

Mary dead-panned, "Well, you almost got yourself killed, so we figured the least we could do was come visit."

292 | PATRICK J. HUGHES

Old Bill grinned, "Mighty thoughtful of you. I'm told recovery will require a daily slice of your apple pie."

As Mary giggled, Overdrive jumped in, "Since the bullshit's already starting to flow, my guess is you're feeling better, huh Dad?"

Old Bill, feigning insult, "That was no bullshit."

Jumbo sidled up to the bed, "Gee gramps, after all those years of you saying it was me, turns out you're the one with a hole in his head. Doc told us they had to drill one to relieve the pressure."

Old Bill winked, "Broke every drill bit they had, but one." Then, after a beat, "What're you doing here, don't you have hay to bale, or something?"

Jumbo made a face, "I'm reporting for duty, remember? Today's July 12th."

Old Bill's brow furrowed, "It is? Damn, that means I missed my weekly card game." He looked around Jumbo, "Hi Lizzie, good to see you. I thought sure you'd kick this dumbass to the curb as soon as he joined the Army."

Lizzie flashed beet-red, "No ... I ... well, it's good to see you, too." The conversation continued like this for a few more minutes, then the nurse insisted they leave.

Seeing Old Bill awake and sharp-as-ever buoyed everyone's spirits. But the drive from Froedtert Hospital to the Army recruiting center was a short one, and the feeling didn't last long. Good byes had always been awkward for Overdrive, so he favored keeping the discomfort brief and upbeat, at least outwardly. He looked Jumbo in the eye, used his left hand to slap his son's shoulder, shook hands firmly with his right, and told his son he loved, and was proud of him. Mary went in for a lengthy hug, held her son's shoulders at arm's length, looked him in the eye, made him promise to write and said she'd do the same, and expressed the same love and pride that her husband had done. When it came Lizzie's turn, Overdrive and Mary stepped away to give them some privacy. They never looked back, but there was no need. The sounds of their oldest son and this wonderful young woman sobbing in each other's arms told them everything they needed to know.

Not a word was spoken during the drive back to Sheboygan County. In the back seat, Lizzie sobbed the entire way home. Mary held it together while serving as navigator until Overdrive escape Milwaukee, but then joined in. With sounds of anguish all around, Overdrive spent the drive home lost in his own thoughts.

* * *

The evening of the next day, the tribe assembled in Council Hall in Wabeno, Wisconsin, for the Potawatomi Tribal Council meeting. The hall filled quickly, after word spread of the meeting's importance, without saying why. Darkwater knew what was to happen, and attended in person to enjoy the show. As one might imagine, it caused quite a stir when he and his fiancée, Robin Thunder, walked in. Until that moment, the tribe at large was under the impression he'd passed away under suspicious circumstances. He and Robin made a point of walking slowly down the center aisle for all to see, on their way to reserved seats in the front row.

The jolt from seeing Darkwater was only a warm up for what was to come. Led by Eternal Oak, the elder of the largest Potawatomi band, the other elders had forced Long Body, the current chairman of tribal council, to agree to make three announcements that evening. As Darkwater and Robin settled into their seats, the hall was abuzz with whispers of anticipation over what was to come. Soon, the lights were alternately dimmed and raised, and the buzz slowly dissipated.

As usual, Long Body called the council to order at the front of the room, and the elders began by dispensing with routine matters. After those were finished, Long Body took the podium and thanked the crowd for coming. Then, he dropped the first bombshell. Effective immediately, he'd be stepping down as chairman. The hall went silent, as if a collective pause were required to process the news. A beat later, the hall broke into a low rumble. Darkwater overheard nearby comments along the lines of it's about time, and felt his first dopamine rush.

Long Body raised his hands and asked for order, and the rumble subsided. Then, came his second bombshell. The elders had unanimously selected Make Wit, the elder of the Little Prairie band, as the new chairman. This triggered an instant roar of approval, and Darkwater felt a new and stronger jolt. Clearly, multiple feel-good hormones were now at work in his body.

Once more, Long Body raised his hands and called for order. It took longer this time, but eventually the hall silenced. That's when Long Body came out with bombshell number three. The tribe had dissolved its partnership with HMR, and would no-longer pursue a casino at the Headwaters of the Milwaukee River location. Pure elation broke out over the crowd. Now literally trembling with joy, Darkwater knew the four Horseman of happy … dopamine, serotonin, endorphins, and oxytocin … were all coursing through his veins in ample doses.

Without further ado, Long Body turned the meeting over to his successor, Make Wit. The new chairman's first official act was to invite Eternal Oak forward, to introduce for the tribe's consideration a new prospective casino site and development partner. Perhaps the most revered member of the tribe, when Eternal Oak spoke, tribal members listened. This night was no exception, and the crowd was won over by his masterful case for a casino in Milwaukee. He emphasized that the new site had no sacred lands, then raised his hands and voice to declare in a reverent tone … there would be no desecration! The hall erupted in a deafening chorus of whistles and cheers.

After concluding his remarks, Eternal Oak introduced the CEO of Vangard Partners, who walked the crowd through the casino marketing study, business plan, design and construction schedule, and proforma estimates of tribal income once the facility was up and running. The CEO emphasized that unlike the tribe's previous partner, Vangard already owned the land and had secured all local and municipal approvals. He told them Vangard was prepared to go to Madison for state approvals as soon as a tribal endorsement was received.

After the CEO finished, Make Wit gave tribal members the opportunity to ask questions and voice their positions. Everyone who rose to speak was supportive of moving forward with Vangard Partners. After everyone had said their peace, Make Wit called for a vote among the elders. Approval was unanimous, when even Long Body came on board. The tribe was on its way out of poverty, no thanks to Rachel Wolf.

* * *

After Wolf's arrest, life gradually returned to normal for the team that brought her down. Ted Ritter's law practice refocused on its longstanding core business of providing holistic cradle-to-grave legal services to dairy farm families. Ted's go-to private investigator, Jason Binder, continued to provide PI services to the region through his private practice. Darkwater Flint set a date for his marriage with Robin Thunder, and returned to his hunting and fishing guide business, which he now runs in partnership with Robin's brother. He also takes on the occasional PI side-gig with Jason, who wished he'd take on more. Peter Nyenhuis continued as the President of Oostburg Bank. After Wolf was convicted of criminal conspiracy with intent to take over the bank, Oostburg Bank successfully sued Wolf in civil court and was awarded compensatory and punitive damages.

Old Bill returned home from the hospital, and his recovery progressed rapidly. The way he explains it, he wore out his welcome after two weeks and the hospital sent him home. During his first week back, Mary checked in on him daily and kept up a steady supply of fresh apple pie. After that, Old Bill started coming out to the farm regularly, like he always had. For the first few weeks, Overdrive kept a close eye on him to make sure he didn't over-exert himself, and recruited the boys to do the same.

Before long, every trip to Reinhold's Grocery,

Art's Service Station, or the various other business establishments in Cascade began to take on an old familiar theme. Without fail, Overdrive or Mary would be approached by yet another village tattle-tale with their harrowing eye-witness account of Old Bill running a stop sign out onto State Hwy 28. Although they took these sightings seriously, and scolded Old Bill each and every time, deep down Overdrive and Mary also viewed them as a sign that Old Bill was well on the way to a full recovery.

For Overdrive and Mary's immediate family, life gradually returned to a new normal after Wolf's downfall. Jumbo's absence left a big hole in their lives, perhaps bigger than they expected. But over time, Mary learned the importance of serving as a communications hub, and they adjusted. She and Jumbo wrote letters back and forth, religiously. Lizzie Flint and Jumbo, even more so. Since Lizzie arriving on horseback was still a common sight at the farm, at the risk of appearing nosy, Mary used these opportunities to compare notes. Then, she'd curate what she knew about Jumbo appropriately, and keep everyone in the family informed. It's safe to say everyone in the family plus Lizzie prayed daily that Jumbo would make it into the military police, and be deployed anywhere but Viet Nam.

As for Overdrive and Mary, they gradually settled back into the natural rhythm of operating a family dairy farm. With this way of life, having a fistful of worries at any given time was inevitable. But merely shedding all the Wolf-related woes, somehow made it all feel much more manageable than before, even in Jumbo's absence. They'd grown from the experience, and were wiser for it. In a sense, the efficiency gained freed them to devote more energy to raising the rest of their children, and reap the rewards of doing so.

In the fall, Joe would enter his senior year in high school. Although still somewhat immature for his age, Overdrive and Mary had a growing admiration for what he could do on the farm. Jumbo's absence had created opportunities for him, and he'd capitalized on them. Kathy would be entering her junior year, and had become quite the young lady. Her beau, Kirk Walcott, had also managed to become fast-friends with Joe, and his eagerness to help out on the farm continued to impress Overdrive and Mary. For her part, Marie had established herself as the family's legacy connection to the ancestors, by proactively learning Welsh, and hounding her grandpa until he taught her how to open the bridge. The Cascade baseball team that John pitched and played shortstop for went undefeated that summer, though one could argue the likes of Adell, Batavia, Beechwood, and Boltenville weren't exactly world-class competition. Being hit by the occasional beanball did not deter David from standing in the batter's box, while John practiced his pitching against the milk house wall. As the summer progressed, he started to swing. Tongues in Cascade are still wagging, over David's low line-drive that bad-hopped into John's groin and caused him to miss a start on the mound.

* * *

One day late that summer, Scully phoned mid-afternoon for Overdrive. The ensuing conversation convinced Overdrive his father had finally fully recovered. After Kathy fetched him, Overdrive picked up and said, "Scully, what's up?"

Scully, in a scolding voice, "Do you know where your father was today?"

Overdrive, eyebrows up at the odd question and tone, "No, not really. We didn't have any hay dry enough to bale, so I gave him the day off."

Scully, teasingly, "Well, if not for me he'd have been strung up by a mob."

Incredulous, Overdrive said, "What're you talking about?"

Scully put a little gravel in his voice, "I'm glad you asked. It seems a resident of Kewaskum was looking for a way to take down an old concrete silo on his property. Someone suggested dynamite, and through word of mouth, he found and hired a demolition expert. This expert set off a blast that leveled the silo and shattered half the windows in town. Guess who that expert was."

Overdrive spat, "Come on Scully. That isn't funny. Don't you bullshit me."

Relishing every word, Scully replied. "This is no bullshit. An angry mob formed, and the constable had your father in custody for his own protection. Not knowing what to do, the constable called the Washington County Sherriff."

Overdrive groaned, "Oh shit, you mean he's in jail?"

Scully, with glee, "No, no ... the Sherriff told the constable to calm down and tell the mob to go home ... you know, tell them that being stupid wasn't a lynching offense anymore, and silo-guy's insurance would cover the windows."

Overdrive snorted, "And that worked?"

Scully laughed, "Not even a little. That's when the

Sherriff sent a cruiser to disburse the crowd, and escort Old Bill to the county line. He also called ahead to the Sheboygan County Sherriff, so the escort could continue all the way to Old Bill's shack … you know, in case anybody gave chase."

Confused, Overdrive blurted, "What does any of this have to do with you?"

Scully, now grim, "Well, the Sheboygan County Sherriff was shorthanded, so he called to ask if I wouldn't mind handling the escort out of my Cascade highway department shed. He figured a highway department vehicle would be official enough for the job at hand. Then, he went on to rant about that riff-raff of an Evans family out by Cascade. And how lately they're treating his department as if it's their own personal police force. You should've heard him … cattle heist, barn-fire threat, personal escort service. I couldn't believe my ears."

Overdrive thought he was being played, but wasn't sure. So, he put a little spin on things to find out, "Well, the Sherriff's got a lot of nerve if that's what he said. He's been all over the papers, radio, and TV taking credit for what we did the night of the cattle heist." Then he paused a beat, half laughed, and said in a conspiratorial tone, "But the Sherriff didn't really say all that, did he?"

Scully laughed, "Well, I might've embellished his remarks somewhat."

Overdrive nodded, "That's what I figured. How's my father doing?"

Scully, in a reassuring tone, "Oh, he's fine. In fact, he's happy as hell to be home safely. A few cars actually followed him and the constable to the village limits, but the Washington County deputy was able to dissuade them from keeping up the chase."

Relieved, Overdrive asked, "Anybody get hurt?"

Scully snorted, "No, just broken glass and your father's wounded pride."

Overdrive sighed, "So, presuming any of this is true, what is it you think I owe you for helping Dad get out of Dodge?"

Scully, with a kid-in-the-candy-store tone, "I'm thinking whenever we run into each other at a watering hole, you buy me a beer."

Overdrive scoffed, "I already do that."

Scully laughed, "I know. But now you know why."

* * *

A few days later, Darkwater was in the area to finish some business with Ted Ritter and Jason Binder. The plan was for Darkwater to stay over with Old Bill at the shack that night, and drive back north the following morning. Old Bill felt it was time to communicate with the ancestors. They'd learned of his injury through Marie, but hadn't heard anything since. Although he wasn't sure if worry was a thing in the spirit world, Old Bill figured it'd be impolite to keep them hanging. Overdrive and Mary agreed, and said they'd been waiting for an opportunity to update the ancestors on the Rachel Wolf saga, and thank them for their assistance in bringing her to justice. They all thought it'd be fun to have Marie open the bridge and do the talking.

That evening at Old Bill's shack, aside from positioning five chairs in the small living area, the adults sat back and watched with pride as Marie made all the preparations for the bridge. With great seriousness, she poured them each a small amount of *Drysien Gwyllt*, explained the sip and whisper ritual, and coached them through the proper pronunciation of *'a fo ben, bid bont'*. This time when Overdrive stumbled over the phrase, Marie got right in his face and very slowly walked him through it, one vowel or consonant at a time.

Soon, the bridge was opened. With an encouraging smile, Old Bill sat back and told Marie to do the talking and interpreting. For the most part, she was able to do so, but here and there Old Bill helped her find the right word, or understand one. The ancestors were thrilled to hear that Old Bill had regained his health, and laughed heartily at his expense over the hole in is head, and especially over his misadventure in Kewaskum.

When the conversation turned to Rachel Wolf, the ancestors were ecstatic to learn the farm, their legacy, was no longer at risk. They asked for more and more details, and relished each and every one. During this part of the conversation, Marie was mostly bug-eyed, since almost all of this information was new to her.

The conversation was nearly over, when Overdrive made the off-hand remark that Wolf had finally gotten her comeuppance. But surprisingly, when Marie translated and passed that along to the ancestors, they exploded. What ensued was a loud rumble of chatter, that grew in ferocity. Apparently, the ancestors were trying to explain something difficult to grasp, and weren't of the same mind about how to do it. Struggling to keep up with the overlapping jumble of words, Marie looked to Old Bill for help.

For the first time all session, Old Bill began speaking directly to the ancestors. Back and forth it went, as if he were seeking clarifications or trying to fill gaps in his understanding. The din of ancestors talking over one another continued for what seemed like forever, and became heated at times. The Welsh spoken was so rapid-fire, Marie was as much in the dark as Overdrive, Mary, and Darkwater. All paid rapt attention to Old Bill, hoping he'd pause at any moment to explain what all the bickering was about.

Finally Old Bill, white as a ghost, turned to them and said, "The ancestors say don't be so sure Wolf got her comeuppance. They say in the past, Wolfs have popped up in unexpected places, and disappeared without explanation in others. That's why people back in the day, our ancestors included, came to believe the Wolfs have some sort of supernatural power ... the ability to possess other living human beings, and live out their lives using them as hosts. They say the only way to get rid of a Wolf permanently, is to kill it before it hops into somebody else. If Rachel has this ability, no jail can hold her."

Overdrive sputtered, "But ... but ... but that's crazy!"

Old Bill looked him in the eye, "No crazier than us speaking to our ancestors."

Five sets of eyes darted around the room, looking from one to another, as they came to grips with what this might mean. Marie was speechless, but the other four muttered a collective, "Sonofabitch!"

THE END

ACKNOWLEDGEMENT

Writing is a solitary activity. Being the way I am, significant blocks of undisturbed time are required to be productive. In this day and age, that's a luxury hard to come by. Sometimes life can get in the way of a writer's best laid plans, and in my world 2022 was a perfect example. Even so, to my amazement, a manuscript I'm proud of was completed almost when hoped for. This never would've happened if not for my wife and partner in life, Paula. Her love, support, encouragement, and understanding pulled me through.

Tim Vane again served as my primary reviewer. As usual, his suggestions to increase the pace and drama were remarkable, and I love the way he delivers tough love with great humor. Special thanks also go to Rose Marie (Zehren) Nelson, a native of Kewaskum, WI. She brought to the attention of my family, information that served as inspiration for the scene involving Old Bill's misadventure in her home town.

Thanks also to my loyal reader community. This novel is the third in the Overdrive Evans series, and shares setting-characters-storyline with the previous two, Headwaters Deception and Headwaters Revenge. Comments from readers received at patrick.j.hughes@outlook.com have inspired plot elements, character evolution, and other aspects of this multi-novel continuing saga. Hearing from readers literally makes my day. It's truly humbling to know people out there care enough about my characters and storyline to send a note. Please keep those emails coming!

ABOUT THE AUTHOR

Patrick J. Hughes

Patrick J. Hughes is a husband, father, writer, and retired research engineer. He was raised on a dairy farm and went on to become the first member of his family to graduate from college, earning two degrees from the University of Wisconsin-Madison and another from Stanford. Writing fiction is his second act, after a long  career fighting climate change while employed at a major research university, large and small consulting firms, and a leading national laboratory. He traveled the world during his career, but never forgot where he came from. That's why the dairy farm setting of the Overdrive Evans series rings true, as well as the farm-family dynamics. He currently resides in Oak Ridge, TN, with his wife, Paula, and together they have two grown sons, Jared and Zach.